SHORTS
3

# Shorts
# 3

## The Macallan/
## Scotland on Sunday
## Short Story Collection

### Selected by Ali Smith

Polygon

Polygon
An imprint of Edinburgh University Press Ltd
22 George Square, Edinburgh

Typeset in Galliard by Hewer Text Ltd, Edinburgh,
and printed and bound in Great Britain by
Bell & Bain Ltd, Glasgow

A CIP record for this book is
available from the British Library

ISBN 0 7486 6287 1 (paperback)

The Publisher acknowledges subsidy from

towards the publication of this volume.

# CONTENTS

# Contents

# FOREWORD

What is it possible to achieve in the space of just 3000 words? In a good short story, the world. The short story is the most elastic, the most adaptable, and the most distilled and essential of forms. It is by nature both social and poetic: its one voice implies many others like its smallness implies all the other stories to be told; it is bound by limited space, and a good story always transcends its bounds. It can be all compression and suggestion, working spatially like poetry, and it can have all the plot and voice and drama and chronology and satisfaction of a novel. It will go straight to the emotions like music. Slight, compacted, multinuanced, it is intellectual and sentient at once, an invitation to the reader and the writer to concentrate, to sense the link between the momentary and the momentous. It will do all this in the space of a few pages.

This year the *Shorts* anthology is a little unusual. To celebrate ten years of the Macallan Scotland on Sunday competition, the winning stories from all the previous years since the competition began in 1991 – when Dilys Rose won with 'A Little Bit of Trust' – are republished here alongside this year's winner, the other five shortlisted stories and the best of the remaining year 2000 entries. This made my task of editing the book pretty tough in one sense; there were well over two thousand entries (the competition grows more popular every year) and usually the editor of *Shorts* can include twenty-four of the best stories from the final long list. I could only choose fourteen; I am still mourning some of the stories I haven't been able to include here. But it makes the collection itself a very interesting one, one which reads both synchronically and diachronically, to some extent giving a fuller picture of the development and direction of Scottish short fiction over the last decade as well as acting as a litmus paper for Scotland's first year after the restitution of the Parliament.

I had over a hundred stories to choose from. Many of them were dark, brooding pieces, in keeping with a black mood surfacing in fiction in Scotland (not unlike the bloody, disaffected anti-kailyard fiction by writers like J. MacDougall Hay and George Douglas Brown at the cusp of the last fin de siècle), in novels as various, as unlike each other, as Toni Davidson's *Scar Culture*, James Robertson's *The Fanatic*, A. L. Kennedy's *Everything You Need*, Michel Faber's *Under the Skin*, John Burnside's *The Mercy Boys* – I could carry on making this list right down the page. Many of the hundred or so stories this year were concerned with self-image; a surprising number of stories dealt with size, appearance, eating habits, greed, self-starvation. This is new. When I helped judge the competition in 1998 this subject was nowhere in sight, and though the winner that year, 'Life Drawing' by Linda Cracknell, was a story of self-image, it was calm and analytical, had none of the guilt or panicked frenzy that accompanied so many of these newer stories I've just read.

Regardless of this, the main thing I noticed in reading this year's stories, along with a very cheering variety of form, was vitality, a tremendous surge of energy. When I chose stories for this collection, I chose in favour of this energy. I notice now, reading the book in one go, that where the energy and that sense of darkness I mentioned earlier combine, it does make for some of the most gripping stories in this book, and where the vitality of voice meets the darkness on terms of sheer strength, or is willing to push at the boundary of form, experiment a little, the stories are extraordinary. As you'll see, the book starts and ends with something traditionally foul (in one case offal, in the other excrement) and what the stories concerned do with these subjects is astonishing, good-natured, transformative, even loving.

'Sheep's Heid and Tonsils' is the apt opener this year, a story that deals with new Scottish self-awareness with proper irreverence and wit. 'Snake House' is a good example of how well-controlled repression in a narrative will give the narrative its dimension. 'Formica (is a Horizontal Surface)' is full of good-hearted circumvention of the age-old divisions. 'Animals', a retelling of the myth of the Scottish split-self, is a work of close-studied craft, leashed violence. 'Dreaming Spires' is funny and energetic, cleverly manic in its version of academic pressure. 'Why You Should Not Put Your Hand Through The Ice' is totally alive as a piece of writing, capturing the alienation of childhood with a kind of grace. 'Life Drawing' won the competition in 1998 with the quiet assurance and the skill it takes to describe the effects of cataclysm well after it's happened. 'The Girl from Quebrada' describes the time before such cataclysm in a story about perfection told to perfection. 'Sleet and Snow' won in 1995. Haunting, beautifully told, it is a great example of how a whole world can be brought to fit the comparative slightness of a story. 'All That Glisters', which won in 1997, gives a different view of grief, expertly executed. The strange unworldly 'Fish' introduced a writer of originality and unusual psychological clarity when it won in 1996. 'When That's Done' examines the psychological from a very different and equally affecting perspective. 'My Father as an Ant' is a metaphor carried to achievement, and is unexpectedly moving. 'Sundays' also takes a familiar scene and remakes it, making it poignant all over again. 'The Neighbours' Return' won in 1999 by taking horror and history and making them unavoidably local.

'Giro Day', an enervating blend of despair and hope, was joint winner in 1992. 'The First of the Month' has an admirable confidence of voice. 'Losing Teeth' takes voice even further, with a style and immediacy that make it completely convincing. 'A Bit of the Map' is comforting and satisfying. 'The Refuge', almost a new kind of myth, is a story of unexpected comforts too. 'Gravity', poetic and stilled, is that rare skilled thing, a story whose texture tells its story. 'The Visit' was joint winner in 1992, a compelling slab of hurt. 'Dead of Winter' is an astute dirty-realist piece of darkness. 'A Little Bit of Trust', winner in 1991, intuits with a fine sense all the spoken and unspoken nuances of cross-culture. 'At the Edge of the Country' is almost comic about the chasms between people, placed right on the edge of understanding. 'Text for the Day' won in 1994 and still reads all right to me, thank God. 'Nessun Dorma' won in 1993 and is a triumph of a story, about everything – art, time, love, loss, this country, the music of what happens. 'Distances' is a beautifully realised, lightly held story about terrible resignation of spirit. And I guarantee that you will never be able to forget the final story in this book, 'The Gift'.

Ali Smith

# Sheep's Heid and Tonsils

## *George Anderson*

His name was Colin but abdy cried him Sheep's Heid McGlumpher.

Helluvanicefella.

That's how he made his roll, the boy. Sheep's heids. He used tae buy up aw the sheep's heids in the district. Fowk dinnae want them these days. Fowk are getting affa bluidy fancy if ye ask me. Willny even eat mince noo, scared o the BSE.

Call it something French and everyone would want it it.

Le Mince.

Le minçaise c'est sur le tatties.

Jocasta, come away in fur yer Boef Minçenaise.

Regard Moi. Regarde Le Française. Pas de Problem.

Oanywye, McGlumpher would sling hunners o sheep's heids into the hold of this old fishing boat he hud – *The Pride o Caerlaverock*. And away he'd sail to the Bewilderd Islands. Hunners o miles oot and bugger all to eat but fish and puffins.

By goad they used to welcome him like a king. A big ceremonial pan o soup, made wi the plumpest and most fetching sheep's heid. The natives ceilidhing into the night. Well as much as they could ceilidh. More of your Norse types than your Scots like. Mair o the swallying and moany coupons than the jiggin aboot ken.

It's the fish.

Faces oan them them like a bluidy haddock maist o the time.

Sheep's Heid made a packet running illegal ruminant nappers. He was the big hero to one and all in the Bewilderds, but the Government were aye oan his case. Sheep Heid's heids were not compliant with EC directive 134 on the size and shape of herbivore heids. Heids that hud no been properly graded were being moved through EC coastal waters. Threats were being made in Brussels. Even when he was at sea, he was haen his heid nipped by the Navy oan the wireless to 'stand to and display heids' or some such.

Ye wid think they had something better tae dae.

Sheep's Heid, as you might imagine, became well and truly scunnered with the whole mullarky. Then he happens to run across this Tonsils Thompson character. Blues singer. Pride o the Broomielaw Delta.

Moon River Thompson they used to call him. Wider than a mile. If it canna be nicked or turned into rhyming slang, then it's nae use tae him.

Used to sing in the pubs. That's when they started calling him Tonsils. Gave it loads. Invented new musical terms the boy. Know how that music has a bit at the toap tells you how to go furrit? Pianissamo, Fortissimo an that? Well Tonsils did it Con Laldy, Laldissimo. Take no Prisoners-issimo.

So Sheep's decided all that effort on the part of Tonsils could not go without fiscal reward in the longterm. Thenk you ferry mech, I'll huv a slice o that, thinks The Heid, an decides to foresake the mutton smuggling and get oan the case as Tonsils' manager. Bit he decided to make one last trip, and he reckoned if Tonsils came alang he would liven up the ceilidh wi a wee bit blues and a smattering of the rock and roll forbye.

Well I'm here tae tell you. It was a bluidy disaster aw roon.

Did Tonsils no 'finn his Celtic roots' oan the Bewilderds?

Heard some old bessom croaking away at some ancient Bewilderd dirge, aboot them being affa cheesed aff wi jist fish and puffins tae eat.

Does the boy no turn into some kind of ethnomusicologist?

'This is the real music that the rest o Scoatlin has lost,' sez the bold Thompson, who is now suffering delusions of adequacy big time. Suffering under the misconception that he is Erchie the original McPuddock of folklore himself. Him that never kent his Alexander Brothers fae his Runrig afore he set sail for the Bewilderds.

Noo of course when Tonsils tried this at his first gig back on the mainland, it wint ower like a cup of cold sick. Bit he worked away at it an afore ye know it, there was big turn oots at the concerts, and the boy wis playing festivals and bigger venues, and touring Canada and Australia and ither places where remarkably large numbers of people suddenly claimed Bewilderd ancestry, and lapped it all up.

The critics startit comin awa wi lines like: 'A puffin-fuelled troubadour unearthing the rich buried treasure of wur nation. . .'

An: 'Thompson's muse parallels the upsurge in our self-awareness as a proud and free nation. He sings a rerr haddy ballad as weel.'

Haddy ballads, that's what they started calling these un-ending bluidy dirges.

Wee bit lassies frae Perth and Bearsden began crooning away aboot how sair their backs were fae humphin haddy boxes. Greetin faced radicals found two or three numbers in the repertoire to their taste. There wis wan aboot the puffin riots of 1857, and anither about the fact that some fowk seemed to get bigger haddys than abdy else.

Haddy ballads with a feminist subtext were soon unearthed.

Meanwhile, back on the Bewilderds, it turns oot Tonsils has sparked aff a back tae wur roots movement. Fowk starts talking about the Culchural Hedge-i-munny they have been suffering from the mainland, makkin them ashamed of their ain wyes. Bedazzling them with the glamour o sheep's heids and ither decadence.

Some daft bit cooncillor, a portly party wi a hoose on the mainland anaw, got up at a meeting and said: 'Fish and puffins wis guid enough fir wur forebears and they should be guid enough for us.'

So was the sheep's heid trade cabbaged?

Does Dolly Parton sleep oan her back?

But Sheep's Heid saw anither dodge, an started exporting puffin eggs and wee strips o dried haddy to the mainland.

This went over big in the delicatessens of Stockbridge and Kelvinside. Supermarkets hud sun-dried puffin silvers in olive oil on the shelves before you could say Nick bluidy Nairn. And did the burger chains no even start offering puffin nuggets wi a wee foil thingumy of fish dip.

This cultural renaissance had quite an effect on the boy Thompson, who never sings oany of that 'American trash' oanymair.

He's cried Haddy Thompson noo.

Pity.

He used to do a rerr 'Long Tall Sally'.

# Snake House

## *Linda Anderson*

N ight adders lay on average twenty-six eggs, Mr Nwosu
tells his wife in a voice that annoys her.

On average, he says again.

Mrs Nwosu does not answer her husband, instead she waves
at the houseboy to sugar her husband's tea.

Mr Nwosu smiles. Of course nothing is ever average, he
says.

Her husband has taken to smiling when he believes himself
to be right. Mrs Nwosu believes he has aquired this habit at
the Clubhouse, where he spends too much time among the
Baturi.

Mrs Nwosu examines the contents of the table rather than
watch her husband dip the sweet bread into his overmilked,
oversugared tea. She does not normally breakfast with her
husband. Instead Mrs Nwosu prefers to breakfast alone after
her husband has left for his job at the Sugar Company.
Unfortunately, the baby snake chose to slither across the
bathroom floor at the precise time Mr Nwosu was having
his morning shower. Her husband had, of course, created a
terrible fuss, yelling repeatedly for the houseboy. When Mrs
Nwosu arrived, awakened by the noise, the tiny snake was
being persuaded into a glass jar for examination purposes. It
was staring out at her husband, looking, Mrs Nwosu thought,

a little hurt by its sudden imprisonment. For a moment Mrs Nwosu was almost sorry for it.

Mrs Nwosu transfers her gaze to the slatted vents of the louvred window where the hiss and swish of the hose suggest the gardener has finally arrived. Mrs Nwosu's attempts to wrestle a garden from this northern clay have had little success. Only the ugliest plants with no scent survive in this bush place. First it was the Harmattan wind with its choking dust; and now, and here a sigh escapes Mrs Nwosu's lips despite herself, now, it is the mud.

Her husband is waving away the houseboy's offer of more tea and has risen from the table. Her sigh has not gone unnoticed. Mr Nwosu is anxious to be away.

Before he goes, he tells her:

There will be more snakes. You must be careful. Night adders are a bit poisonous.

Two days and five snakes later, a group of workmen arrive (on her husband's orders) and start to machete down Mrs Nwosu's scentless zinneas, churning her flowerbeds into the same mud as the drive.

The workmen talk to the houseboy in Hausa and ignore Mrs Nwosu. They shout for water from the hose and proceed to mix concrete on her veranda and smear it into the cracks in the sides of the stone plinth on which the house sits.

Now, Mrs Nwosu thinks, there is nowhere else to go but up.

She measures the space between wooden section and sloping concrete floor with her eye and knows it is enough. Before the workmen leave, they force straggly tobacco plants into her mashed flowerbeds to ward off future snake infestations, confirming Mrs Nwosu's belief that all Hausa people are primitives.

Sitting on her chair on the veranda, Mrs Nwosu does not

watch the men ruin her garden, instead she concentrates on the easy sway of the lush elephant grass that circles the drive. In the distance she can see the permanent houses, dozens of concrete foundations splitting the green waves, exposing their white Baturi bellies to the sun, victims of the eternal 'cash-flow' problem.

Mrs Nwosu remembers how she only agreed to come to the bush on condition that she have a proper house with a garden and perhaps even a swimming pool. Mrs Nwosu thinks once again of the springy lawn of creeping grass, such as she has in her Lagos garden – dotted hibiscis, sweet oleander, graceful jacaranda – then she remembers she is now living in the bush in a temporary house with snakes under her floor.

Madam.

The houseboy's voice interrupts Mrs Nwosu's angry thoughts. She turns annoyed, noticing again that arm, the withered end of which hangs below the sleeve of the uniform khaki shirt she has made him wear. She had not wished to have this boy in the house, arguing that he could not do the work, but her husband had insisted. The boy had lost his arm in the sugar factory, he said. His boss thought it would be the right thing to do. Then let the Baturi employ the boy, she had said.

Well?

Another snake, Madam.

Mrs Nwosu follows the boy into the kitchen where snake number seven is cautiously emerging from under her cooker. This Hausa boy, she notices, is not frightened of snakes. Mrs Nwosu is surprised, even a little impressed by this. She has seen these bush people go mad when they see a snake, poisonous or otherwise, attacking them with sticks and stones.

The snake has paused on its journey across the floor. Mrs Nwosu thinks of killing it, stamping her foot on the annoying little head, detaching it from the body. Instead she fetches the kitchen shovel and allows it to slither on.

Mrs Nwosu tells the houseboy to throw it out the back in the banana trees and returns to her seat on the veranda wishing all her problems could be solved so easily.

That evening, Mrs Nwosu almost forgets the snake nest under her floor, drunk as she is on cold beer, listening to Lagos radio. She thinks of her husband at the Clubhouse, also drinking beer, no doubt telling any white man drunk enough to socialise with an Ibo all his bloody snake stories.

Later, lying inside the billowing cloud that is her mosquito net, Mrs Nwosu dreams she feels the house shift in its bed of clay, opening joints between wooden frame and stonework, passages through which other snakes will seek their freedom. The fan whirrs above her, filling the sails of her dreamboat, its timbers creaking and groaning as the swelling clay pushes them further and further apart.

Mrs Nwosu wakens early, to find her husband lying beside her. She reaches down and examines her thighs, trying to remember. It is then she notices how much like a snake her husband looks. It is remarkable. How did she not notice this before? Those eyes; the mottled skin. Mrs Nwosu reaches out and shudders as warm human flesh touches dry snakeskin. Rising swiftly she goes to the kitchen to order the houseboy to make some morning tea.

The houseboy is not in the kitchen; he is sitting in the back garden among the banana trees, the garden hose emptying into the red earth beside him. Mrs Nwosu watches from the kitchen window as he lifts the soap from the palm leaf and holds it under the running water. Now he is massaging the soap against his stomach with his one good hand and spreading the lather smoothly over his chest and neck, avoiding his head, where clay dye has already turned his black hair to copper. Mrs Nwosu is perturbed by these meticulous cleansing movements, believing as she has that all Hausa people are

8

dirty and lazy. Now it is his legs, one leg then the other, his soap hand pausing briefly between to circle his crotch.

Her houseboy, Mrs Nwosu acknowledges, is not a boy but a man. In fact her husband has already informed her the boy wishes to marry and is looking for a wife.

As if she could do anything about it!

The houseboy is standing now, lather dripping from his manhood. With a towel over his left shoulder, his body appears hard and black and whole.

If it were not for that arm, Mrs Nwosu thinks.

The houseboy has seen her at the window. For a moment their eyes meet, then he drops the towel and slips on the khaki shirt and shorts she has given him to wear.

Today is Saturday and it will rain again, perhaps for the last time. Mrs Nwosu welcomes the smell of home on the rising wind. Her husband has already left for the Clubhouse to drink with his Baturi friends. Mrs Nwosu wonders what he finds to talk about now that the snakes are gone.

The nest under the floor is empty. Her husband has killed twenty-four snakes. He does not know about the one his wife set free. Nor does he know that the last snake is in a pit dug by the houseboy under the largest banana tree. Mrs Nwosu has been feeding it scraps from the kitchen and on these it has grown fat and long, reminding Mrs Nwosu of what her husband has done to her.

The veranda is growing dark with the threat of rain. Mrs Nwosu calls to the houseboy to bring her a beer and settles down to think about what is happening in her belly. The houseboy's black skin glistens with the humid sweat of the rainy season. When he hands her the beer, Mrs Nwosu allows her fingers to touch his, pleased to find the skin warm and damp.

Mrs Nwosu sips her beer. Behind her the houseboy moves

9

through the house, bare feet padding across the concrete floors. Mrs Nwosu allows herself to imagine smaller feet padding across those floors and stops. No. The creeping grass around her Lagos bungalow would be a much better place for a child to play. And there is a nursery on nearby Bilboa Avenue, she reminds herself. She has heard it is very good, run of course by an Ibo woman. Mrs Nwosu imagines herself driving the child to the nursery, going shopping in the big Lagos stores and then perhaps for coffee to a friend's house.

The thought is pleasing.

On the other hand if she stays in the bush the child will have a Hausa woman as a nurse. The child would learn Hausa words. No. She will not have that. Just as she will not turn it into a Baturi, as her husband would wish, priding himself as he does on his British education.

Mrs Nwosu stands up and looks down at her gently swelling belly and silently promises the snake child it will go home.

The path to the permanent houses zigzags through tall drying elephant grass. Mrs Nwosu walks slowly, placing each foot with care. Above her the sky grows darker and around her the rustling wind is moving the grass like a restless ocean. In its voice Mrs Nwosu can hear the sea rush upon the Lagos shore.

The larger foundations were for the Baturi houses, but the Europeans have long since moved to better accommodation on the hill. Mrs Nwosu looks up at the tree-covered hill and for a moment imagines the shade and the cool breeze and that little stone swimming pool, built for the Baturi children; then she makes her way to plot number 33 and sits down under the neem tree that has grown up where her kitchen should be.

Even though she is waiting for him, Mrs Nwosu does not immediately see the houseboy approach, because of the waving grass and the darkening sky. He is carrying the Nido tin close to his chest with his good arm. Mrs Nwosu notices how straight he has become. How tall and straight.

The houseboy places the tin on the concrete and stands up waiting. Mrs Nwosu bends over and slowly opens the lid. The snake is curled and motionless inside. Mrs Nwosu reaches in and touches it and a ripple flows from her finger through the circle of green-brown skin.

The first drops of rain hit Mrs Nwosu's shoulders as she follows the houseboy back through the elephant grass. She smiles at its touch, knowing the next time she tastes rain, she will be home.

Two months later, the Baturi Manager comes to see Mrs Nwosu to offer his condolences on her husband's ghastly accident. He stands on the veranda, hat in hand, the tobacco plants waving behind him. He explains that the Company will of course arrange for her husband's body to be flown to Lagos should she wish. Mrs Nwosu declines his offer, explaining how much her husband liked the bush.

He would wish to be buried here, she tells the Baturi, under the banana trees.

The Baturi looks relieved. After all, the boxed body is already disturbing the workers by its pungent smell.

Behind the house, the houseboy enlarges the snakepit.

As it is Saturday morning, none of the Baturi can come to the funeral service, but they send a local pastor to read a few words over the grave. Mrs Nwosu doesn't mind, after all she and her husband were Christians. The houseboy brings his new wife to his Master's funeral. She is small and very black and, he tells Mrs Nwosu proudly, she is pregnant.

Mrs Nwosu returns to Lagos on the company plane and lives in her bungalow surrounded by a springy lawn of creeping grass. When Osita C. Nwosu is born, the Company increases her pension. The boy has pale skin and eyes that shine green in the sun.

Back in the bush, no one moves into the permanent houses, instead the bush reclaims itself. The shrinking clay of the dry season opens cracks in the concrete foundations wide enough for mating snakes.

The following wet season the houseboy returns to the neem tree. All that remains of the snake is a slither of papery skin clinging to the trunk. Sani removes the stake and watches as the snakeskin catches the breeze; then he takes out a knife and peels a twig from the neem tree to serve as a toothbrush for his newly born son.

# Formica (is a Horizontal Surface)

## *Iain Bahlaj*

B etty wants Formica, she tells Jimmy.
   'No that crappy plain crappy stuff. Ah want the guid
stuff, yi ken? Like aw blue? Thir's blue wans in here n thi look
awfy braw.'

She is sitting in the kitchen, shouting through to the
bathroom, and the *Bella* headline next to her Ikea catalogue
is asking her, *what is the secret of a successful relationship?*

Jimmy is in the bath and cares little about Formica or the
kitchen in general. Jimmy works as a labourer in spite of his
fifty-two years. The reasons for this are complex, but can,
through elimination of minor reasons, be reduced to the
irrefutable fact that Jimmy is, at least according to Betty, 'is
thick is' – something unpleasant – 'in the neck ih a boatle.'

When Betty mentions Formica to her friends she notices them
laughing. This is due to Jimmy's aforementioned stupidity,
and she has to remind her friends that:

'Jimmy'll no be daein it.'

(But he will be.)

'Ah hope no!' they say.

(But he is.)

Betty has a large circle of friends and this little vignette is
repeated whenever she has her kitchen catalogues laid out on

13

coffee tables, bus seats, park benches, a table at the bingo hall, and the canteen at the electronics factory she cleans thrice weekly, from five to seven.

Sometimes at work a new woman will ask 'Why kin yir husband no dae it?'

And Betty will say 'Jimmy! Yi're jokin!'

(But Jimmy *is* doing it.)

And then she'll have to tell the story about the chip-pan and the egg, and how the chip pan 'ver-near blew the whole place ti kingdom come.'

'Yi see, ih *tried* ti *boil* – n that's *his* word – an *egg* in the *chip-pan.*'

'Ah dunno *how* yi pit up wi um!'

Even Jimmy will wonder himself. Sometimes, casting his mind back to his youth, before their years together, he remembers various embarrassing incidents and, almost immediately after remembering these incidents, a horrified voice in his head will tell him that Betty, a face in the crowd from primary to secondary, '*must've* heard aboot it.'

That Betty must have known about the egging of the Protestants, but had forgiven him.

'Yi could've *killed* um,' his own father had said at the time. 'Yi could've killed um, whit yi wir daein? If yi're gonnae egg onybiddy, yi dinnae hard-*boil* it! The laddie's goat a lump oan ih's heid the size ih a golf baw!'

He can laugh now, though, Jimmy. He can laugh now because, looking back with hindsight, he realises that the witty answer, though meaningless at that time, would have been 'Well it least ah boiled it in a normal pan n no a chip-pan!'

(But the truth was, his mother had boiled it, asking him, 'Ir yi wantin mi ti cut yir moarnin egg up fir yi so yi'll git yir soadyirs in!)

His parents are dead now, he reflects, eating his sandwiches, sitting on his horizontal surface of breeze blocks, jeans caked in drying cement. But, like he always says, 'wan's oan thir wiy oot, n another oan the wiy in.'

He tells the story to his grandchildren, the ones on the way in, when they visit. He uses the Protestant with the golf-ball lump's real name, Davey, since he only lives next door and often laughs about the incident, telling Jimmy's grandchildren that he'll get his old adversary back *one* day. Jimmy's grandchildren find the story hilarious and laugh. *With* him, Jimmy tells himself, not *at* him.

(Betty says it's the other way round.)

Betty and Jimmy have one son and one daughter. They both moved away for better jobs. Betty always says that 'It least they tain ma brains n his looks.'

She often drops remarks regarding Jimmy's rugged good looks, comparing him to Clark Gable without the ears, and Jimmy good-naturedly tells her that she is the pretty one, after answering (and misquoting), 'Frankly, my dear, I don't give a fu–'

Betty envies his nonchalance, for like many women, she is concerned with her looks.

So when the grandchildren – girl and boy, both belonging to the daughter – arrive, Betty feels a sense of pride at having their offspring visit them, the antidote to the occasional long, lonely days with only *Bella*, *Woman's Own* and her kitchen catalogues for company.

Jimmy sits them on his knee and leans back in the chair. He gives them twenty-pence pieces as bribes for them to scratch his back. Sometimes they recoil in horror at a wart or liver spot and he tells them they are 'war wounds, fae where the Germans goat mi in the trenches.'

'You shut up!' Betty tells him. 'Yi're fillin thir heids fu ih nonsense.'

15

Jimmy smiles. He knows both his children received National Diplomas from the Technical College; he has their photographs 'wi they dolly hats', imprinted in his memory. He sometimes tells Betty that he 'must've done sumhin right.'

'What ir yi'se gonnae dae wi the hoose noo?' their son-in-law, a nice boy with a good job who's good with the children, asks. He works in the housing industry, as a quantity surveyor, and is often interested in both Jimmy's work and their plans for improving their own house.

'Formica this time,' Betty tells him. 'Ah want a new kitchen, startin wi the bunkers, n ah want thum wi this blue Formica wi wee black specks in it. Hiv yi seen it?'

'Ah hink ah ken what yi're meanin,' the son-in-law says.

'Aye, maw,' says the daughter, 'it's really braw.'

'Well if *he'd* git oaf ih's fat . . .'

She always censors herself due to the presence of the children. This sometimes makes her feel uneasy.

Jimmy feels no need. Jimmy will break wind loudly, asking the children, 'Where's the moose? Did youse hear that moose?'

He tells them he'll 'gie yis a tenner if yi fund it.'

'Well *he*,' Betty says, finding her thread again, 'bettir start daein mair aboot here, ih?'

'What?' Jimmy asks. 'Ah did the waw ootside, ah built half the bloody *garage*, what di yi want mi ti build nixt, the Taj Mahal? The, what's it called? Um, the, *metropolis*?'

'Well ah'll git somebiddy *else* ti dae it,' Betty tells him. 'N it's the *acropolis* ya dunce.'

'Nut, *ah'll* dae it, yi jist need ti tell mi aboot it! N you say pot-ay-to n ah say pot-ah-to so it's the metropolis!'

Their daughter, her husband and their grandchildren will laugh during these arguments, which always end in smiles directed in their direction and icy, but theatrical, glares passing between the couple.

'Your brain's gaun doon the tube!' Jimmy tells her.

'Well it's better thin *bein* wan!' Betty says, and she turns to smile, elated with her victory.

Betty knows that it takes Jimmy a long time to begin a job. This is due to what Betty and her friends from work and the bingo call 'the nag threshold.'

They've started keeping scores over how many nags each of their husbands need in order to 'mobilise thum intae daein sumhin bettir thin sittin aboot scratching thumsels.'

After three weeks Betty looks at her nag diary, a selection of tally marks which take her back, back to her children's SCIAF Black Babies cards. She has confided in her friends, by this time, that 'Jimmy will be daein it, cause the boy thit ah phoned' – she never – 'wantit too much money, n Jimmy's no *that* bad.'

'Ir yi sure?' they say.

She has nagged Jimmy almost eighty times. This includes episodes of nagging, during which the question, 'When ir yi gonnae dae it?', and the order, 'Wid *you* git yir tools oot n git it *done*,' are repeated constantly, mixed and matched, becoming a long, repetitive monologue.

(The rules are that the monologue counts for only one nag.)

Lately she is sensing some weakening in Jimmy's position, and she is right.

Jimmy has been looking at the kitchen. The bunkers are old, he tells his colleagues at work.

'Wi need new wans, this blue n black Formica.'

'Thought yi wir a Celtic fan?' they ask.

'Aye, hiv ti dae sumhin aboot that.'

But they know, and he knows, that he won't. He is looking forward to the job. A voice at the back of his mind is telling that he may not be quite as useless as he himself suspects.

'Did ah no built ma ain waw?' he asks himself in the van,

sitting up the back with the young apprentice, the bricklayers in the front. 'N the brickies ken ah could dae their joab.'

He knew they knew because, each Friday, they put in a ten- or twenty-pound note each, to build up his wages.

'Ah'll git startit it the weekend,' he tells Betty in bed. 'What kind wir yi watin?'

'Blue, wi wee black dots.'

'Well you git thum, ih?'

Betty is soon at the kitchen store, rubbing her hand over the soft smooth surfaces. She walks with her friend Maggie from work, and they look at a succession of young men.

Maggie mentions someone leaving their husband, someone in town. 'Would you ivir leave Jimmy?' she wants to know.

Betty strokes the Formica. 'Why, would you leave Frank?'

Maggie shrugs and blushes slightly.

'Ah dunno.'

'Ah dinnae hink ah'd leave Jimmy, naw! Ah mean, think ih whatsirname, wi a new man, hivin ti break um in!'

'Aye.'

'Ah mean,' Betty continues, 'yi hiv to go through the whole hing aboot no *fartin* in front ih um or no lettin um see yi wi a face like a *witch* or wi a *plook*.'

Maggie shakes her head. 'Nah, nut, couldnae go through aw that again.'

And later in a cafeteria in Asda's, Betty tells Maggie that 'Wi could've done a loat worse. Ah mean, ah look it ma Jimmy n, though ih kin be stupit, n sometimes ah could kill um fir the amoont ih time it takes fir sumhin ti git through ti um, ih's nivir been violent, or an alkie, or a thief. Ih's iy been hard-workin n that tae.'

'Aye,' Maggie says, 'same wi ma Frank.'

*Your Frank?* Betty laughs inside. *He's a dolebirds wis aywis last doon n first oot the pit.*

'Aye, that's right,' she tells Maggie, 'wi could've done a loat worse thin what wi goat. Wi've baith been abroad, saved up, bought oor hooses, n seen the world. N if ah could git ma kitchen bunkers down it'd be great.'

They both pick up their magazines. Maggie has *Bella* and Betty *Woman's Own*. They will swap these magazines, like always, at the weekend bingo.

One article in the current issue of *Woman's Own* concerns cancer and it strikes a chord with Betty. She thinks of the feeling of her own cancer eating away at her body, and the threat of the mastectomy still hanging over her.

It had taken Jimmy to convince her that time. He had to tell her that whether or not she had the mastectomy he'd stick by her. She only asked him once, in a sincere tone which demanded an answer other than 'Right, where's yir insurance premium ah'm gaun to Barbados' or 'Ah'll trade yi in fir wan ih they eighteen-year-auld blonde hings.'

They had been in the bedroom, Jimmy was almost sleeping. Jimmy himself had problems with blood pressure, but sometimes at nights he would seem anaemic, exhausted by another long, hard day.

Betty had said 'Jimmy, wid yi, if ah did hiv ti git it done, want ti leave, cause it'd be awright, like?'

Jimmy only looked confused and said, '*Ih?*'

Jimmy has his tools ready and can see the job in hand, now. He has a grinder, his measuring tape, his ruler. He sees himself as entering a private, spiritual, *male* world; and, as he begins the job, images of cave men enter into his mind for some reason unknown to him.

Betty has the same images. Man as hunter, provider, and woman as mother, nurturer. Like Betty is always saying, she could have done worse, and Jimmy always worked.

'It's no is if ih's that lazy, ah mean, ah hiv ti nag um fir ages, bit whit man di yi no hae ti nag? Thir hisnae been wan invented yit.'

She tells this to every female friend, adding, 'N mibbe it widnae be is much fun is that anyway.'

Now Betty has her Formica bunkers, and Jimmy can say 'That's the last; bloody things,' and throw a tool down in an imitation of rage. Betty will look at the latest job, the latest triumph, and will see it all as an affirmation of something. She even knows the word, having read it in her *Reader's Digest* magazine.

And the Formica is blue with black specks, and silver too. She runs her fingers over it and looks at Jimmy. Jimmy smiles.

'You're terrible.'

'Well, so!'

Jimmy even blushes a little; he always does.

Betty winks and Jimmy says 'Ah'll hae a shower first.'

Betty laughs to herself. Jimmy walks to the bathroom and she hears the water running.

'Wan hing aboot us,' Betty sometimes says to friends when they're joking about sex (after a visit to see The Centurions, say), 'me n Jimmy's love life, it hisnae failed.'

Jimmy himself will sit at work and eat his pieces, and smile at the marital problems of the bricklayers, expressed in explicit detail, telling himself 'Ah'm lucky.'

The Formica is ready, smooth, horizontal.

(The hut he built had a horizontal surface, and the suite he finally caved in and agreed to buy; the carpets were on a horizontal surface.)

Jimmy washes himself quickly, seeing his reflection in the silver tube of the power shower she asked him to buy seven years earlier.

(Which sprays on to the horizontal surface of the bath.)

Betty waits in the kitchen with a spoon ten inches away from her face, looking at her own reflection. She tells herself, 'Well, it's no that bad', and waits for Jimmy.

When the bathroom door is opened both feel the same youthful sense of excitement.

Both think the same word, see the same thing, their minds full of it, the fruits of their labour.

The, blue, black, specks of silver.

Formica.

(It's a horizontal surface.)

# Animals

## *Alan Bissett*

B illy gestures with his cigarette to the roadside, hisses: '*Rabbits!*'

The smoke fleeing his teeth, curling against the glass like little ships reaching the edge of the world. The angry tip of his fag waving. The doomy sound of tyres on tarmac, rolling me back home.

'Wee buggars are everywhere! Must be a factory roon here makin nuthin but bloody rabbits.' He slaps my arm. '*Ih?*'

I don't answer him.

The headlights sliding up and across a corps of furry bodies, still and regimented at the fringe of the dark. Their whiskers twitching, their glassy eyes reflecting the light back at us. They stand their ground, unafraid. Watching. Beyond the traffic-cones, which segregate us from the wildlife, I feel them seething, multiplying, unseen.

Up ahead, our father's funeral looms. Its back arched in a tunnel-shape lined with sickly sodium lights. At the other side: my home town. Billy's town. A place he wears like a scar. A place as familiar and unfamiliar to me as the face of an ape – that awful moment you recognise yourself in its ugliness.

'Goan,' Billy commands, suddenly possessed by the threat the rabbits pose. 'Try an count them.'

I give him the impression that I'm doing so, nodding my

head mutely, but he interrupts, his cackle dry as sticks catching fire: 'Too many, eh! Mair eh them than us!' His lashes blink against the oncoming lights – angelic, demonic – and the Sash tattoo on his hand SURE IT'S OLD AND IT IS BEAUTIFUL and in my stomach car-sickness lurches.

Billy leans over, his voice dropping as if there are creatures in the back, listening.

'Look like they're preparin an invasion or sumhin, eh? Staunin at the side eh the road like that? Ken, sometimes Ah imagine they take ower the world in the middle eh the night . . .'

We go over a bump. A hundred slugs pirouette in my gut. The rise and fall of his smoke-infused voice and the queue of rabbits which stretch into the fields which he has managed to make eerie, as I fumble for a cassette but it's too dark, I hunt, blind, inserting a tape of Orange march music with the volume up, terrifying myself.

Billy laughs a redneck bray. Another animal at the side of the road, bright, ghostly.

Gone.

I ask if he saw Dad before he died.

His face flashes spite like a struck match, then he shrugs, noncommittal. 'Naw. Never did like folk checkin up on him, eh?' Sarcasm curling in the smoke, and a memory stumbling through the corridors of my mind. Billy as a child, running from a belt which streamed from Dad's hand. A quick, crisp, clear image. Like a claw-mark on skin.

'So – *cough!* – ye working the now?'

He changes the subject awkwardly, the same way he used to dance at youth-club discos, jerky and nervous, as if tiny flares are being set off in his fingers, at his joints. 'Cos Ah kin get ye work here, likes.' Billy winks, the lashes flecked with kinship. '*Ken whit Ah'm sayin, ma man?*'

Outside the drunks replicate the rabbits' stares: glassy, fiendishly still. Dad's eyes.

I thank Billy for the offer, tell him there's teaching work where I'm based at the moment, hear him snort derisively, as if I've offered, begged, to tie his shoelaces for him. Smoke dancers unfurling between the hairs of his nose, blasted to bits in the danger-zone of his mouth. His front tooth, yellow, chipped. Billy not brushing right and Dad smacking him on the back of the head and the toothpaste gushing from his mouth, a white ribbon. His tooth hitting the tap. A tiny *chink!* of enamel on chromium.

'Teaching!' He seems to choke on the word. 'Ma wee brither's a *teacher*?'

Billy opens his funeral jacket to reveal a long, silver blade, hanging by a loop.

Ice blossoms on my skin.

'Whit d'ye hink eh that, ih?' he grins. 'Ye ever have tae use *that* in yer teachin?'

The passing headlights washing his shaved head, making the perspiration glisten and his face look pinched and sour, and I wonder if he still sees that girl from Denny Road, the one who used to wear braces, or if he can still bite into a lager-can with his incisors, or if he still does weights, or is it steroids now?

'Whit d'ye hink eh that, ma-brither-the-teacher? Ih?'

In the sullen dark, the knife glints like a giant tooth.

Something dead.

Something undead.

Somehow, I'd expected Dad's eyes to be open.

That web-work of veins, as if a spider had crawled from his cornea, scattering blood with its feet. The white balls revolving, looking for unpolished shoes, stray bits of lint, thoughtlessly left toys. The iris finding, focusing, sharpening. His corpse leaping to life, suddenly enraged and . . .

They're not open.

He isn't rising.

My fingers curl on the edge of the coffin.

And I'm stunned to find: how tamed he looks.

His girth creaking against the wooden sides. His ape-like arms, constricted. His thick legs, which used to stomp the living-room making the cartoons on TV flicker, still. His hair bursting from under his suit, giving him the look of a mountain bear dressed as a civil servant.

The church air growling, soft with death. The shadows of mourners at my back, lips making appropriate noises. But who'll really mourn this man? Friends at the bar, with empty shot-glasses lined and neglected as the children they've left in front of the television? I watch those memories of him, which have swarmed and proliferated like tiny, blind fish at the bottom of the ocean, still themselves, form this obscene whale.

A hollowness inside, where the love never really made a home.

Billy flitting restlessly from one side of the hall to the other.

I stand motionless over Dad's husk, pretending to mumble some last benediction.

Billy biting a piece of sandwich and putting it down and prowling and picking it up, and flicking his eyes like spittle at me, as if he's snarling at an insult I must be whispering in Dad's ear. About him. Surely, about him.

We were daft on nature programmes when we were bairns, me and Billy, loved them the way other kids loved superheroes, footballers. The pair of us jammed in front of the television, the sides of our thighs touching. Excited. Sooking ice-poles to the plastic as glimpses of Africa, Tunisia, Arctic tundras made the concrete scheme outside our window flat, dull: no sharks smashing from its surface, no tigers striding like death-angels on its plains. And turning. And staring at the camera for a heart-stopping second.

God knows how many times he hit us before we noticed the

pattern. Just like on TV. So much like on TV it deserved a narrator. The male home from hunting, displeased by his frolicking cubs. Prowling the room, resentment building in his shoulder-blades, staring at his pride playing there with scattered toys or drawing or singing:

Buy you a diamond ring, my friend,
If it'll make you feel all right.
I'll give you anything, my friend,
If it'll . . .

Then he'd pounce.

The shout itself like a fist from his mouth.

The thrash of limbs and noise and the room revolving, revolving, like a fish in a net and

The bare light-bulb. The filament thin and coloured like heaven.

Going out.

Billy switched the light on.

I was moving plastic farmyard animals in and out of a little stable in the dark, making peace between horse and tiger, making them cuddle, or lie side by side with their legs in the air, and Billy explained it: why Dad did what he did. He looked like he'd been storing it up, or thinking so deeply about it that it that the need to understand had started eating at him, corrupting his insides.

I gazed up at him, worshipful. The lamp spilled oily yellow across the walls, his naked face. He sat down on the bed. The cigarette fumes eddied and turned in the air like suffocating eels. He'd started smoking. That shocked me more than anything that had happened in our house.

'. . . family's nae different tae a pack eh dogs,' Billy was muttering. To me? To himself? Dark lines drawn beneath his eyes. His skin becoming sallow with responsibility, the red-pink of his cheeks undone. 'Like that pack that's always roamin near the chippie?' he said, 'Always fightin each other?'

I nodded. I didn't like those dogs. Thin and hungry and rippling with anger. The envious way they looked at you as you walked from the chippie with your grub.

'. . . must still have that in us fae when *we* used tae be animals, eh? Thae *instincts.*'

*Instincts.* The word sounded like *insect* and *stinks.* I thought it was a funny word. It made me think of a beetle with BO. I kept thinking about it, trying not to laugh, as Billy carried on explaining what it had to do with our dad.

'. . . like some faithers cannae control their instincts . . .'

I had to cover my mouth with my hand, squirming, attempting to look deadly serious.

'. . . the animal in them, ken? They see something smaller and they cannae help themsel. Mind when Ah gave ye a row for tying cans tae that dog's tail?'

I finally laughed out loud, picturing the stray clattering across the ash-park, running faster to escape the noise, its round, brown eyes filling with fear as we followed it, hurling sticks.

Billy had slapped me that night for picking on a defenceless animal.

Dad had slapped me, harder, for something I can't remember now.

Billy crouched there on the bed: thinking distantly about animals and *insect stinks.* His dark eyes lifted to a corner of the room, to a spider hanging bored and still. Its tiny, empty stomach sending tiny-empty-stomach sounds into the world.

Billy was smart. Billy was brave. Billy was my older brother. Whenever Dad went for the two of us, Billy would push me aside, away from the violence of the two of them. His teeth bared. His snarl defiant. He'd take a whipping, of course –

lashed like a cur into the corner – but he knew then, *always* knew, that he wouldn't be powerless forever.

His face, streaming, bright with fury, poked at the top of his spine.

'One day . . .' he whispered up at Dad through a mask of tears, snot. I peeked from behind the door, throat choked with crying. The air thick with their shouts. They retreated, growled at each other. Poised.

Billy's eyes became sleek and sinister, and he hissed, as if slowly mutating into a snake.

'. . . One day Ah'll be big enough tae hit back.'

Billy's huge hand on his wife's shoulder steers her towards me.

Her frame seems tiny as sticks beneath his palm, beneath the Presbyterian church, stuck there in the earth like a tombstone. I feel myself towering above her: a weird surge of power. She gazes up with a lost expression.

'Pleased to meet you,' I say.

'Aye,' she mutters. 'Same.'

'An this is ma eldest laddie!' Billy grins, prowling up and down the line of his family, tapping the boy on the shoulder and making him stand erect. 'Ye want tae meet yer uncle, ih? Ah used tae take care eh yer uncle when he wis your age!' I stand there, on show, not knowing what to say to the boy. His eyes shine at me with dim fury, a mistrust. 'Ye want tae say hello tae him, wee man. Ih?'

'*Say hello then, ya –*'

Billy cuffs him across the back of the head, and he recoils, like a puppy threatened with a cattle-prod. The boy growls, indistinguishable words, and Billy shrugs at me, for whatever reason. As if I understand. His family drifting towards the car, and his toddler lingering, and I watch him, his littleness. His hair is curly and yellow as a flowerhead. He's following a beetle on the pavement, torn between fascination and dislike, trying to decide if the tiny creature is a threat or not. He points it out to his father, who is ignoring him.

Then he stamps on it, laughing monstrously.

And Billy yabbering in a language I hardly understand. His wife and children crowding into the motor, staring, trapped. The fatigued look of sheep penned against the storm. I see faces like that at the school where I teach. Small kids. Brutalised. Lined silent and resentful along the radiators. Skin the colour of rain-clouds. That dazed, identical gaze that lolls in their eyes. I'm starting to develop a migraine. Billy showing me the tattoos spattering down his arms, his voice horse-loud. 'Got this wan done in Amsterdam! Some women ower there!' He checks to see that his wife isn't listening. 'Dae anythin ye want, man! An see this ULSTER SAYS NO? That's fae Londonderry on the Twelfth. Listen, if ye really want me tae get ye some work wi the boys . . .' His words swelling the veins at my temples, as I try to smile, nod, seem sympathetic, while realising, suddenly, like darkness raising, why Billy's face has been haunting me all day.

The inevitability of it chuckling quietly. Amazed I couldn't see those same, harsh features before.

I've forgiven Dad almost everything. Every hurt visited upon us before bedtime, every time we had to explain in school the red-shining stripes across our necks. I've even forgiven what the jury decided he didn't do to Mum.

But Billy. My hero big-brother. Almost too big for the car he's cramming into. Snarling. Raising his hand to the children that squirm and snivel in the back-seat then lowering it.

'See ye later, wee brither, eh? Watch oot for paper-cuts in that school! *An you! Don't you ever speak to me like that again*'

I can't forgive Dad that.

\*      \*      \*

On the drive home, my car-sickness returns. Paranoia itches in my fingers, locked on the steering wheel. The sky opens its mouth ahead, and my gaze roams the hedgerow, and myriad, rabbit eyes blink back, an identical army. Trained, prepared. Waiting for their day.

# Dreaming Spires

*Anne Bree*

H e sweeps round the corner, praying for a space near the exit. Leans out the window and grabs the cardboard ticket. No niceties. The first few times he parked here he smiled at the wee guy in his wooden shed and passed the time of day. But all he ever got was aye. Except for the time he gave old Mavis a lift to a Union meeting. It was afternoon. The lights were on and the street smelt different. Self-conscious, he greeted the wee guy in his wooden shed like a long-lost friend. Hullo! You still here? But all he got was I hope you realise we close at six. Made him feel a right berk. He has considered taking his custom elsewhere but there's nowhere else as handy for McLaren Campus.

He chucks the ticket on to the dashboard then thinks better of it. Sticks it in the top pocket of his sports jacket. He has the whole thing down to a fine art – in and out, £1 for an hour. One minute over costs another whole pound. Miserable bastard, actually, that wee guy in his wooden shed. Yes indeedie.

Mavis was amazed. I wouldn't dream of working on this campus if they didn't provide me with a place to park. Hmph. To be brutally frank she's not likely to get offered classes on McLaren Campus. Dear old Mavis who nods off whenever Mike introduces the economics of top-slicing or the exploitation of research opportunities. Look here, Andy, Mavis said. Would you like me to raise this as an issue with the Union? Ach what's the point? It's the price we pay for amalgamation. Sharing their name with plebs like us is one thing. Sharing their parking spaces is another.

Hah! shouted Mavis almost choking on her nicotine chewing gum. 'When two kingdoms are united the weaker is in greatest hazard of loss; whereas all the honour and advantage of what is done by both is attributed to the greater of the two.' Sometimes Mavis does your head in.

The Dean thought FITS would solve everything. Free Inter-campus Travel Scheme. He tried it once, to placate Mike. Had to get himself to St Jordan's before 8.15 for the privilege of chanking in a minibus all the way back across town. Mad. Couldn't even get a coffee in the College at that time in the morning. Didn't like buses anyway. Always felt as if people were staring in at him. Waiting to chuck bricks. Throw-back to his days in St John Ogilvy's when the entire First Eleven football team slid down under their seats and stayed flat on the floor till the bus crossed over the Craigdyke Road.

The front wheel digs into the dry socket of a puddle, bangs against a rock. Bloody hell. That'll be another trip to Kwikfit. Straddling the potholes he snakes out of the car clutching his acetates to his chest. Lifts one knee to stop them slithering like a deck of cards into the dust. Backsides the door shut and clicks the alarm. Checks his top pocket for the ticket as he hurdles the low metal fence and out into the traffic. Sorry. Yes I see you. What the. Thanks very much. And to you too. And into the empty foyer of the McLaren Tower.

Some building. Everything happens somewhere else. The other side of the block. Up twenty-two floors. In the basement. Wherever he's not. His own students materialise by five past the hour, butterflying through swing doors coatless, chattering to other people who turn away and disappear into the air. Framed colour portraits of staff members hang on the wall. Department of Leisure and Recreational Studies: Professor MacCracken, Dr Moulsworth, Mrs Black (Department Secretary), Anne McGuire, Jim Plunkett. He has never met any of these mystical beings. His portrait is not there. His name barely a dot on a computer print-out.

There is probably a staffroom, but where? Perhaps a pigeon-hole with his name somewhere, overflowing with handy hints for temporary/visiting lecturers. There may even be toilets but he holds on rather than ask. Who would he ask anyway? The phone on the wall downstairs: dial 4333 for janitor. Hey, Willie, guy down in C40 corridor wants the toilet. Naw, says he's a lecturer. O'Brien. Aye, from the College – I mean the new campus. What'll I tell him? Naw sorry, son. Try Café Marcellini. Over the road. Cappuccino's good in there too.

The University Staff Induction Day sounded OK but the brochure turned him right off: Famous Alumni, Energy-saving in the Workplace, The Role of Enterprise Training in a Competitive Business Environment, Coffee and a Chance to Chat.

Lower Ground Floor. Please Stand Clear. Lift Doors Closing. Going Up. Seventh Floor. Please Stand Clear. Lift Doors Opening, says his little electronic friend.

The day the lecture-room door was locked Helga, the German girl, went and found a key. Germans, eh? Today the door is wide and two students are slumped in place. Room hot already. He hangs his jacket over a chair, plugs in the overhead projector and fishes chalk from his trouser pocket. Cathy insists on putting it in a freezer-bag with a metal tie-top. I've never heard of a place that doesn't even supply chalk. Just leave it, Cathy. And was that you up till four o'clock in the morning again? Well who the hell did you think was in the kitchen all night – Jack the Ripper? Do all the other lecturers have to stay up half the night or is it just you? It's known as preparation. Pre–par–a–tion. That's how I keep the nice job that pays our mortgage, capisc'? Maybe you'd like to try paying it out of your commission at the Estella Garden Rip-off Beauty Counter. You're lucky I got the job in the first place, you silly cow. Well all I can say is you'd better get yourself organised before this baby comes. I'll be looking after it all day – I'm not prepared to be up half the night as well. Fine, don't worry, sweetheart – I'll make sure I start lactating in plenty of time.

He ticks the register. They're all in now. All except Martin Coombe and Mary MacIntyre. Anybody know anything about Martin? Hey! Wakey, wakey, all you happy Monday-morning people. Martin Coombe? Anybody seen him recently? This semester? Anybody know where he lives? Anybody know what course he's on? Anybody know what he looks like? Martin Coombe? Oh well. What about Mary MacIntyre?

The door opens. Mary MacIntyre. Raddled. Old thirty-five? Young forty? Very sorry I'm late, Andy. Roads bad. Sorry. Bloody nuisance.

He sifts through acetates. Right. Time flies. Exams next week. I hope you're all up to date with notes and hand-outs? What, Liam? Last week's? You too, Alistair? If I knew where the photocopier was I'd go right now. Will you, Helga? After class? Very kind. Thank you. If you two would turn up to tutorials you wouldn't have these problems. Well, I'm so sorry if the smooth administration of the Safeway staffing roster is being inconvenienced by the requirements of your University course. OK, Asda. Yes I know you need the money. We all have to live.

No, Annabel, the Scottish Historical Background section is not multiple choice. But it is worth 25 per cent of the overall mark, so you might spare a moment or two of your valuable time to read through the hand-outs I sat up half the night preparing for you. Or is that asking too much? Shit. Why did he have to be sarcastic to that poor wee thing? That's the first time she's spoken since she's been here. Have you listened to a word I've been saying, Alan? The exam's on Tuesday. A week tomorrow. Scrawls on the chalkboard: *Introduction to the Arts in Scotland I. Exam no. LRS / ISC.1(2002.479gst) Tuesday 7 May, 9.30–11.30. Room 12.47.*

Hey, have I not given you all this before? Pulls the revolving chalkboard round. I knew it. Still there: *Introduction to the Arts in Scotland* . . . Scrubs it out with screwed-up paper towel. Anyway, it's all in your handbook. Yes, Alan. The handbook you no doubt left in the pub on the first day of semester. Yup, Liam, 33 per cent is a pass. That is right, isn't it, Helga? 33 per cent? My God, you don't know you're born, you lot. Aargh! I'm beginning to sound like my old English teacher. Anyway you'd better all get the finger out. I don't want to have to sit marking resits on my Caribbean cruise. Ha ha. By the way, anyone thought about taking Introduction to the Arts in Scotland II next year? Helga? Good. Anyone else? Mary? Och well, time enough yet.

Right. Where were we? Today I'd like to take a quick shuftie at Scottish architecture. Closing blinds as he talks. Can you manage those lights for me, please, Mary. Switching on the projector. Now maybe you'll recognise some of these build-ings. Yes, indeedie. Here we have the very building in which we are sitting at this moment. McLaren Tower. Circa 1970 and already showing signs of mid-life crisis. Let us now compare and contrast this with a somewhat older University building. No, Andy, not Stirling – gies a break, mate. This is in fact Marischal College, Aberdeen. Built to withstand the test of time. Can we say the same of McLaren Tower?

A sound sidetracks him suddenly. Terrifying as the vixen retching in the night. Or his mother in the hospital. Sorry – can we have light, please, Mary. Boys at the back snuffle with annoyance and shift elbows. At the front wee Annabel Dunbar is phosphorescent. Sweating. One hand clawing at her mouth, the other at her hair. Head twitches, eyes stare. White spume round her lips. Oh God. Drugs? Stroke? What do I do? Am I allowed to touch her? His hands shake. Is she going puke on my good sports jacket? He wills her to get up and leave the room. Takes a half-step towards her as she convulses, falls forward, knocking over her desk. As if stabbed. Mary swooping, covers her body with his jacket. Dear God, is there blood?

Helga trafficwardens the others outside. Coffee? Yes. We have all had a fright. Poor Annabel. But nothing to worry about. One quarter of an hour only. All will be well. Thank you.

He drags himself between desks. Mary stay here with Annabel. I'll get help. Quick as I can. Action-Mans, slow-motion, through swing doors. In emergency use stairs. Plastic legs jerk down to lower ground floor. C40 corridor. Janitor's phone. 4333. Janitor's voice, crackling, idiotic. Who? Mr O'Brien? Hang on, please. On the other line. Bit of an emergency. Shouldn't take long. Why not pop round in person? See what we can do. Down to your left, first right then up a half flight of stairs. Can't miss us.

He runs now, panic oiling his limbs, singeing his bowels. Through swing doors, down corridors lined with empty tutorial rooms, to dead-end: stairways up and down. Choosing up he tries to take three at a time, misses the top step, knuckles the ground with both hands and is propelled head-first through a half-open door. Baffled sounds, dry greyness with a pool of light. A lecture theatre. High-raked students sniggering in the outer gloom. Down in the arena he rises bravely. Is impaled upon a projector-bulb, Times New Roman (24 points) bleeding across his creamy shirt. Sorry. Looking for the janitor. Very sorry. Shrinking from the light he spider-crabs along the wall feeling behind him for the door. A horse, a horse, my kingdom for a horse. Exit across landing. Annabel's face lolls lifeless in his head. Jesus Mary and Joseph help me, please.

Running downward now into another cul-de-sac. Painted brickwork. Bare concrete floor. *Fire Exit. Beware. These Doors Are Alarmed. Emergency Use Only.* Annabel Dunbar the emergency. He bursts the door open with hip and shoulder, crunching the contents of his right trouser pocket against the heavy metal bar. Explodes sideways into sudden daylight. Alarm bells scream then muffle as the door swings over. Haughty girls on the pavement opposite stare pitilessly. At him. The culprit. Like when Miss Murtagh caught him looking for his *Warlord Annual* in the cloakroom of St Patrick's Primary. Surely not stealing. Not Andrew O'Brien? His da hammered him that night. Ears really do ring.

Behind him the door blasts open again, ejecting a second sound-blast. At its vortex a tight-stuffed navy-blue uniform with walkie-talkie. Hey! You! Where d'you think you're off to then, my son? Been up to no good in there, eh? The haughty girls purse their lips. No no, you've got it wrong. I'm staff. O'Brien. It's an emergency. That'll be right. Staff identity card, sir? Carry it on you at all times as per regulations, eh sir? Yes. No. Sports jacket, probably. In classroom. Please can we . . . Classroom number, sir? Classroom number er . . . Oh God. Clutching at straws he feels in trouser pockets. Has been known to stuff his card . . . Pulls out car keys, screwed-up paper towel, and small polythene freezer bag with metal tie top containing something white, chalk-like . . .

By now the navy uniform is laughing uproariously. The haughty girls have turned away. Lost in basement! Wife wraps his chalk in a freezer poke! Lucky I didn't call the police! Oh dear God! Where do they get them from? His eyes sting with the need to kick the ignorant fat face to pulp. Runs instead. Machetes his way down the road, through students, passersby. Oh little Annabel. Mea culpa, mea culpa, mea maxima culpa. On and off pavements, dodging cars, drains, newspaper boards, dog-shit, lamp-posts, coffee ads. Round corner, over cobbles and along the metal rail beside the car park. His car park. His miserable wee guy in his wee wooden shed. His Volkswagen, heart-rendingly familiar. Jump in and drive off it beckons. Don't look back. But that way lies madness. Launches himself across the street. Back into the empty foyer. Back where he started.

Still no janitor. Lift refuses to come. He drags himself, dread-laden, sweat-laden, sweat-sliding, up seven flights. The door is open. Class slumped patiently. No body. No blood. No Annabel Dunbar. Mary soothes.

Annabel's fine. Epileptic seizure. Nothing to worry about, Andy. I used to be a nurse. Liam dialled 999 on his mobile. They popped her round the corner to Casualty just to be on the safe side. Not been taking her pills. Naughty girl.

Thanks, Mary. Liam. Everyone. Whew! Architecture. God. Only fifteen minutes left. Not worth many marks in the exam anyway. Whew! He collapses into a chair. Wipes his face with a paper towel. Hard, green, chalky. The janitor knocks and peers in. Mr O'Brien? Sorry I never got back to you. Ambulance came for a wee girlie who was having a fit and then my colleague Archie had to deal with a suspected break-in. Some nut-case set the alarm off in the basement. Now. What can we do for you, Mr O'Brien?

Five to eleven before the jannie goes off chuckling down the stairs. Where do they get them from, eh? Oh well. Haven't got much done today, eh? Never mind. Make up for it on Thursday. What about last week's notes? says Helga. But Liam and Alistair are off. On their mobiles already. Any plans for to-night? Naw. Been there done that. Pub mebbe. Working late. Well Ah goes to him whatdya mean no overtime an he's given it like that's no what you said yesterday. Party? Naw. Cannae be bothered. Bit of a slag. Their voices echo and spin down the stair-well. Don't worry, Andy, I'll give them their notes on Thursday, says Helga. Bloody don't deserve them, says Mary.

Hey, do you two fancy a coffee? He asks, suddenly daring. Feel I owe you one. Café Marcellini's supposed to be OK.

But Helga has preparation for her next class and Mary is going shopping. Her youngest's birthday on Wednesday. She walks with him to the lift.

Seventh Floor. Please Stand Clear. Lift Doors Closing. Going Down. Here, Andy. Chalk on your face. Oh. Thanks, Mary. Lower Ground Floor. Please stand Clear. Lift Doors Opening.

Hey, d'you want a lift anywhere, Mary? Car's just over there. Doesn't sound like a come-on, does it? You can't be too careful even with the older women. But no thanks. She's only going as far as Sauchiehall Street. Where d'you stay anyway? he asks. Oban. What? Don't tell me you travel from Oban every day? Na-aw. Drive down Monday morning, back up Friday afternoon. Stay with my sister in Maryhill during the week. Spend the weekend washing and cleaning. No rest for the wicked. Well, see you Thursday, Andy. You'll need to pray for us next week, by the way. We don't want resists either. Oh, and Andy – if I make it back next year I might just take your course.

What d'you mean make it back? Course you'll make it.

Well I dunno. Old man's been acting funny lately. My mum died at Christmas there. She wasn't strong but she was good with the kids. Och well, we live in hope.

Momentarily he contemplates going to Café Marcellini on his own. Or wandering down to Boots' to give Cathy a fright. Or even the Gallery of Modern Art. Well – research. When did he last look at a painting? But he's got photocopying to do before his one o'clock class and the College always has scones on a Monday.

He stalls the engine twice coaxing the Volkswagen out across the potholes. That'll be two quid says the guy in the wooden box. You're joking. It's just on the hour now. Look. Eleven on the dot. As per usual. Aye but you came early today. See. Ticket says 09.56. My hands is tied. D'you want a receipt by the way? I take it that's a no.

# Why You Should Not Put Your Hand Through The Ice

*Sophie Cooke*

Her voice is going like a kettle, faster and faster, higher and higher, a squawking song. I do not like her face when she does this. She is waving a spoon, bits of boiling hot soup are spattering off it as she screams.

Lucy yells back at her. She always does. 'Shut up!' Mum slaps her face with the back of the spoon. Bryony is crying with her eyes closed. Her face is slimy and sad. She always cries. Mum is busy shouting in Lucy's face. I slide backwards to the wall with gentle movements. Invisibly I slip from the room; I am a clever little crab, though turning the door handle seemed to take an age.

I can hear them howling from the other side of the door. I pick up my anorak from off the floor and creep out of the back door.

The sun is shining. I pass through the gap in the mossy dyke at the back of the garden and take the path up the hill. It is quite steep, which is good because you don't have to walk far to feel like you've come a long way. The house is quickly far below you – just a little roof in a little garden, grass and Mum's flowers.

She only grows them to dry them. She hangs them upside down and then when she's taken all the juice out of them she arranges them in wreaths and stuff and sells them at the craft fairs to her friends. 'Oh, Mary, you're so clever' they say, and look at me and Lucy and Bryony like we're lucky, arranged beside her.

I turn round and carry on up the path. There are sheep droppings and big stones in it, and short grass either side. I walk hard, getting hot inside my jacket and my head so I stop again. I take off my anorak and tie it round my waist. The glen is goldish green in the late sunshine; the trees down by the river look happy. That's where I used to go; I used to curl up between their roots and feel kind of safe. Now I am thirteen and I'm a good walker so I come up the hills instead. It makes you feel like a bird just flying away.

Up and up I go, over the heathery top. Now I can see the lochan on the other side; the wind is roughening up the surface and reeds are lilting at its edges. I smile. It's not far. I wade down through the heather rustling its bells at my passing.

The near edge of the lochan comes into view again from behind a great hump in the hill, and there's someone there. It is a boy wearing a camouflage jacket and standing with a fishing rod: it is Alan. Standing on a rock, he hasn't seen me yet. I stand still for a while, watching his back. He stands very still, like a tree. Then there is his arc of movement and the swish of the line slicing through the air as he casts, and then he is still again. I like Alan.

I want him to see me so I walk right on, into the side of his field of vision. He looks round. I stand still. We both just stand here, looking across at each other. My arms are down by my sides; my yellow hair is blowing across my face; I wish I didn't have my anorak tied round my waist. Do I look good? He does.

His face is round beneath crumpled reddish-brown hair, his camouflage jacket and his jeans are beautiful upon him. His Def Leppard T-shirt is flapping gently against his body as if it wants to stroke him. He is looking at me and his eyes are like they always are: like he's not a person but an old tree or a big rock and doesn't mind me being there at all.

After a while he grins at me. It is the greatest smile you ever saw. It is like the feeling of the sun on your eyes, nuzzling at your eyelashes, before you fully wake up, before it remembers who you are and you remember too. His smile is like that, something perfect. I turn my head and try to smile back and start walking on and away.

I wonder if he is looking at me as I tramp around the edge of the water. I sit down on a rocky bit. I tug a piece of heather out of the ground and pluck it.

Up here, you wouldn't know there was anywhere else. It is a secret cradle in the sky with just the lochan and its peaty bog, lush with pink and green mosses like cake rot. The wind blows and a buzzard flies. Rocks and water and sky.

Up here, I can feel the numbness. Why don't you cry? says Mum. Because I can't. Not that I say that; I just say nothing.

I glance through my hair and he is still there. A small figure fishing. I look back.

I like the water. One day I will go to the sea and climb in a boat and just sail away. Wide waves and no land in sight, just wind and gulls and jellyfish bobbing by. I'd come ashore and people wouldn't know me and they'd wonder who was I.

Sometimes Mum wonders if I'm her daughter. I've got no feelings, and those horrid little eyes. 'Stop looking at me like that!' she says. Other times, though, she knows exactly who I am. I am her clever little Nesspot and she loves me and I am so pretty. So, it's not all bad. I had better go home. My bum's going numb anyway.

I stand and look over at the fisherboy again. He's still there. I skirt quite widely around him and back up to the brow of the hill. I can feel him watching me for part of the way but I don't look round.

There it is again, the glen, laid out below me. I start down the path. Everything is beautiful and I feel sick. Closer and closer comes the house; lower and lower come I. And I am at the bottom again, with the hills struck up around me in a song that can sometimes go on too long. I like the hills but only because they end the glen if you climb over them. They hold you in and they let you out. If the world was flat you could always see out but would always look back.

I'm at the dyke, past it and crossing the garden. I stop and stand still by the corner of the house.

I can't hear anything from inside so I open the back door and climb the stairs. Lucy opens her bedroom door and comes to stand in the passage, facing me on my ascent. 'You always run away,' she says. She turns round and goes back into her room.

I go to the bathroom, pull down my jeans and sit on the loo. Mummy comes in. She has changed into a clean short-sleeved white shirt. She asks me very gently where I have been and I say 'up the hill'. She looks at me like I am a puppy caught with a sock in its mouth. Seeing as I dislike being with everyone else in the house so much, I needn't sleep in it tonight. Firmly but kindly done. She kisses my head and then she goes out and leaves the bathroom door open behind her.

I finish off and go downstairs. She is waiting. I go outside and she is right behind me all the way, overtaking in time to open the door of the stone shed for me. 'No supper,' she says, and kisses me again. 'Sleep tight.' She closes the door and puts the bolt through. It is still only six o'clock.

The sun is still streaming in through the window which faces out over the dyke. I sit down in the square of light with my back against the wall, head turned upwards to the warmth, back of my head resting on the sill of the window facing into the garden. I close my eyes.

There is a tapping at the sunny window pane. I open my eyes and squint at the person: it is Alan again. I am pleased to see him. I sit still, looking at him until he taps again and then I stand up and climb on to the sunny wooden workbench. Kneeling on it, I push open the tiny top part of the window. It only opens a few inches. I peer down at him through the gap.

He is standing in the field on the other side of the dyke and he gazes up at me without saying anything. The pause lengthens into a dare and so eventually I say 'Hi.' He grins right away. 'Hi, Vanessa,' he says. 'Are you all right?'

'Yes.'

He nods for some time.

'Why are you in the shed?'

I shrug. There's a pause. Then Alan says, 'I heard you got expelled from your boarding school.'

'Yes.'

I look over his shoulder and then back at him.

'I'm a vandal.'

He smiles.

'I defaced the pavilion.'

'What did you write?'

'Just pictures.'

We both look sideways. Then I say, 'They'd given me warnings and stuff.' Alan nods and looks up at my face again.

'Is that why you're in the shed?' I shake my head and don't say anything. I just watch the way his hair blazes in the evening sun, strands of it burning bright like metal wire in the bunsen flame. I seem to watch it for a long time but maybe it is just a few seconds.

'It's not padlocked. I could let you out.'

'No,' I say. 'No, I'm fine.'

He looks away.

I don't want him to go.

'I drew a whale.'

He looks back at me.

'It had eaten loads of people. They were all climbing out

through its skin and being sick on it.' It was a stupid thing to draw.

Alan laughs.

'You didn't paint it on the dinner hall.'

'They call it the refectory there.'

'Do they?'

I nod.

'Your sisters are still there?'

I nod. 'Back to the perfectory in September.'

He grins.

Then he stops smiling. He looks as if he wants to say something; you can see the words making it halfway up his throat and tumbling back.

'I hope you don't miss them,' is what he says.

He was avoiding my eyes but now he looks right at me. I don't react.

There is another small silence.

'I've got a fish for you.'

He holds up a trout. Light from the sky collects on its scales and runs off them.

'Hold your hand out,' he says. I think about it.

I draw back from the window and awkwardly angle my elbow through the gap so that my forearm is dangling out over the dyke. We look funny, my arm and the fish, hanging in the air, both out of place. Alan passes the fish into my hand and waits till I have closed my fingers before letting go. Slowly I reel my arm back in through the window and I look at the handsome trout for a second before laying it on the workbench beside me. I felt his hand touching mine. I look through the window and see him looking at me. Through the dirty glass, it seems that I am under a calm water looking up at him on the other side. He is looking a wee bit worried.

I straighten up so that my face is up at the gap once more

and he grins. Everything is all right. We are back in the same world.

'It's a nice fish,' I say.

'Thanks,' says Alan. 'Please can I let you out?'

'No.'

'Then can I come in?'

I shake my head. He just can't come in here, not really. He would drown in here.

His eyes are moving over my face. He raises his hand very slowly and I stay dead still as if there is a wasp on my nose. But he isn't going for my face at all. He lays his palm under a thick ribbon of my hair that has tumbled out the window. I look at it as he draws his fingers through it. I expect he can feel it in his hands but I can not feel him at all. My dead hair in his live fingers. Only when he reaches a tangle is there a quick jerk of feeling in my scalp.

'Ow.'

'Sorry.'

He is carefully teasing out the knot. He stops before he is finished, though, stops with his suntanned fingers still embroiled in me and looks straight ahead without moving. He is looking into the murky glass and then he looks up at me. At the inches of my face. He looks me in the eyes and he says:

'I really like you, Vanessa.'

I don't know what to do. I can't move and I can't speak, so I don't. I just stay very still and keep breathing. He is looking at me and I don't know how to answer. I don't know anything. I look down at his shoulder. His hand is still in my hair. The cloth of his jacket moves as he pulls his arm away and my hair flaps free again.

I look back at his face. We both stay very still: Alan standing in the field on the other side of the grey stones, me kneeling on the bench in the shed, my hand splayed against the wall and my feet over the edge behind me, hanging in the damp air.

The sun and the sky are behind him and he stands in the whole thing quite surely. He is like a boy, but, me, I am not like a girl.

'I'm sorry you can't come in,' I say. His gold-green eyes spark up and he looks at me gladly although he is not smiling.

'It's okay,' he says, shaking his head.

He stretches out his hand and presses the pad of his forefinger against the glass, watching it with a look of concentration as he runs it down the pane. He looks up again and smiles. I like it when he smiles. I try to smile back.

Anyway, I draw my face back from the window gap and he looks at me lurking there and I look sideways and he departs. He walks like a boy, a graceful lurch, with his fishing rod over his shoulder. I watch him go, a camouflage jacket and a rusty halo.

I turn round to face my shed. It is a little chilly so I pull out the tarpaulin and wrap myself in it like a sausage roll. It feels cold but it will warm up. I stand in it, looking out of the window. Alan is on his way down the road now.

I turn and look out of the other window, into the garden where Mum is stooping in a far-off flowerbed. She has a headscarf to keep her glossy dark hair off her face. She is very pretty, my mother. I love her. I watch her for ages, tending to her plants. Mary, Mary, quite contrary, how does your garden grow?

Lucy and Bryony move past the kitchen window. Mum goes inside; the sky darkens. I lie down on the workbench, all wrapped up but still a little shivery and glad I have got my anorak. I lie on the bench because the concrete floor is colder and not as good.

I have got the trout beside me, it is quite smelly but I like it. It is looking at me. I smile. I look out of the window at the stars. The dirty glass is like a skin of ice now, the water has frozen over and me and the fish are under it looking up at the sky. There is a hole in the ice where Alan ran his warm finger through it, a little line where the sky is blacker and the stars are brighter. Stars.

Sun comes nuzzling at my eyelashes, kiss kiss kiss you're lovely. I wake up. I sit up. My neck aches. I look away from the sun and out across the field where it was burning in the evening.

A leg under a blanket. Something close catches my eye, just below me, on the other side. Over the dyke, a human bundle has appeared like a mushroom in the night. Dark reddish-brown hair and closed eyelids, lips parted, breathing sleep. Cardboard under him and a blanket over the top, pulled up to his chin. How can you be there? Beautiful boy.

I like looking at him. Did he watch me sleeping under the ice when he came in the night? Did he see me through the hole his hand had made? Waiting beside me on the earth. I watch him as the shadow of my shed slowly shortens. It is rolling back towards me and soon the sun will be falling on his face.

The bolt clanks open and Mum is standing in the door in a blue cotton dress. She smiles. I sit still.

'I don't know why you insist on wrapping yourself in that filthy shroud,' she says, striding towards me and kissing me and taking the tarpaulin off my shoulders.

'Come inside and have a bath before breakfast.' She is close to me and smelling of green shampoo. She turns her back and moves towards the door.

I look again at the boy lying in the field and then I follow her.

Later I realised that I had forgotten all about the fish. It was a strangely awful thing to have done.

# Life Drawing

*Linda Cracknell*

I got the job without even taking my clothes off. It never occurred to me there'd be an interview. I imagined you'd get your kit off and give the whole staff a twirl, like a stage audition, them looking on with thumbs and forefingers on chins, clipboards even. And then they'd hold up score-cards, Eurovision-song-contest style.

I answered Trevor's questions.

– No, never done it before; there's a first time for everything!

– I guess it's just a job . . . and I quite like a college atmosphere. Reminds me of being at school.

– Actually I've never tried keeping still for that long. But I'm very patient, and I think a lot – won't get bored.

– I don't think I know anyone here, no.

And the bearded eyes studied me, not undressing me, but trying to see my motivation for a difficult job with crap money.

I have my reasons. Perhaps it was the wording of the ad, the small word 'life' that attracted me when the paper fell open on the public-library desk: 'Models wanted for life drawing. Male and female. £5 per hour.' And what I didn't tell Trevor: a job where I didn't need to speak. OK I'd be naked, there'd be people looking at me, but they wouldn't need to know me.

\*　　\*　　\*

'It's the *pose* you're after,' says Trevor to his class, 'forget light and shade, look at the angle of the arms, the twists here. Amazing what the body can do.' And he points at a part of me as if I'm not in it. I become a machine and that suits me fine.

To start with the students exist to me as a semicircular presence of boards, easels and paint-splattered jeans. I can tell without looking at their faces that they frown and purse their lips. The room is heavy with concentration. Theirs and mine. You just hear the scratch of pencil or charcoal, the shuffle of feet as Trevor approaches and they make way for his superior eye, his chat.

'How's it going?'

'So-so . . . I'm having a bit of trouble with x, y or z/I think x has gone a bit y.'

'OK. Try using marks like these . . .' and he's away, reshaping what they've done, imposing his view on their work. The students grunt, acquiesce, thank him.

And then it's the break and I un-rack myself. I go behind the screen to put on my robe. Can't bear the intimacy of putting clothes *on* in public! Then the hard part – to drink coffee, co-exist as a human in the same room as the students. They're happy to ignore me; they gather around each other's work, chat, bang in and out through the swing-door for loos, coffee, whatever.

When they go out there's a chance to find out what they see when they look at me; how they interpret me. I vary. In some drawings I look too thin, in some too muscular, in others fatter than I would like. Mostly I have no face. There are angles, form, the suggestion of the pattern on the drape behind, but no face. They cannot read me. Thank God. Five minutes shrink to seconds and we're called back by a clap of Trevor's hands. It's a relief to become a machine again.

The studio is quiet when I arrive each morning. Trevor's there, taking small gout-steps around the studio with his nose in a mug, the white beard collecting coffee droplets. His gut pushes against the fisherman's smock, the belly pockets bulging with pencils, paintbrushes, cigarettes.

'Ah, morning, supermodel,' he says when he sees me.

I have no name.

There's a different pose each day. Today it's the couch. It might sound comfy but how would you like it? One buttock clinging to the edge of the couch and the other in fresh air supported by an outstretched leg, the upper body thrust back on to cushions, arms folded above my head. I try to wear a relaxed expression on my face. God knows why.

If I look downwards along my body in this pose, I can see the parting effect of gravity on my breasts, the rise of a not so flat belly and the knee and ankle of the curled leg. The ankle looks so far away, it hardly belongs to me. The dome of ankle bone points at the ceiling. My strange ankle bones. 'Ankle and elbow joints like nipples,' he always said. He lies on his back on the old Indian rug we used to have, with my foot flat in the palm of his hand, as it dangles from my chair. Laughter throws him backwards. Regaining control, his head rises, the eyes return to the foot and its protruding ankle bone, and he shakes his head and smiles.

'Could you put your right foot back a bit?' A student's voice cuts into my thoughts. 'That's it.'

Sorry – that guy on the floor was distracting me. I wrote him a long letter actually. Six months after and I wasn't going to think of him anymore. I told him about my fresh start, told him he was a bastard for leaving me, but that I was going to be OK. I even put it in an envelope, then looked at it, wondering what to do with it. What was the address now? I left it inside my writing pad for a few days in the drawer, then I took it out and burnt it. That was my real new start. There's a small cough nearby and I realise my head is levering backwards, pulled by the tightening neck muscles. I empty my head, relax.

As the days go on, I become more aware of the students, look at them obliquely when they don't realise. I look at their drawings too, but only when they leave the room. You pick it up. I heard some students in the cafeteria complaining about one of the other models, who visited them all during the coffee breaks, squatting down, still naked, 'dangling all his bits on the floor'. They don't want intrusion either.

I don't know their names. I only learnt Nick's because of Trevor getting agitated with him.

'C'mon Nick, man, let's get the feeling for the form going. Fuck all the detail. Here, give me your pencil. B1? Use something softer for Christ's sake.' And after a few minutes I hear long lead lines being stroked on to Nick's paper. 'Get the feeling for the whole body.' Out of the corner of my eye, I see him hand the pencil to Nick. Then he goes on to the next student.

Despite the tuft of goatee, Nick looks young. He's tall and gangly, one of the few students who work standing up, cocking his head to appraise his work with one leg crossed over the other. He reminds me of a cricket.

I make a particular point of looking at Nick's drawing when he leaves the room. From a distance you can tell where Trevor's pencil has been: length and fluidity. The hard long line of the outstretched leg, the other knee foreshortened, curled on to a different plane, the weight of the upper body pressed back. All expressed with a few simple lines. Yes, the pose *felt* like that. I have to move closer to see Nick's work. I see what Trevor means. The faint lines of detail confuse the eye against the sheer spaces of the naked form. The strangest thing is that my face has features worked into it. The eyes stare directly at the viewer; the face is in pain. The forehead puckers; the lips are full and sour. Why was he drawing it? This was defeating the point of the exercise. And though my eyes stare back at me now, I know damn well I never looked in his direction once.

There's a slight shuffle behind me and Nick looks down at me, smiling and pulling at his goatee, the other hand folded on the elbow.

'It's a good pose,' he says.

I pause before I answer, making him wait, wanting to stay in control, give him access to less. 'Fancy swapping?'

And as he laughs, I move on to the next easel, pulling the robe tighter about me.

When I go back to the pose, I feel exposed.

The next day the studio welcomes me with the now familiar rush of turpentine and coffee up my nose. And a new pose. I'm to stand, holding the arms of a chair, leaning into it with my back to some of the class. Trevor says it'll be hard going, I can rest every half hour. I release my hair from its clip so it curtains my face as I stretch forward. The semi-circle of eyes clamp me, start their analysis. I make myself a machine again. The tilt of the upper body in space reminds me of diving. Just a little more forward motion and it would be a tumble towards the big studio window, with its release into a suburban cul-de-sac.

Windows. When the police came, they sat on the sofa, helmets in laps, and I sat on the moss-green velour armchair opposite. The armchair was arranged to give a view through the French windows on to the lawn. It was the first thing that came into my head when they told me; how am I going to mow the lawn? That was his job. The pull start has always been too difficult for me, too stiff.

Back at the studio window, a woman crosses the cul-de-sac with a shopping bag. She stalks down the hill. Even from here I can tell she's frowning, her body says it, with her coat whipping up around her legs in the wind.

My eyes drift to the car park immediately below. A man

leans into the passenger seat of a grey car. I can only see his back, but I know it's him; the greying hair shaved up the back of the neck and the wide beige shirt that I gave him two birthdays ago tucked into straight jeans. Suede boots. He backs out of the car carrying a box and kicks the door shut. I'm ready to rush down the stairs, shake him by the shoulders, scream at him, 'But I thought you were dead. They told me you were dead.' But as he turns towards the building, I see that the buttons are wrong. On the shirt. Dark rather than pale. And the face is too thin; too old; too unkind. My body prickles in fury – tricked again.

'Need a break, supermodel?' And although I'm aware that my arms are trembling and my neck in spasm, I think I'm still in the pose.

'No. I can hold it a bit longer.'

I pick out the dialogue between Trevor and Nick with relief.

'Better, Nick, better . . . much more feel for the overall form, a real sense of movement here. See if you can loosen it up even more. Try these sweeps here.'

During the break, I stretch my arms above my head, circle my head to free the shoulder muscles. I walk around the room to look at the drawings. The proportion of leg to arm has obviously been a problem. The drawings are mostly ugly and I resist the urge to laugh. Nick's drawing stops me. This time there's no face. The drawing is dynamic, more purposeful than the others. The lines are bold, smudged charcoal. He's captured something. The angle of the back and limbs, especially something about the head, suggests a pull upwards. The drawing conveys the pull of shock; a transition out of composure; the spirit in a tangle with the body. I look around the room for Nick but he's not here. How did he dare? I leave the studio for the toilet.

*     *     *

58

By lunchtime I've recovered and am in the cafeteria dropping bits of cress out of a sandwich into the *Daily Mail*.

'Mind if I join you?' Nick plonks himself down opposite me, a plate of sausages and chips in front of him, all goatee and sloping shoulders. His hands are petite on the knife and fork. He sees me looking.

'Concentration makes me hungry – it's my main meal; don't eat much at night.' He loads his fork and then his mouth with chips and ketchup, still chewing when he speaks. 'Trevor says life drawing's important because the naked body's the thing we all recognise most. We react to a live human presence.'

'Oh really.' I ignore the question mark in his voice.

'Yeah, like it's something really fundamental we're looking for? "To be naked is to be oneself, without disguise," said . . .' he looks around for inspiration and then smiles, '. . . some-one!'

'More mystical than a lump of middle-aged human flesh, then?'

'I just wondered how it felt for you, being the focus for all our learning, our . . . discipline. All of us trying to get the greatest insight into human life by studying you.'

I look at him steadily; I have to stake out some fundamental ground here, but he carries on.

'I guess when I look at you with a pencil in my hand I'm looking for what's going on underneath.'

'It's a job. I earn £5 an hour. And no one asks me difficult questions.'

Tomato ketchup slides off the fork in front of his mouth and drips on to the front of his check shirt. He wipes at it with a forefinger and sucks it.

'I guess it'll be a bit of extra for you – on top of your husband's salary?'

I nod, then catch my head. 'No!' Caught out by wanting to

forget again. I don't really have to explain, do I? We fall silent for a moment.

'Your drawings . . .' He looks up from his chips, perhaps happy to be drawn back to the subject. 'Well, maybe you should just be getting the mechanics right. You know, forget all this meaning of life stuff and, well, learn to draw?'

He doesn't respond. It's hard to tell if he even hears.

'What's your name anyway? I guess you're not really called "supermodel"?'

After lunch it's the same pose and there's no curtain of hair that can hide what my body seems to reveal. I am more naked than I've ever felt before. The scratch of each pencil illustrates my pain, outlines my anger. My hands grip the arms of the chair, force me through the minutes and hours to five o'clock.

I get dressed behind the screen. Slowly. I hear the studio empty, measured by the bang of the swing door with the rubber damper missing, the retreat of footsteps and voices up the corridor. I hear the studio fall quiet as the last one leaves.

His board on the easel is empty – he's taken the drawing down. But it doesn't take me long to find his portfolio, leaning against the wall behind where he works. I lay it flat on the floor, kneel down to undo the neatly tied ribbons and unfold the flaps. And there I am. I'm in date order, still acrid with the fixative spray they use to stop the charcoal smudging off. I lay each of the drawings flat on the floor and stand up to look at them. Two of them mock me, display my history to the spectator. Where could I end up? Perhaps framed at a posh exhibition or on the sitting-room wall for his friends and family to admire.

I'm careful with the others – replacing them, still in date order, re-tying the bows. Then I pick up the one with the face. My fingernails shiver on the chalk-feel of the surface. The paper is tough and strong, resistant between my hands. The tear goes diagonally, separating upper and lower torso. But it's not enough; the face still stares back at me. I tear again and again until the pieces are so small they cease to offend. The second drawing is easy: my arms flex confidently until there's a frayed pile at my feet. My hands are black and some of it is probably smeared on my face. I feel triumph and relief.

The swing door bangs, and Trevor is there, looking at me. Then he's standing next to me, looking at the floor by my feet. Without turning, he cups a hand over the top of my shoulder.

'Are you OK, supermodel?'

I feel the salt-heaviness rise at the back of my throat, and the novelty of tears on my face.

# The Girl from Quebrada

## Meaghan Delahunt

*To always be a beginner.* She hears the old man's voice as the boys circle around him, all limbs and angles as they look down into the gash of water. The boys nod. *Entiendo,* they say, even though some of them are too young, really, to understand. *There is the terror of the first time and the overcoming of the terror.* She hears the old man say this. Every day she follows the boys up Quebrada Street. She follows the spine of the street crooked and curving, up and up past the fat *gringas* with meringue faces; she runs past them; her thin legs scythe the fat rich air around them as she runs up and over the rise to where the road falls down to the cliffs. She watches the boys cross themselves three times, bow to the Virgin in the perspex case and wait for the moment to launch themselves into that space between the rocks and the water.

She is drawn to water and to the edges of things. And every day since she can remember she has stood and watched the divers. She watches her brother, the way his knees bend, the way his toes grip the rocks. Afterwards, she taunts him, telling him of her fearlessness, how she could jump in and the sea would save her, how the waves would surround her like a serape, the sea, her friend. She tells her mother and the man they call uncle, *he suffers from fear. Let me do it: the sea is my friend.* But they shake their heads because the divers of

63

Quebrada bring honour and money to the families, and who has ever heard of a girl diver from Quebrada? *It is too dangerous*, the new uncle says. *Stay away from there.*
  *But I can dive. I am a better swimmer.*
  *Stay away, do you hear your uncle?*
  *I hear my uncle.*

When she was younger, in her one good dress, white, with pink sleeves that puffed around her shoulders and a pink sash around the middle, she would wander the plaza of old Acapulco, and she would lean on the arms of tourists forking platters of food into their mouths, she would tug at their elbows and gaze up at them with her large brown eyes as she had been taught to do, and she would chant the two words of English that she knew: *mon-ee* she would say, tugging at them: *piz-za*. And some nights it would be food to share between her mother and her brother, and other nights it would be money. Sometimes there would be nothing. And on those nights her mother would scan the Plaza and send her over to the big tree and the men there, and Esmeralda would put out her hand and close her eyes and in a short while it would be over and her mother would keep watch from a distance and make sure that the men did not take her away too far or hurt her too much. And the things she learnt to do and the things they did to her she never spoke of. In those times by the large tree in the plaza, her eyes shut, the men falling on her like rocks, she kept the image of herself flying out over the Quebrada cliffs; she imagined the details: the crucifix flying around her neck, her smooth entry into the water. In this way she was the girl under the tree and the girl diver of Quebrada and she could endure anything.
  And with those memories of her hand soiled and her dress stuck to her legs, the money heavy in the pocket of her dress, she longed to turn on the uncle.

64

*I know dangerous*, she wanted to say. *And the sea is not dangerous.*

But her mother would slap her if she said that, because they were in a new life now with this uncle. They had hopes now, and this uncle knew nothing of a deserted plaza at night and no money and no food. He had rescued them from the selling of straw toys on the beach, and he was much taken with her young pretty mother. *He was a miracle, this uncle*, her mother often repeated *and they did not deserve him, forget the old days, those days were gone*, her mother said. Those days belonged to the pink and white dress that no longer fitted. *Those days were gone.*

But every time Esmeralda saw this man with her mother, the ways his eyes looked, she felt she could never be certain that those days were behind her.

When her brother Alfonso first joined the young *clavadistas*, she went to watch. From a distance, off the rocks at the bottom of Quebrada, she copied their movements. She practised and they thought she was playing. And they gradually became used to Alfonso's sister, darting like a small fish among them. Old Miguel, once the champion of Quebrada, now trained the squad. Old Miguel remembered the first time he saw that small silver streak in the water, a short distance from his divers. He had watched closely and marvelled at the fearlessness of the child, the expert twirling and somersaulting. He still remembered the shock he felt as the boys emerged from the water and dripped past him that day. The shock of seeing that the stranger in the water was not a boy.

Esmeralda had looked up at him shyly.

Impressed, he asked her how long she had been diving, invited her to stay, to sit with him, to watch the formal training, to listen. And that was how it all began, how she sat and she listened, how she was ready for that moment.

\*   \*   \*

At first he told her about the pain. She did not flinch. He told her how the dive was the flight and the most important part was the take-off. How, if you miscalculated then, the flight would end in disaster. Arms smashed, vertebrae snapped, blood pounding out of eardrums. The life of a cliff diver was beautiful and short, he said. To fly like that was painful, even a good dive was painful, but you got used to it, and the memory of flying was stronger than the memory of pain.

*Yes*, she nodded, her eyes shone.

Some divers were extraordinarily gifted, old Miguel told her, they could watch a person dive only once and imagine themselves curving through that dive and reproduce it. Imagination prepared their muscles and organs, as if they really *had* performed the dive themselves. And this was the key, he told her: *All good divers carry the dive inside, that thing of perfection which never leaves them, the dive which is always out there.*

She came to know and to trust this old man, Miguel, so different from the men in the plaza. He was revered around Quebrada. He had been a champion and was a trainer of champions. Even with arthritis in both hips and his strange rolling walk, he was still known as a champion. After all the fractures and dislocations, he moved only with difficulty, with sticks. He lived at the top of Quebrada Street with his wife Lucia. His wife still took in a little washing and sewing from the neighbourhood. It was said that clothes washed by Lucia were the whitest and the purest because her tears mixed with the washing: tears for each day she had seen her husband leave for the cliffs and for each day she feared that she would never see him again. Esmeralda came to look upon them as her real family. She came to love their old house on Quebrada Street. One wall of the balcony was painted bright pink, and along this wall hung yellow cages with green parrots. In her short life she had never felt such warmth or lived with such colour. Often they would sit together on the balcony, and they would tell her stories from the great time of diving in Acapulco in the thirties, when the American film star and her husband built the Hotel Mirador in full view of the diving platform, when the *gringos* would gawp and applaud and grasp their drinks and toss money and it meant something special then, to be a *clavadista*. Today, Miguel said, it was very different. The time of leaping off Quebrada to woo a girl were long gone. It was very professional now. They had the *clavadistas'* union to protect them; he even had a small pension. His only son had not become a diver. Instead he had a small business selling juice and tortillas. He had done well. *For there was no money in diving*, he told his son. *No money*, he said, *only exhilaration and death.*

Esmeralda nodded. *Entiendo*, she said.

Old Miguel had many theories about diving. *If you can eliminate fear from a diver's mind*, he told her, *then anything is possible.*

'I have no fear,' she turned to him one afternoon.

*But you are not a diver*, he said, testing her.

'But I could be. I want to be.'

*In a different time and place you could have been.* He shook his head sadly.

'Now is the time and place.' She surprised herself with the words.

He looked at her small, determined face. She helped him to stand, and he eased past her with his sticks. *Very well*, he said. *Tomorrow morning at six. Do not be late. A diver cannot afford to misjudge time.*

'I will not be late,' she said, suddenly fearful that the thing she had always wanted was finally coming to meet her.

\*       \*       \*

In the *zocalo*, in the blue and gold church of Our Lady of Solitude, Miguel often saw the Virgin in the candle flames. On the morning of Esmeralda's first day of training, the Virgin appeared to him and he tried to read her expression. It was a sad expression, he decided, and she seemed to cling to the child in her arms more tightly. He crossed himself three times and blessed all that was in that day and walked out into the early sunshine.

He could see Esmeralda practising handstands and cartwheels along the pavement of Costera, dressed in a singlet and shorts, a cap on her head. He saw her thin child's legs scissor the sweep of Acapulco Bay and she looked just like any other boy-child, not like a girl at all, and maybe it was then, he reflected later, maybe it was then he first formed his plan.

In the beginning, they trained around the rocks and off the pier at Playa Calleta, a small beach away from the centre. The sea was calm here, good for beginners, and the waves washed gently up into a small channel, a miniature Quebrada, but without the risk. Miguel instructed her how to dive from a seated, from a kneeling and from a crouching position, pushing off from the rocks, keeping the arms overhead, tucking in her chin on impact, closing and then opening the eyes quickly underwater. Her eyes stung on the days when the pollution was great. He gave her exercises to strengthen her abdomen and her back muscles.

After one month, Miguel took her to the top of the Quebrada cliffs and told her to climb down to the small channel where the divers entered. He told her to float in the small space, nine feet deep, to feel the rhythm of the waves, to know it like the rhythm of blood in her veins, to put her head underwater with her eyes open, to observe where the rocks were, to memorise them. *To know the end point was to know the beginning*, he said. He told her to swim down and touch the bottom with her hands and then to come up without arching her back too much. Again and again he made her practise this movement.

It seemed strange, she thought, that diving, unlike life, had to be learnt backwards. In knowing the end of the dive, really experiencing it, you conquered fear. You knew what to expect. She thought of her nights in the Plaza, the fears that had never left her; how she longed to conquer such fears.

After the early morning lessons with Esmeralda, Miguel would arrive home to sit with Lucia, his *café de ollo* bubbling on the stove and he would shake his head. *To think*, he would say sadly, *at the end of my days, I train the best diver and the best diver is a girl.*

It is not the end of your days Miguel, said Lucia, Drink your coffee now, and rest awhile.

*Was it possible to train like this for nothing?* A plan had been forming but when he eventually confided his plan to Lucia, she was angry.

Why train Esmeralda for a life that could not be hers? she said. What was the point?

*The point?* Miguel put down his coffee cup. *Before the lessons,* he said, *she had only the memories of the Plaza, of a flint-eyed mother and uncles who could leave at any moment.*

And what has she now? Lucia challenged him.

*She has flight and the dream of flight.*

And Lucia moved over to him then, embraced him, kissed her old husband on the forehead.

You are a good man, she said, a good person.

After some months of training, he puts his plan to Esmeralda.

Yes, she says. Cartwheeling with delight. It is a wonderful plan. The dream of my life.

As the time draws closer Miguel starts to worry. Esmeralda has suddenly grown taller. Her body is changing. Miguel feels that he is racing against nature. But Lucia has an idea. From the market she buys swathes of heavy stretch fabric, waterproof lycra. For a week, Miguel hears the whirring of her sewing machine. Next to her machine he sees a faded brochure, from the days of the Hotel Mirador, full of old photographs of men in costume flying through the air.

Gradually, as the months slide by, Esmeralda progresses up the back of the Quebrada cliffs. Her first big dive, from twenty feet, is not good. She is too eager, takes off too soon, contracts her abdomen too late.

When Miguel sees her small thin arm surrender out of the water he smiles to himself. He knows that she will never dive so badly again, that she will never forget the first time, the time of the beginner.

*You came up well,* he encouraged her. *Next time it will be better.*

Forgive me, she said. I forgot everything, and she felt her body ache with tears.

*The ache passes but the lessons remain,* he said gently, as he put a towel around her.

It is December. The evening of the Festival of Guadalupe. The young divers walk in procession down the terraces. Esmeralda's brother holds a flaming torch. She walks down the terraces past the tourists, past men she recognises from the time before she was a diver. She recognises the faces of these *family men* who come year after year to Acapulco and prowl the Plaza when their families are asleep. She shivers at the sight of these men although the night is warm. She sees the tourists pointing at the costumes. For Miguel's young divers are dressed in old-style swimsuits from the 1930s – box-legged, fully covering their torsos, like in the grand days of the Hotel Mirador. They wear red caps. Esmeralda is the smallest diver.

Just that morning, Lucia had cropped her hair close to her head. Underneath the red bathing cap, her scalp itches. Her small breasts chafe against the material. In the costume, she is indistinguishable from the other boys. Even her mother, standing alone, does not recognise her. After much argument earlier in the evening, Miguel persuades his squad. Esmeralda will dive from a height of thirty feet, the lowest height. For display only, not in competition. Reluctantly, they agree.

The older boys are to dive from the highest point. *One hundred and twenty feet.* The best will be chosen to train with the professional *clavadistas* the following season.

The divers swim across the channel, they climb up Quebrada in their red costumes, their gold crucifixes swaying. They bow their heads and pray to the statue of the Virgin in the perspex case. Then the younger divers move carefully down the cliff and take up position. But Esmeralda does not move. She stays standing behind the statue of Guadalupe. The boys shrug. At the last moment, they believe her to be afraid, as they always hoped she would be.

From the terraces below Miguel feels uneasy. Why is Esmeralda not taking up position? Miguel had seen a vision of the Virgin that morning, but her expression revealed nothing. At home, Lucia also feels uneasy. Her knuckles ache and she weeps into her washing and the remnants of the red costume material.

Esmeralda's brother dives last. He is halfway out of the water, triumphant, when something makes him look back up. When he sees her at the top of Quebrada, knees slightly bent in preparation, he signals, shouts up to her, *No, No, imposible!* His arms thrash the water. The crowd looks up.

She stands a long time. She prays for the sea to surround her like a serape, the sea, her friend. She times the waves in her head, reaching inside for the idea of the dive, that thing of perfection, the dive which is always out there.

She prays to the Virgin of Guadalupe to grant her a good flight, the best flight of her life, the flight that the rest of her life must follow.

# Sleet and Snow

## *Chris Dolan*

S he sat on the bed, and he knelt in front of her. He took
her right foot in his hands, which were big enough to go
right round her from ankle to toe, and he pulled like billy-o.
The boots weren't that tight, but his arms ached. He had no
strength left in his grip. It always took him by surprise, this
powerlessness. His arms didn't *feel* weak on a day-to-day basis.
Only when he had to pull at something – like the heavy
saucepan from the bottom of the cupboard, or the loo door
when the carpet rode up and stuck it – then they felt like they
were half-empty. Like his veins were too big for the dregs of
blood that sloshed around inside them.

– What's with the tight shoes anyway, Missus? Trying to
make your feet look thin?

– I've squeezed and squashed every bit of myself half me
life. Why stop wi' me feet?

He used to like that – seeing all that soft flesh crammed into
hard, tight clothes, like a spongy cushion stuffed into a leather
cover. Breasts siphoned into boned bras, buttocks jacked up into
ribbed pants, stomach squeezed into girdles. Then looking
forward to it all springing back into life again at the end of the
day. Now her getting dressed served the opposite purpose – to
make it look as if there was some flesh left beneath the clothes.
That, and to cover up the pain. She had more pain than flesh now.

73

Their lives had become very physical in their old age. All this helping each other on and off with shoes and jerseys, rubbing on ointments, clutching each other on stairs:

– Can't seem to keep our hands off each other these days. Missus.

They both wore the same kinds of clothes, now. Slip-on jerseys and trousers with elastic waists that didn't require the use of strong fingers. She'd laugh and tell him:

– No point in you getting kinky all of a sudden and trying on all my clothes. We're unisex now.

She pulled off the whole geriatric show much better than he could. A dab of lipstick, a water-colour rinse, taking the supporting arm like it was a lady's prerogative and not the result of aching bones. All her life she had been the independent one, doing her own thing whenever it came up her hump. Now she was the lady who expected to be waited upon.

She'd got into his taxi one day outside Central Station wearing a skirt and cardigan and slippers when the snow was piled 6 inches high.

– Where to?

– Eh, Dennistoun. I think.

– Couldn't be a bit more specific, could you?

– Dumbarton Road.

– Dumbarton Road's not in Dennistoun.

– Is there a Dennistoun Road in Dumbarton, then?

– Came out for your ciggies and forgot where you live, did you?

She looked at him for a minute, then threw her head back, laughing.

– And I don't even smoke.

She was English. Chubbier, taller than most women he knew; her hair different. Not blonde, not brunette. Honey, she would tell him later. Honey in some lights, strawberry blonde in others. This was just after the war when you couldn't get a decent pot of jam. Strawberry and honey sounded very tempting.

– So what do we do now then, Missus?

– How do you know me name? And she started laughing again.

It stuck for the rest of their lives. He still called her Missus. Fifty years later there was still something of the stranger about her. Just some missus that stepped off a train into his cab.

When her wheezy laugh had run out of steam – he could have sworn blind it was a smokers' laugh – she didn't open the door to get out, or give him any new instructions, but just sat there, like she was in the living room of her own house. He felt like he was being cheeky, bringing up the subject of where to go.

– That's what they told me. Dumbarton Road, Dennistoun. Or t'other way round.

She stated it like the problem was his.

– Who did?

– These friends of mine.

– Close, are they?

That laughter again, filling up the taxi like a window had been left open.

– They'd bloody better live there. I've been sending their Christmas cards there for ten years.

The row of cabs behind him started blasting their horns. He turned on the engine and moved the car slowly through a red light round the corner. There was something in that decision. Why not just tell her to stop wasting his time? Why go out of his way for a woman who didn't even know where she was going?

The boots finally removed, pyjamas and dressing gown on, she went off out to the loo. He quickly grabbed a handful of tissues to wipe his crotch and the tops of his legs. He'd had a bit of bleeding for a few days now and didn't want her to know. For a start she'd worry her head off. And anyway, he'd already had one operation down there and had no intention of having another. He stuffed the hankies smeared with blood into his pyjama pocket. She came back in and sat in front of the mirror to comb her hair like she'd done every night for the last forty-five years.

– You'll comb that hair out. He used to tell her.

– On the contrary. Combing preserves the hair. You're the one that'll be bald before you're fifty.

Turned out she was wrong. His hair was thicker than hers. But his was grey, and had been since well before fifty. Somehow the combing had helped her keep her colour, though. She wasn't exactly strawberry blonde anymore, but she wasn't grey either. The honey had turned to syrup – a bright thin silvery sheen that perfectly coated the shape of her head, the way their sons' hair did when they were about a year old. She used the brush they had bought for Simon, the first one, forty-six years ago, with soft bristles that straightened the single layer of hair without scratching the skull. Nowadays, all it took was one sweep of the brush over the head, and her hair was sorted. But she did it over and over again, as if her hair was still thick.

He'd never expected to see her old. Every morning in life, he'd gone off in his cab fully expecting her to be gone by the time he got back. She walked into his life in cardigan and slippers and might just as easily walk out of it.

– You just went into the station and got on the first train? He had turned round in the driver's seat to talk to her.

– Don't be daft. The first train out would've taken me straight back to Chorley. I'd just got off the bus from there. Anyway, Glasgow seemed just right. All those nice Scottish people. And then there was Molly and Jim.

– Dumbarton Road, Dennistoun?

– Or t'other way round.

76

– Molly and Jim what?

– Macdonald. Think you can find them?

– You must be joking. Everyone here's called Molly and Jim Macdonald.

– So what now?

He knew it should really have been him asking *her* that. He suggested a hotel, but she'd barely enough money on her for the hire out to Dennistoun. He suggested she go to the police and try and locate the Macdonalds, but she didn't like that idea at all. He wondered if she was on the run.

– Yeh. The Great Escape.

– Who from?

– Me old man. I didn't mean to like. I just upped and offed, before he got home. I was sitting down to do my Christmas cards . . .

– In January?

– Better late than never.

For the next forty years they made a point of sending out their Christmas cards in January, as a kind of celebration. Some years it got even later. She thought you couldn't send out cards until there was snow – it was really the snow she was celebrating. Once, their cards didn't go out until the end of February. This year, she hadn't worked up the energy for it at all yet. It was nearly March now. He had written, addressed and stamped the cards back in December, and was still waiting for her to post them. The fact that she hadn't, worried him. Maybe this was it. The signal. He would find her one of these days hobbling out the door in her slippers and elasticated trousers. He bought her a Damart body stocking, just in case. Not that he wanted her to go, but he didn't want her catching her death either.

In the taxi cab, she'd laid her head back against the window and closed her eyes.

– I'd had enough.

– Of what?

– Don't know rightly. Albert's a gent. Nothing he wouldn't do for me. Works hard, and buys me everything I want. Bought me one of those new Hoovers. First house in the street to have one. Works a treat too. But this morning I took the Hoover and hawked it round the neighbours. Got enough for the bus to Preston, and a ticket to here.

He could see poor Albert getting in from work, finding his wife and Hoover gone. Maybe he never found out she sold it, imagined his wife and Hoover rambling round the country together, leaving him alone in an empty house with dirty carpets.

He never bought her a Hoover. Not even when they became vacuum cleaners and everybody had one. They beat their carpets, hung them out the back, like in the old days. The boys never noticed, until they got married. Then their wives made them see that a house without a proper carpet cleaner is not a home. The girls didn't like their mother-in-law. Thought she neglected her motherly duties. In a way, it kind of kept the family together. The four wives, who had nothing else in common, ganged up, meeting regularly to discuss her shortcomings and how to make up for her to their menfolk. She never noticed. She wasn't what you'd call a woman's woman. It was only when Eddie, their second, split up with his wife that she took the slightest notice of any of her daughters-in-law. She sent her a letter with her birthday card every year, and another with the Christmas card.

He'd started up the engine.

– Where are we going?

– I'll see you all right for the night, at least.

She started to open the door as the car moved off.

– You've got it wrong, mister. I'm not in the market for hows-yer-father.

He stamped on the accelerator, pissed off at that and

thought if she wants to jump, let her. But she closed the door again.

– I'm taking you to my sister's. She'll put you up. But you'll have to give her a sob story. Tell her your old man was thumping you or something. She likes a sad story, does Meg.

Meg died twenty-two years ago last June, and it was almost a relief. She'd been coming round to their house at least twice a week for over twenty-five years, just to make sure he wasn't thumping her. If Missus strained her ankle or whatever, Meg'd ask for all the details. If she jabbed herself on a thorn when she was out in the back doing the rose bushes, Meg looked in the sink and the cutlery drawer for a fork or a skewer with dried blood on it. Whenever he got fed up with it he'd shout a bit. Not at Meg, at her. Then she'd remind him the whole cock-and-bull story about her being bashed up was his idea in the first place.

The brushing routine finished, he helped her off with her dressing gown and into bed. He pulled the duvet back and held her hand to help her balance as she moved first one leg, then the other, on to the bed, and sunk her frail body slowly down on to the sheet. Now they would talk, like they always did.

He'd tried his best never to let their lives get into routines, but with hindsight he had to admit they were riddled with them. Like talking before going to sleep. Every night since they were married, she would ask him about all the places he had been that day, and he would recount his tales, like an explorer back from the North Pole. He told her about the corners of the city he had poked about in in his little black cab, reeling off destinations like a Willy Nelson song: Ruchazie, Arden, Whitecraigs, Shettleston.

Until not so long back, the talking came after sex. Even in their seventies, they had managed a regular session. But it had eventually become a strain on their memories – each of them making love to the bodies they used to have – and on their tired limbs. She never said anything, but he realised how painful any kind of movement was becoming for her. Her moaning began to sound different. He stopped hearing the grunts of pleasure and the slap of spare flesh, and heard instead the scrape and whine of bone and pain. Anyway, his op had put paid to any inclinations in that direction.

So now they just lay side by side, in a way that, if anyone had come in the room, it would have looked like they had just been doing it. She stroked the hair on his chest, as she had always done, and he told her about the day's adventures. Not cabbying any more, of course. He had to retire at 65. But he still drove, taking the grandkids here and there, or just driving around. He sought out streets he had never been hired to go to. He thought if he kept on driving, he might stop himself turning into Albert; coming in at regular times, expecting to find her there, and then one day coming back to an empty house.

He never met Albert. And she never mentioned him. Except once when she had to file for a divorce before they could get married, and he had to sign a paper in a lawyer's office stating that he had had an adulterous affair with Mrs Albert Critchly. Some hope. It had been two years since she stepped into his taxi, and he'd got no more out of her than French kissing. It took another two years before they got married. But poor Albert must have sat appalled in his house in Chorley, his wife running round the country with his Hoover, having it off with Scotsmen.

Her pain was bad tonight. She didn't have to say anything. Grimace or moan or anything like that. He just knew it was bad. She couldn't prop herself up on her elbow any more to face him when they were talking. She lay flat on her back, with her head turned towards him, smiling. Even the smile hurt. He could tell.

– You want a rubbing?

He leaned over her to get her Tupperware box full of
medicines and ointments, but she shook her head and pushed
his arm gently away. It was the pain, he knew that. But, still,
she was quieter these days. More distant, lost in her own
thoughts. He wondered if she was thinking it was time she
went back and explained to poor old Albert Critchly. If he was
still alive. He turned out the light, and lay thinking in the dark.
There was nothing he could do to make her stay. If only she'd
send the damned Christmas cards, he'd feel easier.

She wasn't sleeping either. The pain was keeping her awake.
She didn't move, but her breathing didn't change rhythm. He
wanted to ask her if she was all right, but she got fed up with
him asking that. He lay facing away from her, imagining that if
he turned he'd see that strawberry-blonde woman in cardigan
and slippers. She touched his arm, and it reminded him of
when she'd leant forward and touched his back when he was
driving her that first day to Meg's.

– Thanks, love. She'd said. See? I knew I could depend on
you nice Scottish folk.

Her fingers on his back had felt warm despite the cold. Now
they were cold against his arm, even though the heating was
up full blast.

– You really want to know why I left? she said. Out of the
blue, picking up a conversation started in a taxi half a century
ago.

– There was no point in being there. Albert and Vera. The
Critchlys, 14 Pendle Street, Chorley. Like Jim and Molly
Macdonald. Too many of them.

– And here? John and Vera Murdoch, Ivanhoe Terrace,
Cumbernauld?

– That's what I'm saying. I shouldn't be here. What am I
doing being called Murdoch? I should never've got on that
train. Shouldn't have sold that nice Hoover.

She coughed and laughed, squeezed his arm and turned around, settling into sleep.

The next morning, he woke. As usual, she'd got up before him and brought them both a cup of tea which they never drank. It was snowing outside. Well, sleeting. Big grey flecks of shredded cloud slid down the window pane. He reached out for his cuppa, and nudged her as she lay, still there and grinning that smoky grin of hers, beside him.

– Tea's getting cold, Missus.

He nudged her again, but she was gone.

# All That Glisters

## *Anne Donovan*

Thon wee wifey brung them in, the wan that took us for two days when Mrs McDonald wis aff. She got us tae make Christmas cards wi coloured cardboard and felties, which wis a bit much when we're in second year, but naebody wis gonny say anythin cos it wis better than daein real work. Anyway ah like daein things lik that and made a right neat wee card for ma daddy wi a Christmas tree and a robin and a bit a holly on it.

*That's lovely dear. What's your name?*

*Clare.*

*Would you like to use the glitter pens?*

And she pulled oot the pack fae her bag.

Ah'd never seen them afore. When ah wis in primary four the teacher gied us tubes of glitter but it wis quite messy, hauf the stuff ended up on the flair and it wis hard tae make sure you got the glue in the right places. But these pens were different cos the glue wis mixed in wi the glitter so you could jist draw with them. It wis pure brilliant so it wis. There wis four colours, rid, green, gold and silver, and it took a wee while tae get the hang of it. You had tae be careful when you squeezed the tube so's you didny get a big blob appearin at wanst, but efter a few goes ah wis up an runnin.

And when ah'd finished somethin amazin hud happened.

83

Ah canny explain whit it wis but the glitter jist brought everythin tae life, gleamin and glisterin agin the flat cardboard. It wis like the difference between a Christmas tree skinklin wi fairy lights an wan lyin deid an daurk in a corner.

Ma daddy wis dead chuffed. He pit the card on the bedside table and smiled.

*Fair brightens up this room, hen.*

It's good tae find sumpn that cheers him up even a wee bit because ma daddy's really sick. He's had a cough fur as long as ah can remember, and he husny worked fur years, but these past three month he canny even get oot his bed. Ah hear him coughin in the night sometimes and it's different fae the way he used tae cough, comes fae deeper inside him somehow, seems tae rack his hale body fae inside oot. When ah come in fae school ah go and sit wi him and tell him aboot whit's happened that day, but hauf the time he looks away fae me and stares at a patch on the downie cover where there's a coffee stain that ma ma canny wash oot. He used tae work strippin oot buildins and he wis breathin in stour aw day, sometimes it wis that bad he'd come hame wi his hair and his claes clartit wi it. He used tae kid on he wis a ghost and walk in the hoose wi his airms stretched oot afore him and ah'd rin and hide unner the stair, watchin him walk by wi the faint powdery whiteness floatin roon his heid.

He never knew there wis asbestos in the dust, never knew a thing aboot it then; nane of them did. Noo he's an expert on it, read up aw these books tae try and unnerstaun it fur the compensation case. Before he got really sick he used tae talk aboot it sometimes.

*You see, hen, the word asbestos comes fae a Greek word that means indestructible. That's how they use it fur fireproofm – the fire canny destroy it.*

*You mean if you wore an asbestos suit you could walk through fire and it widny hurt you?*

*Aye. In the aulden days they used tae bury the royals in it. They cried it the funeral dress of kings.*

The next day the wee wumman let me use the pens again. Sometimes when you think somethin's brilliant it disny last, you get fed up wi it dead quick an don't know why you wanted it in the first place. But the pens wereny like that, it wis even better than the first time cos ah knew whit tae dae wi them. Yesterday ah'd put the glitter on quite thick in a solid block a colour, but today ah found a different way a daein it almost by accident. Ah'd drawn a leaf shape and coloured it green but a bit squirted oot intae a big blob, so ah blotted it and when ah took the paper away the shape that wis left wis nicer than the wan ah'd made deliberately. The outline wis blurred and the glitter wis finer and lighter, the colour of the card showin through so it looked as if sumbdy'd sprinkled it, steidy ladelin it on: it looked crackin. The teacher thought so too.

*It's lovely, Clare. It's more . . . subtle.*

Subtle, ah liked that word.

Ah tellt ma daddy aboot it that night efter school, sittin on the chair beside his bed. He seemed a bit better than usual, mair alert, listenin tae what ah hud tae say, but his skin wis a terrible colour and his cheeks were hollow.

*What did she mean, subtle, hen. How wis it subtle?*

Ah tried tae think of the words tae explain it, but ah couldny. Ah looked at ma fingers which were covered in glitter glue and then at ma daddy's haun lyin on the bed-cover, bones stickn oot and veins showin through. Ah took his haun in mines and turnt it roon so his palm faced upward.

*Look, Daddy.*

Ah showed him the middle finger of ma right haun, which wis thick wi solid gold, then pressed doon on his palm. The imprint of ma finger left sparkly wee trails a light.

He smiled, a wavery wee smile.

*Aye, hen. Subtle.*

That night ah lay awake fur a while imaginin aw the things ah could dae wi the glitter pens. Ah really wanted tae make sumpn fur ma daddy's Christmas wi them. The tips of ma fingers were still covered in glitter, and they sparkled in the daurk! Ah pressed ma fingers aw ower the bedclothes so they gleamed in the light fae the streetlamps ootside, then ah fell intae a deep glistery sleep.

£3.49 for a pack of four. And ah hud wan ninety-three in ma purse.

Ah lifted the pack and walked to the check-oot.

*Much are they?*

*Three forty-nine.*

*Aye but much are they each?*

The wumman at the till hud dyed jet-black hair and nae eyebrows.

*We don't sell them individually.*

She spat oot the word *individually* as if it wis sumpn disgusting.

*Aye but you'll get mair fur them. Look, you can have wan ninety-three fur two.*

*Ah've already tellt you that we don't sell them individually, ah canny split the pack.*

Ah could see there wis nae point in arguin wi her so ah turnt roon and walked towards the shelf tae pit them back. If Donna'd been wi me, she'd just have knocked them. She's aye takin sweeties an rubbers an wee things lik that. She's that casual aboot it, she can jist walk past a shelf and wheech sumpn intae her pocket afore anybdy notices, never gets caught. And she's that innocent lookin, wi her blonde frizzy curls an her neat school uniform naebdy wid guess tae look at her she wis a tea-leaf.

She's aye on tae me tae dae it, but ah canny. Ah suppose it's cos of ma ma and da: they're dead agin thievin. Donna widny rob hooses or steal sumpn oot yer purse but she disny think stealin oot a shop is stealin. A lot of folk think lik that. Donna's big brother Jimmy wanst tried tae explain tae me that it wis OK tae steal ooty shops cos they made such big profits that they were really stealin affy us (the workin classes he cries us though he husny worked a day in his life) and they're aw insured anyway so it disny matter, and even though ah can see the sense in whit Jimmy's sayin, well, ma daddy says stealin is stealin, and ah canny go against his word.

In the end ah sellt ma dinner tickets tae big Maggie Hughes and all week ah wis starvin for ah only hud an apple or a biscuit ma ma gied me fur a playpiece. But on Friday it wis worth it when ah went doon the shops at lunchtime tae buy the pens. It wis a different wumman that served me and she smiled as she pit them in a wee plastic poke.

*Are you gonny make Christmas decorations, hen?*
*Ah'm no sure.*
*Ah got some fur ma wee boy an he loved them.*
*Aye they're dead good. Thanks.*

Ah couldny wait tae show them tae ma da, but as soon as ah opened the door of the hoose ah knew there wis sumpn wrang. It wis that quiet, nae telly, nae radio on in the kitchen. Ma mammy wis sittin on the settee in the livinroom. Her face wis white and there were big black lines under her eyes.

*Mammy, whit's . . .*
*C'mere hen, sit doon beside me.*

She held her weddin ring between the thumb and first finger of her right haun, twistin it roon as she spoke and ah saw how loose it wis on her finger. No long ago it wis that tight she couldny get it aff.

*Clare, yer daddy had a bad turn jist this afternoon and we had tae go tae the hospital wi him. Ah'm awful sorry hen, ah don't know how tae tell you, but yer daddy's died.*

Ah knew it wis comin, ah think ah'd known since ah walked intae the hoose, but when she said the words the coldness shot through me till ah felt ma bones shiverin and ah heard a voice, far away in anither room, shoutin but the shouts were muffled as if in a fog, and the voice wis shoutin: *naw, naw, naw!*
And ah knew it wis ma voice.
We sat there, ma mammy and me, her airms roon me, till ah felt the warmth of her body gradually dissolve the ice of mine. Then she spoke, quiet and soft.
*Now hen, you know that this is fur the best: no fur us but fur yer daddy.*
Blue veins criss-crossed the back of her haun. Why were veins blue when blood wis red?
*You know yer daddy'd no been well fur a long time. He wis in a lot of pain, and he wisny gonny get better. At least this way he didny suffer as much. He's at peace noo.*
We sat for a long time, no speakin, just haudin hauns.

The funeral wis on the Wednesday and the days inbetween were a blur of folk comin an goin, of makin sandwiches an drinkin mugs of stewed tea, sayin rosaries an pourin oot glasses of whisky for men in overcoats. His body came hame tae the hoose and wis pit in their bedroom. Ma mammy slept in the bed settee in the livin room wi ma auntie Pauline.
*Are you sure that you want tae see him?*
Ah wis sure. Ah couldny bear the fact we'd never said goodbye and kept goin ower and ower in ma mind whit ah'd have said tae him if ah'd known he wis gonny die so soon. Ah wis feart as well, right enough. Ah'd never seen a deid body afore, and ah didny know whit tae expect, but he looked as if he wis asleep, better, in fact than he'd looked when he wis alive: his face had mair colour, wis less yella lookin an lined. Ah sat wi him fur a while in the room, no sayin anythin, no even thinkin really, jist sittin. Ah felt that his goin wis incomplete

and ah wanted tae dae sumpn fur him, but that's daft, whit can you dae when sumbdy's deid? Ah wondered if ah should ask ma mammy but she wis that withdrawn intae hersel, so busy wi the arrangements that ah didny like tae. She still smiled at me but it wis a watery far-away smile and when she kissed me goodnight ah felt she wis haudin me away fae her.

On the Wednesday mornin ah got up early, got dressed and went through tae the kitchen. Ma auntie Pauline wis sittin at the table havin a cuppa tea and a fag and when she looked up her face froze over.

*Whit the hell dae you think you're doin? Go and get changed this minute.*

*But these are ma best claes.*

*You canny wear red tae a funeral. You have tae show respect fur the deid.*

*But these were ma daddy's favourites. He said ah looked brilliant in this.*

Ah mind his face when ah came intae the room a couple of month ago, after ma mammy'd bought me this outfit fur ma birthday: a red skirt and a zip-up jaicket wi red tights tae match.

*You're a sight fur sore eyes hen.*

*That sounds horrible, daddy.*

He smiled at me.

*It disny mean that hen, it means you look that nice that you would make sore eyes feel better. Gie's a twirl, princess.*

And ah birled roon on wan leg, laughin.

*Those claes are no suitable for a funeral.*

*Ah'm gonny ask ma mammy.*

Ah turned to go oot the room.

*Don't you dare disturb your mother on a day like this tae ask her aboot claes. Have you no sense? Clare, you're no a baby; it's time you grew up and showed same consideration for other folk.*

*Get back in that room and put on your school skirt and sweat-shirt and your navy blue coat. And ah don't want to hear another word aboot this.*

In the bedroom ah threw masel intae a corner and howled ma heid aff. The tears kept comin and comin till ah felt ah wis squeezed dry and would never be able tae shed anither tear. Ah took off the red claes and changed intae ma grey school skirt and sweatshirt and pit ma navy blue coat ower it. Ah looked at masel in the full-length mirror in the middle of the wardrobe and saw this dull drab figure, skin aw peely-wally. Ma daddy would have hated tae see me like this but ah didny dare go against ma auntie's word.

The only bit of me that had any life aboot it wis ma eyes fur the tears had washed them clean and clear. A sunbeam came through the windae and ah watched the dustspecks dancin in its light. There was a hair on the collar of ma coat and it lit up intae a rainbow of colours. As ah picked it up and held it in ma fingers an idea came tae me. Ah went tae ma schoolbag which had been left lyin in the corner of the room since Friday, took oot ma pack of glitter pens and unwrapped them. Ah took the gold wan, squeezin the glitter on ma fingers then rubbin it intae ma hair, then added silver and red and green. The strands of hair stood oot roon ma heid like a halo, glisterin and dancin in the light. Ah covered the dull cloth so it was bleezin wi light, patterns scattered across it, even pit some on ma tights and ma shoes. Then ah pressed ma glittery fingers on ma face, feelin ma cheek bones and eyebrows and the soft flesh of ma mouth and the delicate skin of ma eyelids. And ah felt sad for a moment as ah thought of the deid flesh of ma daddy, lyin alone in the cold church. Then ah stood and looked in the mirror at the glowin figure afore me and ah smiled.

Subtle, daddy?

Aye hen, subtle.

# Fish

*Michel Faber*

These days, Janet let her daughter sleep in the bed with her. It wasn't what child psychologists would have said was best, but there weren't any child psychologists anymore, and her daughter needed help just the same. Janet had tried forcing Kif Kif to sleep alone, but the little girl would wake screaming with nightmares about God knows what – sharks, probably. Now she was sleeping dreamlessly, cradled in the curve of Janet's waist as Janet lay smoking, head and shoulders propped up on the pillows. All around the bed, the fly-wire was stretched taut from floor to ceiling, the support struts and entrance zipper glowing in the light from Janet's bedside candle. She shut her eyes against the tick-tick-ticking against the wire and tried to prepare for sleep by concentrating on smoking, sucking on the Wee Willem, but it was no use; there was always the anxiety that something would be eating through the wire, through the canvas of the zipper, or that someone would have quietly jimmied the boards off the windows and holes in the walls, and you would open your eyes to find . . .

She opened her eyes. Nothing had changed. There were still the same thirty or forty little fish (newly spawned wrasse perhaps? – it was difficult to tell in the dark) hovering in the air, bumbling against the fly-wire, trying to get in. Individual fish would bob off from the cluster, floating up to bump against the ceiling from which the fly-wire was hung. Janet drew another cigar from the box on her lap, wishing it were a cigarette, craving a cigarette. But of course, there were no cigarettes anymore, either. They had been one of the first things to run out after the Great Reversal.

At the striking of the match, the fish scattered, and the room was alive with shining little bodies, flitting against the furniture, knocking ornaments off shelves, disappearing into dark corners. Almost immediately, however, they began to swim back to the same part of the fly-wire they had been worrying at before, and the tick-tick-ticking began again. Kif Kif squirmed in her sleep, digging her hard little six-year-old's shoulderblades into Janet's side.

'It's all right, darling,' murmured Janet, stroking her daughter through the blankets. 'Nothing to be afraid of.' Blinking against the smoke from her own cigar, Janet wished she had a large enough ration of matches to strike them one after the other.

In the morning Janet and Kif Kif dressed up in their camouflage to leave the house. The fish, which now lay gaping and dead on the floors of every room, had gained entrance, as Janet had suspected, through the narrow gap between front door and hall floor. The little plank of wood which Kif Kif put there nightly, wedged between the door and two large nails driven into the floor, had been levered out of place from the outside sometime during the night. This paltry act of vandalism happened every week or so; the devotees of the Church of Armageddon (the 'Army' for short) knew well enough that it could cause nothing worse than annoyance, but they didn't like to pass a house by without attempting, however feebly, to advance their cause. As far as major attacks went, Janet and Kif Kif had been lucky. Only once in the last year had they returned to their house to find that all the boards had been hammered or jimmied off the orifices and taken away, all the windows and doors unhinged, and all the food and clothing taken. The bedroom wall had been daubed with one of the graffiti slogans characteristic of the Army: THE FIRST SHALL BECOME LAST! On that occasion, Kif Kif had kept guard with her machete while Janet laboured to restore the defences. By late afternoon the five-year-old was splattered with fish blood and muck, although she hadn't been attacked by anything very dangerous. Most of the fish she had wounded had swum away, to die inside the deserted buildings and gutted cars where they sheltered, but some had been hacked too severely to do anything but wobble slowly to the ground and die twitching on the crumbling asphalt. When Kif Kif had suggested that these fish should be gathered up and taken to the Soup Kitchen for use as food, Janet hadn't been able to keep the tears in, hearing a suggestion like that from the fear-shaken little girl, and she had pressed her daughter's soiled body to her own as she explained that it was a very good and sensible idea in theory but that it would attract predators on the way there.

Today Janet and Kif Kif locked the door behind them, as always as quietly as possible, for sound sounded so much louder these days than it had sounded in the days when there were things like cars, factories and people going. The million sea creatures moved noiselessly. Schools of barracuda swept without warning in and out of broken windows. Starfish wriggled on the bonnets of rusty cars. Octopi cartwheeled in slow motion through the air, their tentacles touching briefly on the tips of barbed-wire fences and the tops of awnings. Even the shriek of a shark attacking would be obscenely silent, so there was actually no point in keeping your ears cocked, though you always did. At a cautious trot Janet and Kif Kif put a zig-zag of streets between them and their house, in the hope that if they should be observed by the Army along the way, the location of the house would at least not be obvious. It was possible, of course, that one day the Army would no longer be itinerant, and would concentrate on each occupied house they chanced to find, patiently devoting their attentions to it, taking advantage of every occasion when it was left unoccupied, however briefly, until at last its inhabitants had been killed by what they preferred to call The Holy Reclamation Of Nature. Then again, it was also possible that one day the Army would amend its religion to permit its devotees to do the killing themselves, rather than waiting for The Holy Reclamation Of Nature to do it.

'Far enough now,' said Janet, her breath clouding the dry, grey air.

Kif Kif threw the plastic bag of dead wrasse into the gutter, where it burst open on the sharp edge of a broken camera tripod. A large eel floated out of a sewerhole nearby and slid through the air towards the spillage.

'Hungry?'

'Uh-huh.'

Coming back from the Soup Kitchen, feeling warm and sprightly with the city's only hot meal in their stomachs, Janet and Kif Kif leapt and skipped towards home. Small fish of all colours and shapes cluttered the air around them, frightened out of their foraging places by the commotion. Carp nibbled at the plankton nestled inside an exposed automobile engine. Barracuda circled a small dolphin which had become tangled in a shop awning and starved to death there. A manta ray of moderate size floated over their ducked heads and settled against the wall of a factory. Slowly it slid along a line of newly painted graffiti (ANY CRETURE THAT CAN READ THIS, YOU'RE DAYS ON EARTH ARE NUMBER'D!) obscuring the words one by one. Janet repeated the slogan to her daughter on request.

'He's reading it,' smirked Kif Kif, making Janet laugh. They both knew the ray had mistaken the moist paint for something edible, and would be lying maw-up on the ground by tomorrow morning, whereupon it would probably, if found by the Army, be eaten in turn. Since it was highly unlikely that the nomadic Church of Armageddon had any equivalent of the secret underground Soup Kitchen which kept Janet, Kif Kif and the other unbelievers alive, it seemed to subsist by fishing. Army nets could be seen occasionally, spanned between buildings in intricate layers. It was rumoured that the Army scorned to eat the tinned and packaged food they carried off from the houses they broke open to let in Holy Nature's predators, but merely confiscated it in order to deprive unbelievers of any unfair advantage against God's will. Hoards of unused food had certainly been found in odd places, in which event it was, of course, conveyed to the Soup Kitchen and either cooked there or distributed among the Survivors – a term which neatly excluded the Church of Armageddon, being crucially at odds with the ultimate aims of that religion. There was hardly a public building in the city that was not marked with their commonest graffito: LET THE DRY LAND DISAPPEAR!

'A bit quieter, Kif.' They were nearing the home streets. An acrid warm breeze started up, smelling of large, half-eaten fish. Janet's nose wrinkled with distaste. She reached out for Kif Kif and gathered her to her waist as she walked.

'Sorry it's so nasty,' she said, but, looking down at the child's abstracted, placid face, she realised the apology was wasted, as Kif Kif obviously hadn't noticed the smell.

Janet's mood soured as she considered that her daughter had grown up in a world which stank to high heaven. Kif Kif had never smelled air untainted by decay. She'd never seen a growing fruit or a flower, as every form of vegetation was immediately eaten by the fish before if even came to bud. She lived shut up in an unheated, poorly-lit prison, trembling and twitching with nightmares every night. Even now, as they walked along the deserted street, any of a hundred broken windows might suddenly spew out a long, slick streak of grey, and then what could you do? Janet had only heard from other Survivors what it was like to just stand there while a huge shark, its jaw locked open, glided through the air towards the smallest prey. The Army certainly wasn't wrong in thinking the world was no longer intended for human beings. Kif Kif with her dinky little machete against the hatred of all creation . . .

'Mummy, look!'

Janet was summoned out of her brooding with a jerk she could feel in her bowels.

'What? What?'

Kif Kif was pointing over the roofs of the houses, halfway across the city. Horrified, Janet watched the blue-black killer whale emerging from the low grey clouds, followed by another whale, and another, and another. They hung huge in the sky like black zeppelins, and the air seemed to grow claustrophobically dense with their displacement of it. Janet was nauseous with fear, and would have sunk to her knees but for the grip she had on Kif Kif's shoulders. At her back there was nothing that could offer safety, only more crumbling streets, more fragile, half-broken buildings: a mile of ground a whale could cover in less than a minute and, beyond that, the empty sea, where humans, unfairly, had not been granted the ability to breathe underwater. The killer whales began to move towards Janet and Kif Kif's part of the city. Their tails swept the air lazily. They kept together. They were attacking.

A hundred metres or so from the street where Janet and Kif Kif stood, there towered an old building which, though dwarfed by the broken, skeletal office blocks around it, had survived extraordinarily intact, marble statues and all. The foremost whale weaved through the office blocks with a grace that belied its massive size, and passed very close by the old building, almost clipping it with its aeroplane wing of a tail. Then it loomed on, its shadow spilling across the streets straight towards Kif Kif and Janet. By the time it reached the street where they stood it was swimming about thirty metres above the ground, the motion of its tail blowing their hair all around their faces. Directly overhead, blotting out the sun with its monstrous bulk, it opened its mouth. A thousand needlesharp teeth swung down like the hatch of an aeroplane. Water clattered on the asphalt: saliva in the wind. Janet screamed.

But the whale glided over them altogether, its great shadow smothering them as it passed.

'It's coming back! It's coming back!' shrieked Janet as, whirling around, she watched the whale describe a slow semicircle and cruise towards them again. Once more, however, it passed them over, and slid by the old building, while the other whales floated in rough formation nearby. Turning again, it swam back towards Janet and Kif Kif, but in a smaller arc this time, so that its shadow did not even reach the street where they stood. The third time it returned to the old building, it did not pass it by. Some decision seemed to have been made deep in the creature's brain, and with a final sweep of its tail it hurled itself straight at its target, ramming into the stonework with its massive head. Amid the noise of a muffled thunderclap, the old building shuddered, stones falling out of their pattern in small clusters. A pale statue swayed on its perch and toppled to the street below, smashing unseen and unheard. The other whales, following the example of their leader, attacked the building with him, ramming and ramming it until its woodwork flew off in beam-sized splinters and its stonework crumbled and its crucifixes cartwheeled down through the air and its bells rang with chaotic lack of rhythm. At last the tower fell in on itself with the tremendous racket that only collapsing buildings make. For an attenuated minute the whales circled the ruin, then they swam off towards another part of the city, their tails beating up clouds of shimmering debris.

Janet let out her breath shudderingly, then gasped at the pain of frozen muscles thawing. She wasn't really very grateful to be alive; life had been conceded too far beyond the extremity of terror, where she could no longer recognise it for what it was. To be unconscious in the long gullet of a whale: that would have been *real* mercy, not this ghastly approximation of survival. Only, she must *pretend* to be alive, *pretend* to have hope, spirit, feeling, for the sake of her daughter, so that her daughter wouldn't give up. She must be strong for her daughter, comfort her, get her home to bed, carry her there if need be. Janet looked down at Kif Kif for the first time, and was shocked to observe that the child's face was radiant. 'Oh, Mummy!' marvelled the little girl. 'Wasn't it amazing?'

'Amazing?' echoed Janet incredulously. 'Amazing?' Anger started up deep inside her like convulsions, getting more violent as she let go her hold on it, until she was shaking with fury.

'Amazing!?' she yelled at last, and began to hit Kif Kif, flailing at her with the flats of her hands. The child ducked under the blows, crying out, but doing some flailing herself, and not without effect either. In a few moments they were in a real tussle, pulling each other's clothes and hair, until a warning shout from Kif Kif ended it. Janet found herself being pulled along the street by the wrist.

'Come *on*!' shouted the panting child crossly. 'Stupid!'

Janet stumbled along, stumbling partly because she was too tall to be led properly by a six-year-old. She glanced over her shoulder to see what the child had spotted before her: a school of moray eel gathering twenty yards away, attracted by the commotion of the fight and the smell of human flesh. Janet gained her stride, scooped up her unprotesting daughter in her arms and ran and ran.

In bed that night, safe behind the fly-wire, Janet tried to explain why she had been so angry, but had little success.

'I thought you were terrified of sharks and big fish like that,' she said lamely, hugging the slightly alien child tight to her side. 'You have nightmares every night . . .'

Kif Kif pawed sleepily at an itchy cheek and nose.

'I have nightmares about other stuff,' she said.

# When That's Done

## *Jim Glen*

I had the book out as usual, the one I was on, but it was hard going. A lot of words, like *heuristic*, which I thought I should know but didn't. Or maybe did once and so that was worrying, made you wonder how you can forget the meanings of words. But of course I was only reading the book at that time so when Anderson popped his head round the door, I wouldn't just be sitting there gazing into space like I had nothing else to do.

Something else you wondered was why these places were aye so hot. Did nobody feel any personal liability for the heating bill and so they just kept it cranked up? Or was there maybe an actual requirement in law, something in writing somewhere that said a certain minimum temperature had to always be maintained? What I was meaning though was: I know you can't exactly have places *cold* but if you thought about it, in that heat and the folk passing in and out every day, spreading their germs, their bugs or whatever, it just made you think. Made you wonder.

. . . *it has merit as a heuristic device*. God almighty.

Anderson gave me the nod and we walked the short distance through to his office, where I took my usual seat in the corner, his over by the window. Then there was the minute or so before he started up. His usual way: So how have things been?

Fine, I said. Fine.

Good.

Then we were quiet again. Always a kind of false start, this neutral exchange of pleasantries just to get the ball gently rolling, that sort of thing. I could see that now so it didn't bother me, not the way it used to. Used to drive me near demented, him sitting there saying nothing, doing nothing, hardly moving a muscle even, and me aye thinking: Here it comes, any minute now, the *big yin*, though it was only a feeling I got, I hadn't any real idea of what I was on about, just a weird sensation that something momentous was about to happen, some life-changing event right before my eyes.

But like I said, at first I couldn't bear it so it was aye me that broke the silence. These days though it can just as easily be him.

We were talking last time about the group, he said.

Aye.

It looks like we'll not be starting for a month or so. Easter even.

Right.

You're still interested?

Aye, if you think.

It's important we get the composition right. There have to be . . . points of connection, he said. And a balance. Age and sex, that sort of thing.

You mean the same but different?

He smiled. That sort of thing.

Then it went quiet again and the cynical side of me got to thinking: Here, this guy's getting paid a mint for saying next to nothing and I have to spend my days yakking away ten to the dozen. An ill-divided world right enough, and a wee laugh, maybe more a smirk escaped, caused him to raise his eyebrows, though he didn't pursue the matter.

I've been thinking about institutions, he said.

Aye right. Institutions.

They seem to make you unhappy. Ill at ease.

You mean in the concrete sense or the abstract? I said.

Either. Or both.

This had come right out the blue, this thing about *institutions*, but then I thought: Aye, maybe you could be on to something here, for what I'd just said about the concrete and the abstract, Christ it had only been the day before I was standing looking out the window as ever, across the rain-puddled roof down into that part of the courtyard where you aye see the detritus being whipped around in the wind, the sweetie-papers, crisp packets and the like, and I was regarding again the sad, sad state of the place; the peeling window-frames and the battered doors; a patch of charred brickwork where some wee bastard had lit a fire and I was thinking: Well, whoever it was had been right enough for you could see the whole place needed tearing down, starting over again, or better still why no just forget it, no even bother at all? So that's how it struck me that he'd hit on something. That was what I was on about, what we were both on about; how the concrete and the abstract merge to the extent that the two become one and the same, inseparable.

You've got a point, I said.

And it got me to thinking about the book, funnily enough, the chapter I'd just finished reading, being largely a critique on Marxist theory and the way in which actions by groups have an outcome that is to some extent predictable, based on models of group behaviour which become institutionalised and that such institutions can thereafter be changed by action of a radical nature. The fact that Marx himself had stated in his *eighteenth Brumaire* that: *Men make their own history* and it was *under circumstances directly encountered, given and transmitted from the past.*

I thought about mentioning this to Anderson, just in the

passing, but when I thought about it again, I realised I couldn't be arsed.

There was just me at the bus stop and a couple of giggly lasses, thirteen or thereabouts. I didn't know them. I had my paper but a fair breeze had got up around the shelter, started flapping the pages about so that I had to fold it up into a tight wee square, rectangle or whatever, an effort that was hardly worth it.

After a while this young guy turned up, wearing a Walkman, and after him a woman carrying her messages, *Farm Foods* on the side of the bag, stuff for the freezer.

Mister have ye got a light? one of the lasses asked.

Naw sorry, hen, I said. She just tutted with that smacking sound of the tongue, the way youngsters do to indicate how useless you are, and went off to try the guy with the Walkman. But I was fine, I was okay about it. Nothing was going to happen.

Thinking back to that time, a year ago now or a bit more even. Granted there were a lot more folk around then; in fact, the place had been heaving, not just the bus shelter but all the comings and goings on the street with folk having just finished their work or whatever, trying to get themselves home and it suddenly occurred to me: this *endless wash of humanity*, I remember thinking those exact words, this *endless wash of humanity*. Spewing out everywhere it was, from shops and pubs and offices and schools and God knows where, spilling out on to the streets, battering itself ceaselessly, day in day out, against . . . against . . . against . . . and then I just lost the power to think anymore, to keep a hold of where I was going and that's when the panting started, slow at first with wee sharp intakes but enough to let me know something was up and I was trying to control it, keep it right down so that nobody would see, nobody would know what was happening but the panting got heavier and so they did begin to notice but in the way that folk do when they suddenly find themselves around something they don't want to know about, they were getting edgy themselves and annoyed even that you were being a disturbance to their lives, so I had to get right away from that place all together and I just started walking, it didn't matter where, the head down and gulping huge lungfuls of air until I thought it would pass but the thing was it didn't, it *didn't* pass, it just got worse and so what I had to do in the end, what I actually had to do, was I had to phone her to come and get me. Phone her to actually come and get me. Like a bairn that had suddenly found itself lost.

The lassie had got her light for the pair of them were now puffing away good style. Ach well, I thought, it's their funeral. Then I saw the bus I was waiting for, the 44 stuck at the lights behind a car. I had the exact fare ready in my pocket so that all I had to do was drop it into the machine and grab my ticket. It was the middle of the afternoon and I was hoping it would be quiet, thinking I might even go upstairs, a thing I had always done when I was wee. You aye sat up the front when you could, for there was a wee periscope affair with a mirror above it. It was how the driver kept an eye on the top deck but, equally, you could keep an eye on him. It was a bit of fun looking down into his cabin, watching him watching the road, and I was wondering if the buses still had them.

So how did it go? she said.

Ach okay.

I reckoned the lamb would take another five minutes at the most, with ten to rest. I'd crushed a whole bulb of garlic over the top with some fresh rosemary from the tub, so the smell was unbelievable, made you want to not actually eat the thing but just stand there looking at it, breathing it in.

So it went okay?

I looked at her. Aye.

It's just that sometimes it doesn't.

Christ, look it went okay; watch out the road, I said for I knew the spuds would be just about done and when I checked them with the knife they were. I grabbed the oven gloves and drained the pot. I'd almost let them boil dry so I sniffed the air, tried to catch any burntness that might be there, but, no, they were fine. I finished them off with some lemon juice and a sprig of thyme, left them to steam for a while.

But do you think it's helping?

God knows. Have ye seen the corkscrew?

It's where ye left it.

I went through the front room and right enough, it was still lying on the table from the night before. Back in the kitchen she was up at the cooker, stirring at the soup she'd made. I started opening the wine.

You want some of this first? she said.

Aye, great.

She ladled the soup into a couple of bowls, took them through. After the wine was opened, I took out the lamb, left it to rest by the sink. What about the wee fella? I asked.

She shouted through that he was getting his tea at his pal's.

Fair enough, I thought. Doesnae like lamb anyway.

When we'd sat down at the table with the soups, she went right back to the subject of Anderson, asked me if there was any sign of when it might be ending.

I shrugged, said, Who knows? I was still thinking about the meat lying ben the kitchen. It's no like cooking a roast, I told her. Ye can easy tell when that's done.

I was hoping she might have laughed at that but she didn't.

But does he no say things? she said. Suggest things it might be?

Aye, sort of but no like . . . I mean, if ye've a pain in your side then ye go to your GP and he'll maybe say, Aye it's this or it's that, right? But Anderson's no like that. I don't think it works that way.

So how do you know if you're getting anywhere?

Well . . . and I was wanting to tell her something, anything would have done. Maybe that business over the concrete and the abstract. Or about how men make their own history. Even getting the bus okay but that would have sounded daft. What I said though was, I think you're supposed to find out for yersel. I think it has merit as a heuristic device.

She just looked at me.

Aw nothing, I said. Just something I was reading, that's all. Something I thought I'd forgot but I hadnae. I started pouring the two of us some wine and had a wee chuckle to myself. I could see she was still eying me quizzically but I knew she wasn't going to say anything. In a minute or two we'd be on to something else, maybe how her work had gone or what the wee fella had been up to. Anything. Anything at all, it wouldn't matter.

(With acknowledgements to John Tosh,
*The Pursuit of History*, Longman, 2000.)

# My Father as an Ant

## *Diana Hendry*

**M**y mother liked to remind my father that he was only an ant. She did this whenever she thought he was getting above himself or was about to be carried away by yet another expensive dream of grandeur.

We'd had chandeliers, ballroom size in our modest hall, a billiards table (a big mahogany job, fit for a London club and with a baize smooth as a Wimbledon lawn) taking over the dining room, and now, suddenly, it was oil paintings.

I never could see my father as an ant, although I tried. He was a big man, not easy in his body. Often I thought it must be very tiring always carrying that bulk about and having such a heavy tread that people always knew you were coming. And I rather pitied him being weighed down like that. Perhaps he might have liked being an ant, nimble and skittish on however many legs ants have. And indistinguishable from all other ants. But I couldn't shrink him. I could get as far as a beetle or a spider – because you can tell one beetle/spider from another – but not an ant. No, I saw him more as a stranded whale or a walrus perhaps (he had a moustache), lumbering about our house and making the best of things but not exactly at home.

So I was glad of the oil paintings. They told me what was in my father's mind. Actually the chandeliers and the billiards table told you too. (My father was off waltzing somewhere or, dressed in his DJs, was shooting an elegant cue, a cheroot in his teeth, as he potted the red, the green, the blue.) But the oil paintings gave you more to go on. You could walk inside them like a room and spend a long time wandering about and looking.

The oil paintings were the closest I ever got to my father; for he was a silent man and didn't know what to do with daughters, though sometimes, I remember, he would take my nose between his knuckles and try to lengthen it. He wanted to make it as long as my mother's and that was affectionate in a way, though I would have preferred to keep my snub. Still, I succumbed. He was so large and lonely. The least I could do was lend him my nose.

Perhaps the oil paintings also allowed my mother to look into my father's mind and maybe she didn't like what she saw. But I don't think so. Whatever my mother had in her mind it wasn't *The Alps at Sunset* and she couldn't conceive of them existing in anyone else's. Oil paintings, to my mother, belonged in art galleries or in stately homes and when she heard the price of *The Alps*, she told my father just how many people he could feed with that amount of money and my father looked briefly ashamed and she reminded him he was only an ant.

I gazed at the rosy glow on the peaks and suffered a frisson of excitement: they were so sinful those oily Alps. Just as looking into someone's mind was like seeing them naked. I didn't know any fancy literary terms then, like 'landscapes of the mind'; I thought that somehow or other my father had grown those mountains in his head and I puzzled over them. Over why he should do it. They were so cold and icy. So unhomely without a human being in sight and nothing green growing. The sunset didn't improve them. The sunset was just like the smile on someone's face who doesn't really like you.

I didn't know then that, to my father, *The Alps at Sunset*

hanging on our living-room wall, in a discreet pale-grey frame, was a status symbol, an announcement of wealth, and that to choose a painting of mountains – used by the painter to display his skill with light – showed a classy, but respectable good taste. Yet part of me thinks this isn't right and that my father did, truly, grow the mountains in his head.

And then I think that the ways of misunderstanding someone are endless and that as my father spoke so rarely, he was open to every kind of misinterpretation. And mostly we were happy to accept the character reading of him given by my mother. She never told *us* he was an ant. She told us he was a good, honest, hard-working, ambitious and determined man, and we were lucky to have such a man as our father.

Fastened into his laundered shirts, his heavy suits, his laced-up leather shoes and stranded in his armchair by the fire, my father drew my nose down between his knuckles and said nothing.

He brought a second oil painting home. I think his painting sprees – like all his other extravagances – were very carefully planned, but he never told my mother in advance. For fear of being diminished into an ant perhaps. I've no doubt he needed to feel dinosaur size in order to slam down that amount of money on the counter of some art gallery. And there was another element to it. My father liked to surprise us. Actually, surprising people is quite easy if you rarely talk, but my father chose surprising surprises. For instance my mother told the tale of how once, before they were married, he arrived at the station to meet her with a dog in his arms. And I remember how one day he got us all in the car to drive to London and then told us he'd sold our house.

Anyway, about the oil paintings. My father would arrive home with this large parcel wrapped in cloth and paper and string and looking shamefaced (which was just a pose because we all knew he was a determined man and currently obsessed by paintings), set the parcel down and wait for my mother to exclaim that he had ideas above his station and was only an ant.

The second oil painting was quite different from the first. It was small and dark but set in a great gilt frame. It featured a monk and a traveller with a knapsack on his back, seated at what looked like a monastery table drinking goblets of wine. The traveller looked rather like my father, only thinner and easier in his body, and I supposed he and the monk must have been talking about journeys. Journeys of the heart and the feet.

My mother liked this painting even less than the first. The Alps were cold and white. This painting was dark and gloomy. It remained my favourite; I suppose because it told part of a story, and you could make the rest of it up as you liked and think of all the places the traveller might be going (or indeed why he was going at all) and what advice the monk was giving him. It hung in the breakfast room and nobody looked at it much because you had to look very close to see what it was about.

My father really got into his stride then and the next painting was enormous and took up the whole wall of the landing. It was of Spanish women, potting and you'd never have thought my father would have such women in his head along with the monk and the Alps, the chandeliers and the billiards table, but evidently he had.

The women were as curvaceous as the pots they were making. They all sat round a table and they had lush thick dark hair piled on their heads but escaping in curls and tendrils. They had warm complexions and large bosoms and I remember that the one in the forefront had a yellow dress like sunshine and you could see her nicely sandalled ankle underneath.

You'd have thought this painting was colourful enough for

my mother to like it, but she didn't. 'Foreign women,' she said in the same tone she used for her ant works. And nor did she see the point of the pots when pyrex was just in and easily bought at the shops.

The Spanish women worried me too. There was a kind of alarming vitality about them that didn't quite fit in with our house and our way of life, and sometimes I'd dream of my father, in his very correct business suit with the waistcoat, dancing on the table with the Spanish potters, and I hoped that if he was planning to do any such thing he might go and consult the monk first.

By now our house, with the chandeliers and the billiards table and the oil paintings, was looking very grand indeed. And there was a new three-piece suite and one of the first televisions with doors to cover the screen.

My father still looked large and lonely and uncomfortable, and in the morning he sat in his dressing room – beached again, only this time in a wicker chair – thinking something over for hours. My mother said it was business, but I wasn't so sure. I thought he had more pictures growing in his head or that the pictures hadn't quite done what he'd wanted them to do. They remained pictures on the walls, pictures in his head. He couldn't go travelling to the Alps or dance with the Spanish women. He sat in his chair shrinking into an ant.

# Sundays

*George Inglis*

S he could feel the damp of his sweat against her arm. Him
lying there sweating and reeking of whisky, the stale smell
of it wafting into the room with every breath he took. Large
heaves of his intake of breath and the low rumble of his snores
as it escaped the confines of his lungs, mingling with the rotten
smell coming from his stomach. And her feeling tender.

The monotony of it all threatened to overwhelm her. Every
Sunday the same. Waking in the early morning and lying there
beside him as he continued to sleep for hours yet, sweating
and snoring and reeking of booze.

Then, when he did wake, he'd have a hunger on him that
drove him to the frying pan and the smell of bacon would fill
the air and the eggs spluttering madly in the hot fat. He'd be
happy standing by the cooker, humming away to himself some
song from last night when they'd danced in each other's arms,
kidding with the weans, teasing them and laughing with them.
Them laughing, too, at the happy father cooking for them and
joking with them.

She would make light of it, too, joining in with the general
mood of things. Smiling at the weans, trying not to look at
him.

She'd have been up for hours, bathed and fresh smelling,
dressed and fed; some toast and coffee. A few hours to herself

in the quiet of the Sunday morning. A few hours' reading whatever book she was reading at the time, seeking a point of contact. The weans still sleeping, mimicking their father with their slumbers.

The bacon teased her with its smell and she would have some with the rest of them. Eat two breakfasts on a Sunday, hers and theirs.

Then the day would continue on its predictable course. Her washing and ironing the weans' clothes for school in the morning, him off to the pub to top up the night before's intake and round off the weekend, the weans out to play if the weather was good or sitting in front of the telly if it wasn't.

Then the Sunday dinner, roast beef and Yorkshire pudding, roast tatties, boiled tatties, some cabbage, and then some trifle with plenty cream topping, all prepared and ready for him coming home from the pub with another hunger on him and he would sit and eat the lot, kidding with the weans again, teasing them and baiting them, and them loving all of it. And he would eat anything the weans left and then sit on the couch and fall asleep until some time around eight o'clock or half past when she was bathing the weans, and the house was full of the smell of shampoo and soap and talcum powder and splashes and giggles.

He would wake and yawn and come through to the bath-room, the stale smell on his breath again and towel the weans dry with his rough hands, putting his mouth to their bellies and blowing, making rude farting noises that made them laugh and squirm and want more. And he would carry them through to their room, slinging them over his shoulders like sacks of tatties, kidding on he was staggering under the weight and making them squeal with delight and fear.

Then he would dump them down on their beds so as they would bounce back up in the air, arms and legs flailing about, shrieking with excitement, tears coming to their eyes. They'll never sleep, you know, she'd say, not after all that excitement. And he would laugh and bounce the weans in the air again and again and again until they were breathless and dizzy and he too was puffing, his face red.

Ach, they'll be fine, he'd say, and bounce them one last time for good measure then collapse on one of the beds himself, lying there breathing hard, his whisky reek filling the air, sweat forming on his brow, while the weans did the same, heaving in lung-fulls of air, pulling the long strands of their wet hair from their red faces, lying spread-eagled on their beds, arms and legs by their sides like starfish.

Right, she would say, get yourselves into bed; you've school in the morning.

Will Daddy read us a story? asking her as though he wasn't there.

No, she'd say, it's getting late; you've school in the morning, knowing he would read them a story anyway and them knowing he would too.

Of course I'll read yous a story, he'd say, but not for too long: you've school in the morning.

And she would tuck them up in bed, giving their hair a quick brush, while he got a book from the bookcase in the corner, asking them what one they would like, knowing all the time it would be the same one they always wanted him to read because they liked the voices he put on for all the different characters. And he was good at the voices, even made her laugh at times.

Then the weans would be giggling again at the voices he did until sleep came over them and they lay there with their heads to the side and their mouths open. Catching flies, he always said.

Then the kettle would be on and the two of them would sit in the kitchen, her tired and him too, and they'd talk about the week ahead, what was to be done at work and at home, then he would talk about some of the guys in the pub and the things they said and did, and she would talk about so-and-so along the road and so-and-so in the next street, and sometimes their stories would converge with one of the guys in the pub being married to so-and-so from along the road and it was funny how they each got different impressions about their spouses from the guy in the pub and so-and-so from along the road.

Then he would yawn and rub his head and scratch his belly and say he was off to bed and she would say I'll be there in a minute, but she would make sure he was asleep before she went to bed. Until then she would sit and relax and read her book in peace, her feet up by the fire, the house quiet around her, the silence hugging her like a mother hugging her daughter, pulling her tight, hurting her with love.

# The Neighbours' Return

## *Michael Mail*

I t was remarkable how quickly things seemed to return to normal in Kierscen. The war had been over hardly forty-eight hours before the butcher Sleider reinstalled his famous ornamental shopfront beneath the free Polish flags which grew from every building on the main street. Although everyone joked that his meat was pre-war, there wasn't a dry eye in the village. The next day, the old stamps appeared in the Post Office. The '39 face of President Moscicki beamed confidently in a range of colours despite the fact that he was dying in Switzerland. They were quickly replaced by drab yellowish ones issued by the mysterious Provisional Government. It was said that the glue tasted of vodka.

The occasional shot could still be heard in the surrounding areas, which ensured that people didn't venture too far in those first weeks. Partisans were still coming in from the forests. Some couldn't believe it wouldn't all just come rolling back as suddenly as it had rolled away.

The Russians by and large stayed away from our village. Except when they lured Wojciech's cow on to the road and it ended up making the supreme sacrifice to the 'great liberators'. They preferred the town of Liebling with its three pubs. All the pubs were owned by one man, Kasprzycki, who was said to be the first millionnaire in post-war Poland.

Someone picked up the word 'reconstruction' from the radio and it clunked round the village as if saying the word was half the task. No one was sure exactly what needed to be reconstructed. Certainly, there was the Church. All sorts of unlikely people were terrified at the thought that there wasn't a place to avoid going to on a Sunday. Only two of the five walls had survived the direct hit by stray Russian shells and it became a source of pride that rebuilding began almost straight away. The Cathedral at Cracow had been used to hide most of the silverware and iconography, which were speedily returned, remaining in the town hall for the next two years.

People revelled in the rediscovered delights, soon to be lost again, of uninhibited conversation. In the absence of any form of distracting entertainment, gossip became a favoured pastime. Of course there were the war heroes whose exploits were loudly proclaimed. Like Fleveritz's son Miklos, who'd escaped to the East and came back a tank commander in the Russian army. But there were the other kind of stories, told in whispers and nods. You would think that some people would never venture into the street again. Yet everyone did, the brave and the foolish, the virtuous and the corrupt, the saviours and the sinners. Another word soon became fashionable – reconciliation. Somehow we wouldn't spend too long on who did what in the war. It was as if the act of survival itself justified absolution. The war years became almost a taboo subject. The optimists talked about the future and the pessimists about the Russians.

Then one day something happened that broke the mirage. Something happened that no one expected. Jews got off the bus.

Before the war many Jews lived in Kierscen. The Great Synagogue dominated the southern neighbourhoods where they lived. One day they were gathered together and marched out. Sometime in '43 and that was that. Soon their homes had been moved into, their businesses taken over. There wasn't a villager who hadn't benefited in some way from the discreet looting that went on after they'd gone. Furniture, cutlery, chickens, farm machinery. Everyone became richer.

No one talked about the round-up of the Jews to this day. Yet it hung over the place like a dread. Dread of the day now arrived. When some would come back.

Gershon Steinhart and his son Yozef got off the bus from Warsaw. It was the bizarrest sight. They looked normal. As if they'd been on a three-year shopping trip to the capital. Steinhart was dressed in a sombre black suit that appeared well worn. He could have been a tax inspector or an under-taker. Yozef was also in plain attire: blue trousers and a lighter blue shirt, his hair in neat waves across his forehead.

From the beginning, we had all understood the arrange-ments for the Jews. More so than the Jews themselves. The camp being built for them in Platow was well known. You couldn't miss it. A huge ugly factory on the edge of the town. Some had family who had helped with the construction. They knew its purpose from the start. Everyone did.

It was just a matter of when they would be taken. The restrictions against them began with the occupation. What type of work they could do. Where they could live. They had to wear badges to identify themselves. Then one day a third of the village disappeared into the night. We all heard the commotion, shouting, crying; many came out on to the streets to watch the spectacle. Some stayed at home and locked their doors.

Those who risked sneaking into the emptied neighbour-hood just after the Germans got the richest pickings. By the next morning it was like Christmas. The streets filled with families looking as if they'd just come back from tea with their favourite auntie who'd decided to give them all her possessions. It was like a big jumble sale.

And then the arguments started. Some just moved straight into the vacant houses. You could see fires lit the very next night. It was eerie to witness, as if their ghostly owners had returned. A huge fight broke out over the engineer Levy's property with its prime setting at the end of main street. It was famous for being the first house with a balcony and the Mayor was determined no one else would get their hands on it. It was quickly realised that there would have to be a secret meeting to sort out the various claims being made. In a few weeks it was all resolved and the once Jewish neighbourhood was smoothly occupied. The Mayor got the Levy house.

There were also lots of stories about Jews hiding away treasures. Dontiech got a whole field ploughed up ready for planting on the basis of one rumour everyone became convinced he'd started.

No one really thought about the end of the war. It was hard to at the time. And of course no one thought that any Jews would survive. Then that bus arrived from Warsaw.

Steinhart had been a grocer in the town. He wasn't someone people knew much about. The Jews by and large kept themselves to themselves. There was an understanding about the extent to which the two communities could or could not mix. It had been like that for centuries. Of course there was a lot more mixing going on than people would have you believe. Especially among the young. Politics got everyone talking to each other. And there was the gambling – an indiscriminate passion. If you visited Tinzer Lake in the summer it was clear which part of the lakeshore was taken up by which community. But the island in the middle was a no-man's land, common ground. It was like a free zone where all sorts of things that would never be countenanced in the village went on, and not a few secret romances were begun under the cover of its leafy terrain and permissive ambience. Both sides knew each other well. It wasn't like there was a lot of tension. People just got on with their lives. Everyone bought their bread from old Mama Greenstein's. She was the mother of the town not just the Jewish quarter.

What shocked everyone was how well Steinhart appeared. Initially no one knew who he was. It was only when he went into the Post Office and asked if any letters had been kept for him that the story of his return got out. It chased round the town like a storm. Was he the first of many? Were they all coming back? Maybe the Jews of Kierscen had been treated differently. Maybe they were used as slave labour and had survived. What did Steinhart know?

And what about his home, all the homes, everything that had been owned by the Jews parcelled out to their grateful neighbours. There wasn't a family that hadn't benefited in some way from the bonanza. Even the priest, Father Lubomirski, suddenly procured an ornate rug for his chambers, which it was said, somewhat mischievously, had been taken from Rabbi Wilmeier's place. Would it all have to be returned?

Steinhart was now heading slowly down the main street. The way he walked suggested he wasn't trying particularly to recognise or be recognised. His face was set rigidly forward and he was holding his son Yozef's hand tightly. Yozef's look contrasted his father's. He was smiling at people. But it wasn't a happy smile. It was more like a request. For a moment I thought about the huge welcome-home party they had given Miklos, Fleveritz's son, decked out in his splendid Russian uniform, beaming like he'd won the war by himself. The whole village turned out as if Miklos was everyone's son, a bit of all of us. And you felt this strange sense, that he *had* somehow actually saved the town.

*   *   *

They were heading towards the old Jewish district. It would just be a matter of time before Steinhart would arrive at the door of what was once his home and was now lived in by the butcher Sleider. Sleider had left his former flat above his shop and had been in that house now for over two years. The assumed permanence of his occupancy was further underlined by the slaughterhouse he had built out the back.

Steinhart's journey was being discreetly monitored by all the townspeople. It was like watching a lit fuse meander towards its end. Someone said that he should be spoken to. Reasoned with. We should find out what happened to all the Jews. But no one would volunteer. Someone else said he should be arrested but no one could think why. Fleveritz said it was an official matter and the Mayor should take charge. He disappeared and we assumed he had gone off to get him.

On Praga Street, Steinhart suddenly stopped. Mrs Porwuit was walking up the street and he started talking to her. Soon he was moving on again and Mrs Porwuit was quickly pounced on and interrogated. She didn't reveal much. He'd asked about the clock tower that had stood on the street corner. It had been dismantled and taken by retreating Germans scattering grenades as they ran. She'd asked him about Mama Greenstein but he didn't know.

Steinhart reached the front of the Great Synagogue, now more a ruin than anything else. It had been the most impressive building in the village, much to the annoyance of the Catholic Church, which had successfully lobbied to have the main steeple reduced by fifteen feet to make it lower than its own. The gold lettering that had once adorned its façade had long been stripped away, but the Hebrew and Polish words could still be made out: 'Let mercy roll down like waters and justice like a mighty stream.' They walked around the building and then entered through a side passage. There couldn't have been much to see, but they were there for quite a while. It was being used for storage and what hadn't been taken was rotting away. Maybe they prayed.

People were now waiting for Fleveritz to come back with the Mayor. We gained a bit more intelligence from Mrs Kolchak, who'd sometimes bought food from Steinhart's store. He was a quiet man. His wife mainly served in the shop. And they had two daughters as well as the son. He was in his late forties and Yozef probably eight or nine. Someone said the Mayor was in Cracow. There was a growing sense of panic. Sleider had closed his butcher shop and rushed home.

Steinhart emerged from the Synagogue and carried on southward. Rembertow Street had been the location of the central market and would normally have been bustling with people. The quietness must have been startling for them. But he would surely have known how everything had changed. Now there were only Polish faces in these streets. Surely he didn't expect to come back and find things the same. Return to his home. Go into his kitchen and prepare hot water on the stove. Surely he knew. So what was he doing? That was the baffling thing. Was he simply going home?

They were just a few roads away. In streets that would be very familiar to Yozef. He would have played football with other boys on the rough piece of ground by Poniatowski Avenue. In the winter, he would have sledged down the steep hill on Torun Road, careful to miss the huge hole halfway down that would scupper the less experienced or the careless. Now for both of them, memories would be enveloping. Walking down the same streets that they had been marched out of on that cold spring night. Into the blackness.

Finally, they arrived in front of Sleider's house. Steinhart scrutinised the outside for a moment before, incredibly, taking out a key. It seemed to fit and he turned it but he couldn't open the door. He turned the key again and you could see the door give up some of its resistance yet still it remained closed.

He started knocking, then banging. There was an urgency, an aggressiveness in his manner that contrasted sharply with his careful, ponderous progress through the village. As if his mild demeanour had been corroded by the journey. Yozef looked as if he could fill the street with tears. Then suddenly, like a shock, the door opened and they were gone.

What happened to Steinhart and his son became another concluding fable straight out of the war. Lost in the haze of stories, some true, some less so. It turned out that Fleveritz's son Miklos had spent the war years working in a brothel somewhere in Soviet Asia. Soon no one was sure what really happened to them. Some said they were passing through on their way to Lublin and had caught the next bus out of town, others that they were communist agents. A few even disputed that they had actually got off the bus. No doubt their disappearance was a relief to many.

Their last sighting was the two of them standing in that doorway. Being welcomed in by Sleider. Apparently he had given them a tour of the house. One can only imagine their surprise at seeing the place almost exactly as they had left it. Then he took them out the back.

No more Jews returned to Kierscen. The see-saw of Polish history swung Russian and Red. A joke circulated the village that the engineer Levy had survived the war and was now Mayor of Tel Aviv.

# Giro Day

## *Morag McDowell*

S he sat on the pavement pressing her back against the cold
green-tiled wall, her skinny legs pressed against her chest.
The ground was freezing her bum and messing up her skirt.
People stared at her, the sort of people you see in the afternoon in Saracen St, old men with shopping trolleys and
women like her mum with prams and Tesco bags wearing
high-heeled shoes. She tried to think of something obscene to
shout at them if they spoke to her. Nothing too bad of course;
she didn't want to create a commotion for he might hear her
from inside and it was important to let him come out in his
own time for today was Giro Day, when there was money, lots
of it, and sweets and videos and other special things just there
for the taking. She hunched her shoulders and bent her face
into the collar of her coat, partly because it was only February,
and too cold to sit still for long and partly because it was 1.30
and she couldn't go into school the next day with the note she
knew he would write her if someone saw her sitting on the
front steps of the Viking's Head when she was supposed to be
indisposed. That was the word he always used and it impressed
her, made her sound like a lady. 'Anna was absent from school
yesterday as she was indisposed,' he would write in his
beautiful handwriting with all the whorls and curves making
it look like something more than it actually was. She loved the

words he used, so many of them bubbling out along with the laughs and jokes and the coins and notes he sometimes pulled out of his pocket and gave to her on days like today.

There was a sudden noise and a rush of warmth escaping into the street as the doors swung open. She heard the deep rumble of male voices and smelled the familiar dense air different from that in the street, rich with smoke and beer and the scent of many people pressed together in one room. Sometimes she would jump up when someone came out and try to see through the space before the doors swung shut again but all she ever got were glimpses of a dimly-lit world and sometimes a face glowing suddenly for a few seconds in the flare from a lit match, but it was never his face – he was always hidden away and she knew it was forbidden for her to enter, so she waited.

He was longer than usual, she knew, for she had heard the second bell ring which meant it was past two. A few feet away the traffic churned past – double-decker buses grinding their way up to the depot and cars in bright clean colours using the street as a through road to somewhere else. She was thinking about that morning at school when the teacher had told them about another country in a place called the Southern Hemisphere where there were jungles and cities and deserts where men still lived and the stars were different and even the sky itself seemed bigger. He had said more but as usual she hadn't been listening – she'd been thinking about a new place where she'd live in a desert or a house with a garden and kangaroos jumping past the fence. Perhaps there was a pub there where she would sit baking in the sun instead of freezing her bum off. She closed her eyes and thought of the sky in the Southern Hemisphere spread like an ocean above her and she wanted to fly up there and dive through it until she landed in a strange country like the one behind the swing doors, vast and limitless in its secrets.

She had thought of something to ask him. It was a game they played – she would think of questions – Did the Pope have to go to school, why were bananas yellow and if the gym teacher Miss Watts was a woman why did she have a black moustache? They could be about anything or anyone but he always had to have an answer and even if it was stranger than anything she had ever heard before she would let herself believe him, for he had never disappointed her and he knew more than the people at school. She breathed in deeply and the coldness in the air made her gasp. She touched the tip of her nose with her fingertips. It was numb. Although she looked like her mother she had a nose like her father, or so her grandmother said.

'Ye've a nose like yer father – and yer just as cheeky . . .' she would say, her face fond and sad and her mother would roll her eyes and sigh impatiently, but she was always pleased to hear it, for there was no one else in the world she would rather be like. It was getting cold though.

'Half an a half an one for yerself, Bob.'

He slapped a five pound note on the bartop, then wished he hadn't. A bit obvious. Jim Boy, think ye'd never seen money before. Bob said nothing but nodded in acknowledgement, took the note and started pouring. Didn't feel like he'd been there two hours – didn't feel like one hour – felt like he'd just come in, breathing steam stamping his boots on the wooden floor worn black and smooth with age, nodding at the lads.

'Cauld day outside, eh? Can't stop for long . . .'

'Got the housework to finish, have you?'

Funny, ha ha they all smiled – friendly bunch of bastards.

'Beats ye up if her dinner's not ready, does she?'

Roars of laughter and he'd bought a round. That was what had started it. He'd only stopped for one, but he had to go in before getting the messages – couldn't walk into the Viking's Head with Tesco bags and blow the street cred forever, so he'd gone in just to sample the atmosphere. It was busy for a Thursday afternoon – noise fair bouncing off the yellowed walls, and everywhere warm steamy air stinking of damp clothes and whisky breath. He let it wash over him in pleasant waves. He'd never liked this place before – bit of a working man's pisspot, now there's a misnomer if ever there was one, and he'd felt out of place at first until one day he'd seen his face in the mirror above the bar and not even realised it was his own. It was sallow, dreamy as though he'd just woken up, needing a shave, and it blended perfectly. To his surprise he hadn't panicked, just ordered another drink and smiled up at his reflection in belated recognition. Didn't seem like two hours. He drank the short Bob had set in front of him then lifted the half pint and downed it in one. Felt better than he had in weeks, leaning into the bar, smiling at faces he thought he recognised, feeling the change clinking heavy in his trouser pocket, patting occasionally the thin wad of notes on the inside of his jacket. He should go now, if he went now there would still be enough left – just, but it was warm and someone was just starting on a funny story that no one was listening to, so it was easy to let the muscles of his face relax into a cheesy grin, close his eyes tight and bellow with laughter with every-one else. It felt like old times.

If he went now, it wouldn't be bad. She'd just be waiting to make dinner – mince, oven chips and Pampers, yum yum, and then he'd pay the gas bill, mind he'd forgotten about that – probably not enough left now to cover everything, what the fuck did he go and buy a round for . . .

'Same again Bob . . .'

Bob's face was white and ghastly looking like a dead slug, but he took care of his customers. There was always a slate at Bob's till Giro Day.

'Celebrating something are we?'

'Whit's it tae you?'

Hadn't meant it to come out like that, his voice cold and angry, but Bob just turned away, murmuring 'Nothing at all, Jim Boy, nothing at all . . .'

He turned away from the bar. Big Davie was talking now. He couldn't remember when Davie had started to look like a waxwork of himself, his face blotchy red and white, hands chubby pink and wrinkle free, nose and fingers yellow at the tips as though he had been dipped in a preserving solution that didn't work properly.

'Did ye hear about Minty?'

His right eyebrow arched dramatically and he took a quick puff of his cigarette.

'Superglued his hand to the counter at the DHSS an said he wisnae movin' till they gave him his rights. When the police came he told them it wis a protest against Thatcherism. Naebody had the heart tae tell him she wisnae there any more. Fire Brigade had tae saw off the desk top an carry it wi him intae the ambulance.'

He shook his head.

'He's a sad case . . . Mind ye, they've sent him tae wan i the best psychiatrists in Scotland. Jist think whit a yuppie would pay tae endure whit he's gettin' free. Talkin' of yuppies – how's Jim Boy today?'

He smiled at the insult, habitual ever since they'd caught him reading a copy of *The Times* in the park one afternoon. Big Davie looked over at him questioningly and made an operatic drinking gesture with his arm.

'Thanks Davie, but I've got to go.'

Davie walked past him to the bar.

'Don't be such an old woman, sit down and enjoy a pint.'

He took the drink and walked back towards the table, the glass held unnaturally high in his hand, his body floating between the chairs and elbows and shoulders shaking with laughter. He couldn't work out what was so funny. It seemed odd to him. Maybe he'd been this way before, but it was too long ago to remember like everything else in his head except the walk from here to the house and the Post Office and her face white and blank but still managing to project just the right amount of bloody-minded mute suffering. The girl looked like her mostly, same sharp blue eyes, same red hair, same laugh from what he remembered – he always wished she didn't look and sound so much like her mother.

He blinked as Davie's stubby yellow fingers waved before his eyes.

'Penny for them, Jim Boy . . .'

'Nothin' worth tellin . . .'

'Life and soul of the party aren't we?'

He drank back a third of the beer.

'So how's Mary?'

Big Davie shrugged.

'Mer sarcastic every day, goin' on at me about money an' houses an' how she wants her place in the sun . . . place in the sun, I ask you. Ah think it's the change of life . . .'

'What is?'

'That's makin' her talk all this crap.'

'At least she talks to you . . .'

As soon as he said it he wished he hadn't. Davie looked at him seriously.

'No gettin' on together?'

'Ach am only jokin'. He shrugged and smiled ruefully, 'Got to be grateful for small mercies . . .'

He drank the rest of his beer. It was the sort of joke he'd never, laughed at. One of the boys now aren't you Jim? He felt Davie poking his arm.

'Never mind Jim, at least ye've still got one female fan.'

He put down his drink and saw Davie wink in the direction of the door. Someone had just left and the doors swung to and fro blowing the cold air in. He felt it on his face and saw her white face and saw a halo of red curls bobbing about, then disappearing altogether.

'Shit . . .'

Davie looked at him, puzzled. 'Everything all right, Jim Boy?'

He shook his head and stood up. At least he could still walk straight – probably.

'Sure Davie, everything's fine and dandy. Here.' He threw three pound coins on the table. 'Get one for yerself . . .'

'Don't be daft . . .'

But he had already turned away and was pushing his way towards the door. Silly little cow, waiting for him like that, standing on the pavement like some kind of street urchin. Walk straight he thought, smile, walk straight, take care, be cheerful . . . one day, he thought, one day I'll walk out of here and keep on walking and never come back – I'll emigrate, go to Australia, build bridges, dig ditches, shear bloody sheep, anything till I've made a few bob, then I'll send for them and it'll be better again. All it takes is a few bob. One day but not today, Jim, for it's Giro Day and you'd better get your lazy arse back home while there's still some of it left . . . He pushed the doors open and the cold air bit, sobering him instantly.

She had wanted to surprise him, but it didn't work. He just stood there in his boots that he wore for going round the building sites, swaying a bit as though an invisible wind were blowing him this way and that, not saying hello or smiling, just waiting for her to get up.

'Ye shouldn't wait out here like that. Ye'll catch cold.'

She jumped up and took his hand and began to tell him about school, about the Southern Hemisphere and the world that lay beneath it. He looked at the pavement and listened. When she asked the question it sounded stupid, not the way she had hoped.

'Is it true the sky's a different shape down there?'

He shrugged and looked down the street. 'Don't know . . .'
She tried again. 'Haven't you been there then, Dad?'

'Never have been, never will be.'

The finality of it silenced her for a moment. She thought
again of diving through the deep blue like Wonderwoman, her
body like an arrow, outstretched arms with small fists parting
the clouds and her hair blown out like a slipstream behind her.
Then she had an idea.

'One day I'll go there and find out for myself . . .'

She was scared for a moment that he'd laugh. He'd never
done before, but something in his face made her think he
might.

'So you will darlin', so you will.'

He squeezed her to him for a minute then they turned
together and began to walk down the street. She realised they
were going straight home, not via the shops and she wondered
what had changed for it was Giro Day, when there was money
and sweets and special things just there for the taking.

# The First of the Month

## *Hannah McGill*

O n the evening of the day that Iris and Lilly die I go and
see Carl Cotton's band play. In the morning as I'm
leaving his room I notice his fingers against the white pillow-
slip, bloodied up to the knuckle. I don't mention it, but I
immediately begin to feel it, the heaviness at the pit of my
stomach, the pain.

On the street I meet Dominic, who is wearing a bright-red
shirt. I tell him I have never seen him in red before. He says
that he is celebrating the imminent dawn of a new era of
socialism. I look at him blankly, realising that it's the first of
the month and I have barely given a thought to the general
election. We go for coffee, though I am damp and dirty and
sticking to yesterday's clothes in the new sunshine. In the café
toilet I buy Tampax from a slot machine and clean up the mess
as best I can. Sitting down at our table I feel myself spread
across the chair as if I were made of something less solid than
flesh; I feel all hips and haunches, all womb, my whole body
centring on that low ache. I remove a clot of mascara from the
inner corner of my eye as the waiter takes our order and
Dominic asks me what is wrong.

'Iris and Lilly died.'
'Your two old ladies?'

'Yes. Both on the same day, isn't that odd? It seems that Iris just made up her mind that things wouldn't be much fun without Lilly, folded her arms and breathed her last.'

'I am sorry, Sarah-Jane.'

'Oh, you know.'

'Have you been up all night?'

I think about this, recalling various positions, various requests, various exclamations. I woke up at some stage, so I must have slept. 'No,' I say, 'I slept a bit.'

'Who with?'

Dominic is being sly.

'Cotton.'

Dominic wrinkles his beaky nose at me. 'Oh, I say, what an honour. He's been after that for a while.'

'Allegedly.'

'And you?'

'He dedicated a song to me. I felt indebted. It was just . . . convenient.'

The coffee comes. Dominic tells the waiter, 'She has no heart.' The waiter smiles beautifully at me and says, 'Who needs a heart when a heart can be broken?'

'Oh, you're such a show-off. Get away with you and stop flaunting your intellect.' Dominic scolds, tearing a sugar sachet. 'You shouldn't be wearing blue, by the way, on a day like today. Someone might see you and subconsciously absorb that image of blueness, only for it to resurface just when they're standing in the booth with the ballot paper.'

The waiter looks down at himself as if just remembering what he's wearing and says, 'When I lived at home our polling station was in the chip shop.'

'You're joking?' I say.

'No, it's true. There were even pictures of it in the papers because it was so weird.'

'And was that the formative experience that inspired you to

136

enter the heady world of catering yourself? Did you anticipate finding yourself at the epicentre of world politics, serving fried-egg sandwiches?' Dominic asks. I draw circles in a pool of coffee, smiling.

'I must remember to vote,' the waiter muses. As he speaks, the sun breaks through cloud and dazzles the white-walled room. We all laugh as if this is the punchline to a joke, and Dominic proposes a toast with his coffee cup to the new, just republic that the dawn and Peter Snow will herald. I ask him where he has obtained this new-found faith in Tony Blair's Labour party and he tells me, 'I decided last night, while you were no doubt engaged in some kind of tussle with that pock-marked creature over there, that blind optimism was the only reasonable way to approach the whole undignified affair.'

I follow his eyes and see that sure enough Carl Cotton has entered the café with another boy.

I spent last Tuesday afternoon as I have spent many of my Tuesday afternoons, reading to Iris and Lilly in the Silver Birches Rest Home. There are no silver birches in the vicinity. Lilly dozed in her chair and Iris looked out of the window. The Rector's Wife was open in front of me. I made an uncertain start. Iris twisted her hands in her lap and turned to me, eyes watery behind great pink-tinged glasses. She was seventy-nine, the nurses thought. Lilly was seventy-six.

'Lilly's been unwell. She's quite washed out.' Iris leaned towards me, confidentially. 'You'll keep an eye, won't you? An eye on her. A pretty young thing like you must have so many other places to go, people to see. But if you'd keep an eye . . . I'd be grateful.'

'I will. I . . . shall I read, Iris?'

'She's sleeping. She wouldn't want to miss any.'

'No.'

'Ah . . . it's not how they said it would be.' Her voice was a whisper as she turned back to the window. Sunlight moved on the dirty pane and the television in the next room suddenly blared bright voices. Lilly stirred but did not wake. On the floor, the bananas I had brought as a gift spilled out of their brown paper bag. The room was almost unbearably hot; my hands were moist and the air was thick and sleepy. At first the smell had bothered me, the smell of stale clothes and un-washed skin and old food, but now I barely noticed it, and when I did, when after a visit I caught a whiff of it on my clothes, I was reminded of Iris and Lilly and I felt nothing but affection.

Lilly's hands, sound asleep in her lap, were like Chinese paper. I had touched them, and felt how dry and delicate they were. She had tiny fingers, but they still wore their rings, so they must have been small always.

I peeled a banana for Iris and gave it to her in bits that left a wet powderish deposit on my fingers. She sucked the pieces like sweets as Lilly's wheezy snores marked time and Joanna Trollope rested unread in my lap. I moved the book to the table, afraid that it would slide from me and hit the floor. I couldn't, at that torpid moment, conceive of anything ever being that loud or sudden again. I remembered the interminable Sunday afternoons of my childhood when I would lie slumped against my father's chest while he watched football in front of the fire, muzzy-headed and sluggish and eventually fractious, half-hearing the commentator's monotone, feeling the uncomfortable thud of my father's heartbeat and the prickle of heat on my skin as the kitchen smells of hot laundry and cooking meat mingled in the drowsy air.

'Carl.'

'Hi . . .' He looks to the side, then down, circling his pretty head, not quite looking at me. I am, as always in these situations, a little amazed by the notion that I am facing someone who only hours before was breathing all over me, panting on me, occupying me. My eye darts involuntarily to his fingers; they're clean. I picture him at the tap, scrubbing, running brownish water down the drain. It seems like witch-craft, to have marked him like that. Will he trail me now like a cat after catnip, dazed and adoring, hexed? A real smile troubles my fake one for a moment as I picture it. Carl crouches down by my chair and his friend, whom I know vaguely from occasional drug transactions, exchanges gruff words with Dominic whilst kicking the leg of the table. Dominic stops being arch.

'Haven't you been home?' Carl asks, quietly, washed hand by his mouth, looking around as if he expects to see his mother watching us.

'Do I look like I have? Dominic waylaid me.'

'You left your cigarettes.' He looks at me now; I'm re-minded of his eyes, the eyes everyone always talks about, and I stop wanting him to go away quite so much.

'Did you bring them?'

He shrugs. 'Didn't know I was going to see you. Do you want one of mine?' He takes a packet from the top pocket of his shirt and shakes out two. He taps his on the table a long time before lighting it, looking like a little boy playing cow-boys. He's beautiful, Carl Cotton, that's the thing, that's why I honoured Iris and Lilly with such an energetic wake last night. He has the kind of remarkable configuration of features normally confined, in my experience, to celluloid and maga-zine pages; his eyelashes are half an inch long and his nose is as neatly sculpted as that of a china shepherdess. A delicate boy, only a little taller than me and slender, so slender that in bed he made me feel enormous and clumsy, like one of those awkward mediaeval Madonnas clutching a spindly, wise-eyed Christ child. I always liked boys like that, little boys. I went out with a big man once, a foot taller than me and twice my weight, or almost, and he crushed me. He crushed all the air out of me and I couldn't move him about like I wanted to.

I draw hard on my cigarette; Carl smokes a different brand from me, a fashionably cheap one, and the taste is unfamiliar and harsh. At the next table a moon-faced baby watches me wisely. I mouth 'Hello'. The baby stares and frowns. Too loud, Dominic asks Carl if he's voted yet. Carl turns from me to show Dominic his dumbly lovely eyes and say, 'Don't see the point. I'm not even registered, I don't think.'

'I can see you want to leave, dear. Are you meeting a boy?'

'Actually, Iris, I just really want a cigarette.'

'Oh, dear. A smoker. Are you a smoker?' Her face creased with concern, she laid a light hand on my knee. 'My husband wouldn't have let you in the house.'

'But I thought he smoked a pipe!' I pictured this dead husband, stern and small and rattish with fading ginger hair and liver-spotted hands to match hers. Suddenly I couldn't remember if she had shown me a photograph of him or if I had just constructed this image of him from what she had told me. I could almost smell him, sharp sweat and dry tobacco, old man smells. She laughed.

'He did, but he wouldn't have a woman smoke in the house.'

Carl Cotton has, as Dominic said, been after me for a while. He has a thing about my face. I am not used to this and find it strange. I was never pretty, but some shift has occurred, some accident of space and skin; I'll never be one of those delicate rose-petal girls, but I have acquired a certain power. What used to bulge now curves, and cheekbones have emerged and eyebrows arch interestingly, and all of a sudden people look my way as if I have a light over my head. I am not at ease with it, not yet; my reflection still shocks me as if I've had a

particularly drastic haircut. I am like someone who has unexpectedly grown an extra hand; I know it'll probably be
useful, but I haven't accustomed myself to it, yet not learnt
how to use it. Last night, though, my mourning dress clung
about me in a sleek, slatey way, slimmed and sharpened me
and made a statue of me. Carl bought me gin and tonic and its
glassy sparkle cooled the flush on my face, but he didn't
understand the novelty of my position, because he has always
been beautiful. He wakes up beautiful, exists all day in a
cocoon of beauty, and goes to bed at night still beautiful.
Adolescence held no horrors for him; the whole town watched
him make an effortless transition from pretty child to handsome youth without the intervention of spots or puppy fat. He
still has a child's skin, absolutely smooth, and that combined
with the lightness of him, his airy bird-boned delicacy, his five-
foot-six, that lent an innocence to acts that might have seemed
sordid with somebody else. He was so clean, he tasted of
nothing and had a baby's smell, a slight powdery sweetness in
the bends of his body. He was like a thing newly made.

I raise my eyebrows at Dominic, who I can see is teetering
on the brink of some embarrassingly erudite tirade about
democracy, and I tell him that I need to go home and get
clean. Carl moves smoothly to face me again and his smile is
languorous and hopeful. His eyes touch my hips, my stomach,
my breasts, with which he was too rough. I can feel bruising,
tenderness. I will look in the mirror later on in sickly afternoon
sunshine and see red reminders of his fingernails. It's not that
he was violent, just over enthusiastic. Like a dog jumping on
to a settee and making itself comfortable without thought for
the upholstery.

'You going out tonight, Sarah-Jane?'

'Watching the election.'

He rolls his eyes and smiles indulgently. 'You going to
vote?'

'Not old enough. I'm only seventeen, remember? I missed out by a week.'

The waiter passes with a little pot of baby food which he has microwaved for the moon-faced baby. The mother looks overwhelmed with gratitude, as if the waiter has done this for her unbidden. The baby reaches out a fat small hand and I feel a little weak.

When I left on Tuesday Lilly was still asleep and I never saw her awake again. I don't know the details. I didn't really ask. She'd been ill a long time and she didn't suffer, they said. With Iris I think it was more dramatic. That would be typical of Iris. A fall, an attack, clamour, a noisy death.

I sit up with Dominic to watch the polls come in. The pain has settled in my belly, curled up tight and made a home, and we are opening the fifth bottle of wine as Michael Portillo loses his seat.

'I haven't seen so much red,' says Dominic as the scarlet bands flash feverishly at the bottom of the screen, 'since I last gave blood.' I know very well that Dominic has never given blood. The next morning I go into town to buy something to wear at the funerals; I am sick with sleeplessness and drink but everyone on the bus is smiling.

# Losing Teeth

## *Hannah McGill*

'Have you been at school?' the woman asked, leaning in on the child with eyes wide. She had stringy blonde hair scraped up into a ponytail and she wore earrings that dangled and caught the light; perhaps they were supposed to look like flowers or bunches of grapes. Nothing about her could have been called beautiful, but she was trying to be kind. The child nodded distractedly, not looking at her, holding on to the back of her father's chair and looking around the room.

'It's fucking great,' the father said. 'She brings home these bits of paper with blobs of paint on and her name in the corner and you have to go, "That's lovely, yeah." '

The bearded man across the table sniggered into his coffee cup. 'Lucky they have short memories at that age so you can chuck the thing in the bin when they've gone to bed and they won't remember in the morning.'

The woman rolled her big eyes at them in reprimand and then looked back at the little girl, who was chewing thoughtfully on her hair and gazing at the bearded man. 'Ssh – oh, they wouldn't do that, would they? You'd remember, wouldn't you? Your pictures? She knows what you're talking about, Rob.'

The little girl swung herself around the back of her father's chair, changed hands and swung back again, still silent.

'She does not.'

The bearded man called the waiter over and ordered coffee. The waiter raised his eyebrows at the little girl as he passed, and she looked at him with interest. He had blue hair, bright blue, and he was wearing a bright-pink shirt. She watched him hurry back to the counter, looking at his little notebook with a puzzled face, and to no one in particular, perhaps to him although he was now busy at the coffee machine, she said, 'I had two biscuits at milk time today because Holly couldn't eat hers.'

'What did you say, love?' asked the wide-eyed woman.

'Holly couldn't eat hers.'

'Her what?'

The child didn't reply; she wanted the blue-haired waiter to come back. She had been promised orange juice when they left the house, when she'd cried, but she'd seen no evidence of it as yet. She put her finger in her mouth to count her teeth again.

'Did she have a sore tummy?' asked the woman.

A lady had come in and was talking to the waiter over the counter. The café was very small, and they had taken the nearest table to the counter, so the little girl was close enough to see behind it and to hear the waiter talking. She edged towards him, looking. He must have put something in his hair, she thought, to make it blue. She didn't think that people could really have that colour hair. The new lady had black hair, and big dark eyes with a lot of black around them. She leaned very close to the waiter and they talked through big smiles.

'He wouldn't even have to know.'

'Oh, Michael. This is such a small town.'

It's not a small town, thought the little girl, it's a big town. She thought of the distance to school, and of the buses to Granny's house. The town is so big, she thought, that you might not even be able to walk across it in a day. Just when you think it's going to stop, there's another street you never saw before, another bright parade of shops, another road, button to press, reach up on tiptoe, wait for the green man, don't run in case you fall down. Most people in the town won't ever even meet each other.

'He knows the score as well as I do,' the bearded man was saying, 'the funding's just not there.' The girl's father was twisting round in his seat, though, not listening, looking over and frowning, waiting for coffee that was cooling on the counter as the waiter talked. Other people were waiting too, looking with impatient faces, a boy with a camera round his neck, a girl with red hair. The blue waiter and the dark-haired girl kept talking, talking over each other as if they were trying to sing a round, like at nursery, London's burning, London's burning, if you're the last group to start you end up singing on your own, 'Fire, fire,' and everyone looks.

'Look at her. Melanie! Jesus, you know, something's not right there. Look at her staring. Looks like the village idiot.'

Melanie was her name; people always said, 'What a pretty name!' It sounded like melons, melony. Some people said Mel. She didn't like that.

'Takes after her mother. Big blue eyes and an empty fucking head.'

The blue waiter had his hand over the lady's hand now and she was laughing, pulling away, and he was saying 'Chrissy, Chrissy . . .'

'Mike, we decided . . .'

'You decided.'

'All right then, I decided . . .'

Chrissy. Christmas. After Christ because it's his birthday. Kissy, kissy.

'Melanie!'

Melanie thought she would prefer to be called Laura or Kelly. Laura Hodge and Kelly McKay sat together at school and the teacher sometimes said they were twins because they both had yellow hair and they always went to the toilet together. Miss Croft said to them, 'Does it take two of you?', but she said it with a smile and she always let them go. Melanie's father was angry now, because of the coffee. The blue waiter was biting the lady's fingers; she almost looked cross, but she was still smiling. Melanie had once liked biting people's fingers too. The taste and texture of skin had been interesting to her, and she had been curious to find out whether she could draw blood, though the idea of doing so had made her shudder. She never did, and she was glad, and her mother had finally screamed and told her never to bite again and that she was a little savage. Savage was like a tiger, and it was like an advert on TV for perfume where a lady crawled on the ground. Sssavage. In a whisper. Melanie tried it out. Ssss. The waiter went past her, carrying coffee, in a hurry, in too much of a hurry, spilling.

'Not before time,' said the bearded man. The boy and girl with the camera between them got up and left, shaking their heads and laughing. From the counter the dark-haired lady smiled; she was straightening her coat, brushing herself down, about to leave too. Seeing this, the waiter went to her and stood close and they spoke too softly for Melanie to hear.

'Don't blame him, though,' the bearded man said thickly. 'Bloody lovely.'

'Too young for you,' said Melanie's father.

'Maybe if I started dressing like a faggot . . .'

The door swung shut behind the lady. Unexpectedly, the blue boy turned to smile at Melanie. She smiled back. 'I wanted some orange juice,' she said accusingly. He came closer to hear her better and she repeated herself.

'Well, I can get you some orange juice,' he said. He went over to a little fridge behind the counter and took out a carton. Once Melanie had been to a café where the orange juice bubbled in a big fishtank thing. He poured it into a red cup. Melanie wished he would use a proper glass. He gave her the cup and crouched down so their heads were level. Forgetting to say thank you, she asked, 'Is your hair real?'

'Is yours?' he asked.

She touched her own head and giggled. 'Of course.'

'Ha! I made you smile.'

She tightened her mouth, trying not to smile more.

'You can touch it, if you like. To see if it's real.' He inclined his head, an invitation. She was hesitant. 'Normally of course I only let very important people touch it – princes, princesses, lion tamers. But I'll make an exception for you.'

Not knowing what an exception was, she touched his hair. It felt real.

'My hair is golden,' she said.

'Looks mud coloured to me.'

She knitted her brow. 'It's golden. Mud's brown.'

'You just don't play in the right kind of mud.'

'Do you play in mud?'

'It has been known.'

'I don't like mud.'

'Everyone likes mud.'

'Once Kelly McKay trod mud into the Reading Area. Miss Croft made her clean it up. She had to scrub on her knees like Cinderella.' Melanie said this almost in a whisper, but he didn't seem to be listening anyway; he'd turned away, was looking towards the door. The orange juice had bits in it. She caught them on her tongue. They felt like little pieces of skin. The blue waiter had black hairs in his nose. She imagined his whole face being hairy on the inside, as if he was a bear turned inside out.

Her father called her again.

'Look at her chatting up the bloody waiter. I told you she takes after her mother.'

The blue boy looked back at her, but vaguely, with a distant look. 'Unhappy face,' she said, reaching out to sketch an exaggerated frown over his real one with her finger, and making him smile. She saw the gap.

'Where is your tooth?'

'I don't know.'

'When did it come out?'

'Six months ago. Someone hit me.'

'Hit you?'

'A boy hit me.'

'Why?'

'Oh . . . I said the wrong thing.'

Melanie thought about this. Some more people had come in and were talking noisily, laughing, moving chairs. 'Did you stop being friends with him?' she asked.

'I never really was his friend, to tell you the truth.'

'Will a new one grow?'

The blue boy didn't answer; he looked around the café as if he'd just remembered it was there. Then he turned back to Melanie and said, confidentially, 'I'll have to go now, but it's been very nice talking to you. Your hair is prettier than any mud I've ever seen.'

'Thank you,' she said.

'Leave him alone, will you?' said Melanie's father to her as the waiter hurried over to the new tableful of people clutching his little notebook. 'Christ. Come here. Oh, been making orders for yourself, have you? How much will that set me back?'

'He gave me it.'

'I bet he did. Sit up here. Put that down. You've got it on your dress . . . What did Steve say?'

The bearded man said, 'I told him, "This is meant to be a fucking collective." He said, "It's meant to be a business as well."'

'Jesus.'

'I told you.'

'You know the situation as well as I do, though; the funding's just not there.'

'Doesn't give Steve the right to act the fucking dictator.'

The woman sighed, and shifted forward to rest her loose bosom on her arms. 'Steve's just trying to do his job, same as you.'

The bearded man turned on her angrily and hissed, 'Who asked for your opinion?'

'I'm just saying . . .'

'Well, don't, because what you say rarely makes a lot of sense.'

The woman looked down at the tabletop and rubbed her jaw. It never seemed to sit quite right, and one back tooth still felt loose to her, though he told her it was her imagination. Behind the counter, the waiter pressed his eyes with the heels of his hands until he saw stars and counted the hours and half-hours between him and the bus home, while Melanie pulled herself up on to her father's lap and curled into his chest, feeling the springiness of hair behind his shirt and knowing that he wouldn't let her sit there long.

# A Bit of the Map

## Seonaid McGill

W e were the only ones who saw her get off the boat that morning. We were the only ones who weren't waiting for anything.

Bleak March, undecided for days, with a weak light that never touches the chill on the sea or even makes an effort to lift the skin of glower from the dense sky. Everyone wrapped in scarves and hats. Gloves stuffed in pockets. Raw, chapped hands waving, grabbing. Questions whipped about by the engines' low rumble. Enough cigarettes on the go to give a fair run to the queasy, oily stink of the boat's innards. We stood apart, me and Lizzie, and nobody noticed us. We'd gone beyond the 'poor wee souls' stage and, without even grazing the sides of acceptance, dropped straight into invisibility.

But invisible people are lucky when it comes to looking. She slipped off the boat; straight, thin, eyes washed sea glass clean, and we saw her. We were the only ones. No one came to meet her; no car waited up on the road; no jerky hands in the air tried to attract her attention; she just walked away. Didn't seem to expect anyone, didn't hesitate for a minute.

And we saw her; step lightly over the low wooden fence, tick the heel of her shoe with a smooth leather finger, hoist her bag a little higher. She didn't dart the curious looks of a stranger; she didn't stop to check directions; she didn't turn to see where she had come from; she just walked straight on to where she was going.

'Did you see that woman off the boat?' Lizzie said on the way back.

We'd moved off before the others. If anyone had spoken to us they'd have wanted to know where our dad was and I'd get red from the lie I was about to tell. Or, even worse, Lizzie would just open her mouth and everyone would see exactly what was in her head.

'Shut up, Lizzie.'

I was twelve that March and filled with spite. Even I couldn't tell why I was that way: I just was. Every time Lizzie spoke to me I wanted to kick her knobby legs or swear at her. Lizzie was nine and she didn't even notice. She just kept on going until I wanted to kick her so much it was almost unbearable. I hadn't yet, but it was only a matter of time.

'I've seen her before you know.' Lizzie dodged up the road, bobbing and bouncing, the hems of her too-short jeans sticking out like funnels around her bony ankes and the sole of one gym shoe spitting and flapping at the dust.

'I said shut up. You haven't see her before, or anyone else. You're just like me. You don't know anyone.'

'I do. I know her. I know I know her.'

Lizzie was way ahead now. Lucky for her, I thought, kicking the loose stones on the road instead. She was singing. One of those annoying songs that don't have a real tune or words, just a noise beeping out of Lizzie's mouth.

'Think Dad'll be up yet?' She shouted back at me between beeps. 'I think he might be.'

'Well if you know why are you asking me? Anyway, there's no way he's up: he was up all night.'

As it turned out, this one time, I was wrong. He was up, wandering around, green looking and slick with hangover.

When he bent down to kiss the top of my head, his breath was the stale goo in the bottom of an empty whisky glass.

Our dad, waiting all his life for a big, sick Mercedes to slide into his garage and release the magic he knew he had in his hands. That was his dream. The silent purring engine, the smooth leather seats, the power to go anywhere, to take you out of whatever you'd got yourself into. But a garage on an island where cars are run to rust and then abandoned to the elements wasn't a magnet for Mercedes. Still, it was the only dream he had and it was quite a small dream, no harm in it, except the only way my dad could enjoy it was in the company of a whisky bottle at four in the morning.

'We saw someone we know down at the boat, Dad.' Lizzie plaited the fringes on the old, doggy smelling blanket round his shoulders.

'Did you? That's nice, love.'

It wasn't that he wasn't interested, it was just that he didn't really know how to be. He'd never got the way of it, the knack of being about us, the remembering to listen. He used to try harder, but even that effort seemed too much now and when he stopped bothering I don't think me and Lizzie really noticed. It was like someone who wasn't there much, went away forever. You knew that they'd gone but it didn't make a lot of difference because their being there hadn't made much difference either.

He did take us to see a film once, in the town hall, about a baby that was stolen by seals. He was excited, went on and on about how he used to tell our mum she looked like a seal maiden and how we'd know what he meant when we saw the film. We weren't too convinced about this, considering neither of us could even remember our mum, but we were going to get an ice cream afterwards and he was sober, so we didn't really care.

But the film just made him sad and he forgot all about the

ice cream and just took us straight home, all quiet and sour about his mouth. Shouted at us to get into our nighties, slammed doors and went to look for the big, sick Mercedes all by himself in the kitchen, all night long.

And now that was mostly what he did all the time: drank and dreamed and told Lizzie she looked like our mum. And that was hard to believe, because if that was what a seal maiden looked like, then no wonder seals went around trying to steal humans.

'She looked like the seal maiden, Dad. The woman off the boat. She looked like the seal maiden.' Lizzie never gave up.

'You don't see many of those, Lizzie,' Dad said, looking around for his cigarettes, which were sticking, like crushed fingers, out of the top pocket of his shirt. 'No, it's a lucky girl who sees a seal maiden: they can teach you a thing or two.'

I could see where this was going. Dad was a drunk who cried and whined at the injustice of it all, but hungover he was even worse: knew everything and wanted to share his wisdom with the world.

''mon, Lizzie, I'll take you down the beach. We'll get some shells.' I didn't feel like getting any wiser that day.

Our beach wasn't on any postcards. The seaweed was too seaweedy, the sand too wet and the sky hung over it like a fat, grey belly. It didn't have enough of anything, and too much of everything that wasn't wanted when it came to beaches.

Even the path down was mean: a narrow, broken scar of loose stones and sharp, whipping grass. All day and all night that grass whispered malevolently to the beach and the beach hummed back. An endless, sinister dialogue.

Lizzie didn't mind. She bounced along, jeans flapping, sole flapping, arms waving, bucket banging off her knees. I was a bit more careful. That was another thing about that March: I was more careful, less bouncy and flappy, more pulled together. And like the spite, I didn't know where it had come from.

It was just above the beach that we saw her. Down on the sand at the water's edge, drawing shapes with a stick and walking back slowly to let the tide wash them away. Draw, walk, wash, a solitary dance on a dismal day.

Lizzie shrieked.

'There's the woman off the boat, the one I know.'

'Ssh, you don't know anything, Lizzie, or you wouldn't be shouting and bellowing at the top of your voice at a stranger on the beach.'

Lizzie's voice went quiet, but her face didn't. She looked like Dad on his ninth glass when he suddenly realised the Mercedes was always going to be a beat-up old transit van.

I pulled her down into the long, sharp grass and together we watched the woman dance with the waves.

She was way down on the beach and we were way up on the path, but I knew her pale eyes. I knew they looked like the sea after a storm, washed clean of all memory. And I knew she knew we were there. And that we were the people she didn't have to look for when she got off the boat.

Not once did she look up. She just went on dancing. The waves got meaner and her movements wider, then suddenly she stopped, dropped the stick and turned towards our huddle on the path. She raised her hand, and for a second I thought she was going to wave.

Lizzie broke first. Jumping to her feet she ran, skidding down the stones, arms wide, mouth a perfect 'O', right up to the woman. And when I expected her to stop short, she didn't. She just kept running, right into her arms. I thought then, that Lizzie did know her after all. And what was strange was that it wasn't strange at all.

I didn't run; running wasn't something I was doing that March either. I walked, slowly, carefully, taking my time to rehearse the words I would say when I reached them. How I would take Lizzie's hand and apologise to the woman, and how we would turn away and the things I'd do to Lizzie when we got home.

But even from a distance I could see there was nothing to say. Lizzie stood with the woman and her faded drawings as if she was meant to be there, as if this was what was supposed to happen. And they were waiting for me.

'Becky?' The woman's voice was low, but so loud that the gulls wheeled, shocked, above us and the whole beach was filled with the sound.

I wasn't surprised she knew my name. I think I would have been more surprised if she hadn't. And when she touched my hair, I didn't mind, and I always minded when people touched me that March.

We walked, and she talked. Not looking at me, but out towards the sea. She talked about the spite and the pulled-together feeling and the loneliness and not belonging. She talked about our dad and the big, sick Mercedes. She talked about making soup and washing hair. She talked about loving people. She talked about knowing where to go and always seeing that place ahead and never doubting that you'd get there. She talked about my whole life that had been and that was going to be. And while she talked I felt that warm way you do just before you don't remember going to sleep: one minute your head's full of worry and wishing, the next you're some-where far away and you don't care anymore.

Lizzie was ahead of us, beeping her songs. But this time there were words. Something about seals and babies and maidens. And I thought I remembered.

'You're the seal maiden?'

She laughed.

'No. If I had a lifetime to be here I couldn't teach you what a seal maiden could. The seal maidens don't lose what belongs to them; they hold on forever. Whatever happens they never let go.'

'But sometimes you find what you've lost. Sometimes it just turns up again and it wasn't lost at all.' I don't know why I said this. I just wanted her to go on talking, to stop staring out at the hard water, to take away the sadness.

'I thought that too,' she said at last. 'But it's not true. If you've really lost something you can't go back and find it, because even if it's there it isn't the same. All I can give you is a bit of the map to take you a little further forward, and maybe that's all you need now, Becky. The rest you can do yourself.'

I looked along the beach, and for the first time ever I wished I was Lizzie: beeping and bouncing and flapping through the waves. Sticky with sand and knowing nothing about spite and being careful and pulled together. Lizzie didn't need a map: she always knew where she was going.

'Don't go.' I could hear panic in my voice, a wheedling, teary edge. I sounded little and pleady and, even as I was speaking, my own voice shocked me.

The woman bent to pick up another stick and didn't look at me. 'I've got to go. I can't stay with you. This is just like a visit, to move you on a little when you needed me.'

'So, you'll come again? For Lizzie?'

'No. Lizzie won't need me. Lizzie has you. You have more of the map now, and once you know the way, you'll come back and take Lizzie.'

'But what if I can't find the way on my own? What if I can't take Lizzie?'

'You will. You will find the way. And you will take Lizzie.'

She did go; she talked all the afternoon away, but she did go. And she never came back. For a long time we went to the boat to look for her and we asked people if they'd seen her and they looked at us as if we were daft. And after a while I began to think we were. But then, when it came to moving forward, I could, and I could because I had a little bit of the map, the bit she'd given me. I did find the rest for myself eventually, and I

157

did come back for Lizzie and I did take her with me and she had part of her own map to add to mine.

Our dad never stopped dreaming about the Mercedes, right up until the day he died, slumped over our kitchen table. We left the island and went on to have a different life that didn't have boats to wait for and beaches to walk on. And all the way we carried the map with us.

She said it was a gift.

I didn't understand then. Was reading the map a gift? Or was giving the map a gift? But now my own daughters are waiting for me and, I know, it's both.

# The Refuge

*Farquhar McLay*

I n my dream the Green Lady came. The green in her coat
nearly all faded now. She came to me from another age, in a
green coat and hat, with a pencil and notebook. The last of her
species, come to check on me in my new domicile. I heard the
rat-tat-tat of her pencil on the door, Maya calling. She rushed in,
eager to be at me, ready for any and every awfulness. Dirt and
disorder were the enemy. Her eyes beaded as she neared her
quarry. She knew me of old, had me summed up and pigeon-
holed in a jiffy, this grinning, lantern-jawed skulker in the bed.
The Katz brothers, to whom I owed a lot of money, would never
look for me here. But the Green Lady knew where to find me.
She knew the kind of habitation I'd be at. She plucked the fag
from my mouth and put in a thermometer. Her little warm
hands wandered all over my poor decrepit body. Her tone was
sharp but strangely reassuring. One felt in good hands.

'We'll have to see about you,' she said.

After a tough struggle a young man pushed the door open just
enough to poke his head through.

'Anybody there?' he called.

'What's that?' I said, raising myself in the bed.

'Sanitary!' he shouted. He thrust in a hand which held some
kind of ID.

'That's OK,' I said. 'Come right in.'

'The door seems to be jammed,' he said.

'You have to push,' I answered in a brittle voice. 'I'd help but I'm not up to it.'

The young man launched a further assault on the door and burst in, slightly dishevelled and out of breath. He clawed his way with a few grunts and curses through a mass of entanglements. For some moments he stared at the mountain of junk he'd just penetrated. He looked disgusted. For some moments he stood there, shaking his head, eager that his disgust should not go unnoted. I watched him between a shirt and a towel on my washing line, which curtained off the corner of the room where I slept. He carried a briefcase in one hand and a pair of wellies in the other.

'I'm over here,' I said, waving.

He swung round, peering into the gloom. He advanced slowly, taking great care where he put his feet, till at last he ducked under the line. He was a podgy character in a pinstripe suit. His eyes darted about suspiciously. He put down his wellies and flashed his ID once again.

'Sanitary,' he said, a note of disapprobation in his voice.

'Very good,' I said.

He gave me a long look. 'It's a right mess you've got here. I don't think I've ever seen anything quite like this.'

'It's none of my doing,' I said. 'It's all Buirett's stuff.'

'Buirett? Who's he?'

'The previous tenant,' I explained. 'I've only been here a few days.'

'A few days, eh?' He picked up his wellies and waltzed up and down for a while, studying Buirett's fortifications from various angles. Finally he came to a halt in front of the sink and rubbed a hole in the dirt on the window pane. 'We've had complaints.'

'I don't wonder,' I said.

'Rats,' he said. 'People have seen rats on the stair.'

'It doesn't surprise me,' I said.

He scuffed some rubble from under his feet. He put down his wellies. 'It's just asking for trouble, you know, a mess like this.'

'You better believe it,' I said. 'It's telling on my health.'

I watched as the sanitary man put the wellies on the floor and opened the briefcase. He took out some newspapers and spread them on the floor. He put down the briefcase. He removed his shoes and stepped on to the newspaper in his stockinged feet. He slid out of his jacket and let it lie beside the briefcase on the newspaper. He fetched a white boiler-suit out of the briefcase along with a pair of plastic-coated work gloves. He got into the boilersuit, buttoning it up to the neck. He took two crepe bandages out of the briefcase and bound up the lower part of each trouser leg in a tight puttee. He then stepped deftly off the newspaper straight into his waiting wellie boots.

My next-door neighbour is Clara. She is a large lady with a large dog, a recalcitrant, unkempt brute the name of Marcus. It was early on a quiet Sunday morning when I first ran into them, although I was aware of them before that, hearing Clara through the wall in altercation with the dog, or seeing her from the window, hurtling along behind the galloping Marcus. I had just returned from the shop at the corner with some rolls and a packet of fags. She was on the landing as I came up, bent over, trying to steady the excited dog while she attached the lead.

I tried to slink into the flat unnoticed but Marcus wasn't having any. In a moment I was pinned against the bannister and Clara was screaming at him to remember his manners.

When after a while she got Marcus calmed down somewhat, and into a sitting posture, from which he looked ready to spring at the slightest provocation, she asked me straight out if I'd seen any rats. I said I had not. She seemed surprised. She said Mr Buirett used to put stuff down to kill them. He used to carry them down in a shovel to the bin after dark. 'I take it you never knew Mr Buirett?' she said.

'I never had the pleasure, no.'

'It's really very sad when you come to think about it. People tormented him so. I suppose it was the way he let things get to him. We were neighbours for eighteen years and never once was there any unpleasantness. Eighteen years, if you want to know, and not one angry word, not till towards the end, anyhow, when things got a bit out of hand, so to speak – you know, when the whole thing got to him. But he wasn't to blame for that, was he? That was nobody's fault. Just the way he was made, I'd say. It was just the worry getting to him. Mind you, he was always very civil, and very fond of Marcus. Twice a week he'd leave a polythene carrier hanging there on the door handle, full of goodies for Marcus. He'd never knock. Never wanted any fuss. Dear me, it's sad, very sad. Too bad you never met him. I'm sure you'd have got on. I'm sure you'd have lots in common. A very quiet little man. Wouldn't open his door unless he knew you. Never let anybody in. Not even me. In all those years he never once asked me in. But a very nice man. Don't let anyone tell you different.'

The sanitary man looked ready for action. I leant over on one elbow in the bed.

'Would you mind shutting that door?' I said. 'There's one helluva draught coming up that stair.'

He went back to the door and pushed it shut. It swung back. He pushed it again. It still didn't shut. He started twisting at the handle, then turned to me:

'Your lock's jiggered,' he said.

'I know,' I said. 'Jemmied open one time too many, I suppose.'

I lay back with my hands behind my head.

The sanitary man thought he understood and nodded.

'Been burgled, have you? You should get yourself an Ingersoll 10 lever automatic deadlock. They won't jemmy that so easy.'

He put a couple of bricks against the door, then returned to his briefcase.

'What happened to the Green Lady?' I enquired.

He looked up. 'The what?'

'When you said "sanitary", you know. That used to be the Green Lady,' I said.

He was rummaging in the briefcase. He brought out a chisel, then a little hammer. He said: 'I might have to lift a couple of boards.'

It seemed incredible. A functionary of such importance forgotten already – even in her own department! She was an institution in the slums. A woman in a green trench coat, maybe a little severe of aspect, carrying a leather attaché-case. She was the terror of the slums in her day. Liked to catch the poor with their vermin showing. Examined every corner in the house, looked in cupboards, under beds, drew her middle finger over surfaces, ordered windows to be washed, stairs to be scrubbed, and always made great play with the pencil and notebook. Only the unwary opened their doors. A sanitary inspector and nurse combined. She inspected children's heads for nits, and cavity beds for bugs. Easing me out of my shirt to check the healing appendectomy. I loved the feel of her hands on my body.

'We'll have to see about you,' she would say.

The sanitary man was preoccupied. He was putting on his work gloves, pressing each finger into its separate groove with great deliberation.

'I'll just have a look round,' he said. 'See what's what.'

He made a tour of the room, still kneading his gloves into position. He was peering into this corner and that. He even had a quick squint under the bed I was lying in. And as I observed him I thought I saw something of the Green Lady look: severe distaste, disgust that such dirt should be in the world, and censure for the one that harboured it. I was certainly in disgrace. And I was reminded that it was under a bed forty years back, in Warwick Street at the brewery end, a Green Lady dug out the find of a lifetime – a rag-shrouded foetus. The highwater mark of her career. She gave evidence at the trial, got complimented by the judge, had her picture in all the papers.

The sanitary man took a small can from the briefcase, levered up the lid with his chisel, peeped in at the contents, and slowly made his way to the bulwark behind the door. He put the can on the floor. He made a few turns round the heap, still undecided about the best point of entry. He dragged out some cardboard boxes, then a couple of oil drums, then some loose boards, and lastly a railway sleeper.

There was everything in that heap. It started at the back wall with cardboard boxes which contained Mr Buirett's personal papers and paperback library. They were stacked four deep and went almost to the ceiling. There was an iron bed standing on its end. There was a double wardrobe minus its doors. There were two rolled-up carpets leaning on the wardrobe. There was a supermarket trolley, a bike frame, a mildewed mattress, a TV with its face bashed in. There was a pickaxe and a shovel, bricks, sand, mortar, slates and half a tiled fireplace. There were skirting boards, floorboards, railway sleepers, cast-iron guttering, half a hose pipe. There were paint tins and oil drums. There was potato peel and coal ash and tea leaves. There were chicken bones, crusts of bread, pot plants, rotting potatoes. There was a tattered brocade pouffe with its entrails showing, a chair seat with a back but no legs, a cobbler's last and a life jacket. But that was only what you could see on the surface at a quick glance. Water seeped from the centre in several places. There were mushrooms growing.

'I expect she's been phased out,' I said.

'What's that?'

'The Green Lady,' I said. 'I expect she's been phased out.'

'I wouldn't know,' he said, putting a little stick in the can and giving it a stir.

'She was in the sanitary, just like you.'

He gripped the can firmly with both hands. Then he lowered his head and with a violent breenge disappeared into the heart of the barricade. I could hear him squelching about in the filthy depths, where the creepie-crawlies meshed and pullulated. A brave man. The Green Lady of the foetuses herself might have baulked.


Clara, I soon gathered, was about the only friend Simon Buirett had. In fact, when he snuffed it most of his neighbours breathed a sigh of relief. His DIY-home improvement schemes had kept them in a state of permanent trauma. Some were still in counselling.

Yes, Simon went to work on the flat with a vengeance. To begin with, he pulled down the dividing wall between the bedroom and the living-room, providing himself immediately with a ready supply of bricks. They were dotted all over the apartment in neatly-stacked piles. Reclining on two such piles was the bedroom door. It served me as a table.

Nor did he stop at that. He uprooted the lavatory pan and refitted it, along with its compact, dual-flush, easy-action cistern, right there in the living-room. It was in perfect working order. To keep it company he disconnected the bathtub and fetched it along as well. It remained as he positioned it, upside down, the capstone on a rectangular wall of crudely cemented bricks, about two foot high, with a narrow entrance at one end, making it a little house-within-a-house, where Simon Montague Buirett sought refuge, as snug as a tortoise in its shell, from the demons that menaced him.

Another amenity was the Buirett shelving system. When he needed a shelf Simon didn't trust to brackets and planks, he just howked out a couple of bricks here and there. The walls were riddled with these little niches, sometimes lined at the back with mirror glass, so that wherever you happened to be in the house you caught a pair of eyes peeping in at you – your own. At least you hoped they were.

Simon had bricked up the bathroom window, likewise the window in the bedroom, and was getting ready to start on the living-room when he had a paralytic seizure, and after that his heart gave out. He had one surviving relative, Anne-Marie, a paediatrician in Newcastle. She put the sale of the flat in the hands of a lawyer. But prospective buyers took one look and hurried away badly shaken. Thanks to Simon's demons, and his pertinacity in building strongholds against them, the flat was now a total write-off. I could squat there for life un-disturbed if I so fancied.

The sanitary man emerged. He was pressing the lid back on to the can.

'Everything OK?' I asked.

He nodded, tight-lipped, and seated himself on a pile of bricks.

'I put down some stuff,' he said, holding up the can for me to see. 'This will do the trick, I guarantee it. It's the Depart-ment's own formula. It never fails.'

I watched as he pulled off his wellies and undid the puttees. Then he went on to the newspaper again and went through his earlier routine in reverse. When he was back in his pin-stripe suit, with the wellies in one hand and the briefcase in the other, he turned to the window and took a peek through the hole in the grime.

Just at that moment there was a stir on the landing, then an angry shout, and suddenly Marcus came plunging through the door. He headed, trailing his leash, straight for the Buirett heap.

Clara followed him in, yelling that she would have his life. But in a moment Marcus was quite forgotten as the full range and complexion of Mr Buirett's changes impacted on Clara's vision. For a moment she stood open-mouthed and speechless, large and formidable in her blue floral dress.

She put a hand to her open mouth, and slowly rested her great meaty posteriors on the edge of my bed.

'My God!' she gasped. 'Who'd have believed it? It was beyond his strength, a penance like this.'

She shook her head in pained disbelief. She'd heard stories of course, but was never one to give credence to neighbours' tittle-tattle. They were saying there was a crime in his past, of a sexual nature. There were people after him. Of course she always took his part when the others ganged up on him. She liked fair play, always had. She couldn't stand by and watch people taking liberties, but look at the thanks she got. And her bedroom just the other side of that wall! It hadn't been very considerate of Mr Buirett; she didn't mind saying it. It was hard not to feel let down.

At the door the sanitary man said: 'I'll leave the can with you, if you want to put some more down in a week or so. I don't think it'll be necessary. It's our own formula. You'll be all clear in no time, I guarantee it.'

Clara went on to the heap to reclaim Marcus. After a tussle she dragged the dog clear. She looked down at her blue suede bootees, sodden and mired by a decomposed mixture of coal ash, tea leaves and potato peelings.

'I'm sorry about that,' I said, indicating her shoes. 'I'll be clearing the whole place out of course. But it may take a while. I've not been keeping too well, you see.'

'Yes, yes,' Clara said. 'Mr Buirett was the same. Never looked after himself. Never ate enough. And the worry – nothing but worry. It got to him in the end.'

Clara continued to pay me visits. Usually she fetched along small victuals like a rhubarb tart or a piece of Madeira cake. I was always very grateful for these tasty offerings – I was especially fond of the ginger dessert cake moistened with rum, which was my Saturday treat. I got to look forward to her visits. I even got to like Marcus, who never tired nosing around in Buirett's earthworks.

Often in the twilight Clara would sit by me on the bed, and together we'd contemplate the Buirett heap. With a consoling smile she'd say: 'You're a slow worker, that's for sure. Still I think I can see some improvement. Yes. I think I can definitely say it's not what it was. I hope you realise they'll have no problem selling this flat, now you've made a start.' Then, scrutinising her face and neck in Mr Buirett's little wall-mirrors, she'd laugh and say: 'Just think. You'll be the last bit of refuse to go down that stair, does that frighten you?'

It frightened me, and we both knew it. We'd need the Buirett heap a long while yet.

# Gravity

## *Donald Paterson*

Yet again, he tells me a story: hands on the blanket, white hair on the greasy pillow. Not the same story as the ones he's told me before, not the same as the ones he'll tell me next.

The soup I made for him lies untouched on the bedside table and I empty the bedpan and straighten the sheets the best I can, not that he's weighing much now. While he talks the sun falls down the sky and away from the window, leaving the leafless trees all cold and shadow. While he talks I watch the black crows drag themselves by and the first sparkles of frost settling on the black park. While he talks I listen, but, I imagine, not so closely as I listened months ago when these stories began, when he first lay down in the bed and didn't get up, and decided it was time to tell these stories to me.

All the stories take place here on this farm, and they cover the eighty-odd years backwards and forwards. They have a seriousness, a weightiness to them as they drop from his mouth, stumbling to my ears. Stories of a lifetime full of stories: things that happened; other things that happened. To begin with, I looked for clues, waiting for the meaning to appear, looking for the strand that tied all the stories together. After a while I stopped that search, confused. I couldn't see how one story was descended from another so I stopped trying to work it out. Now I just listen and as often as not I'm just thinking about myself, not him, while he speaks.

And anyway, I think, I still think, what I should be doing is just looking after him, not trying to understand the shape of what has happened to him. He can only pull me in so far, as I circle round him lying dreaming on that bed, the glass of water never touched near his left hand.

'When I was six or so,' he says, his voice like grey dust, 'or maybe seven or it was six I think – I know that Lizzie was still here then because she was here when we had that horse – so six, then – that's when it happened – this thing – I still remember it – even now I feel myself falling and how when I landed – that never goes – I never forget when I landed and underneath – was that my fault? – You maybe think – how can he remember so many seasons ago? – with so much in between – how can he put in his mind a thing that sounds like nothing – about jumping – falling from a wall and landing on the stony farm track? – but it's still a real thing – tell *him* that – tell him yes I *can* remember and tell him I had things happen to me long before ever anything happened to him.'

What do I do while he talks? Watch, watch the darkness drop and sort through his words to find the story, like sieving flour to let the fine white dust drift through and down and keep the clogging lumps apart.

I do not know what else it is that I should do. I know that when the story ends it will have, as always: 'Tell him – tell him – unless he comes – unless he comes and *I* can tell him . . .' I do not know what more I can do than half listen, sort, remember. No need to understand. All the help that I can give is now this matter of reporting, or waiting for *him* to come to see his old father, and if he comes my task is complete and I can walk downstairs and out the door, down the beech-lined path and out the red gate, down the road to town and out of these stories. And is it worth it even to tell these stories, and, if not, is it worth it trying to remember them? Should I even listen when my own life moves on, dragged who knows what way?

I can hear the brown earth in his voice.

'I went out one morning – afternoon it was – I'd had my piece in the farmhouse – my mother, alive then – her hands shaking though and the cough always at the top of her chest – the sadness in her eyes – as if she knew – and maybe yes she did – it wasn't long – I knew that – I did know that and I was only six then – still I knew she'd be gone soon – I went out to the farm and all the clouds were gone and all the sky – the sky was clear – the clouds were gone – the sun – you hear? – a bright and shining sun that lit our farm – when I was small I thought our farm was all there was – and me in it – the sun had brightened all the farm while I'd been in the house – as if – as if – while I was in, the farm had been pulled – what – an inch? a foot? nearer to the sun – towards that warmth and light – tell him I remember – happy – clear – it was – younger then – my life was younger and when the sun shone – tell him to come and see me – tell him I want to tell him how I ran out with the heat on my head – out to the farm and I was meant to go and help old Iain – the Highlander – with the mucking out – or something – yes the mucking out – but no – I wanted still to be under the sun – with the sun pulling me nearer and nearer.'

So many of his stories begin this way, a gradual broadening out from the farmhouse, that I hardly need to take this in. I think of all the other stories I'd heard, of his mother and her cancer, of Lizzie, who was ten years older and who married the next farm and went away to the strange other side of the world in a ship and who died who knows how many thousand miles away by drowning with nobody family near to help her, of the father and his big-grained hands and the strength that let him work until the candles in the window were lit to let him drag his body home. And of the way he left school with a swear at the headmaster, and his youth, and of course about Amy and how hard it was to draw her in. Some massiveness about him did in the end attract her, despite herself and her doctor father. She'd lived here forty years or more, as joined to him as that hand scratching at the sheet, but when she died, the child long gone, the old man lay down in his bed and let the whole farm fall away, further and further from the sun.

And what he speaks about is his son. The stories that he tells are all about the farm but they're all about his son. The son who left with gambling on his heels and ran who knows where and who never wrote at all. Sometimes when I'm in the kitchen downstairs I see somebody walking up the track, stumbling in the rutted ground, and I hope it's the boy come back, made a man. I roll my blouse sleeves down and put aside the sharp knife and the green vegetables and go keenly to the door and open it to let the fresh air fall in. Because if this is to be his son come back, then I can leave. I want to leave this accountability, close the cupboard doors and let the grey dust settle. He tells me all the stories but how can I ever know what he is talking of? I bring him food, clean the windows that he'll never again look out of, listen to him, and if I listen to him until the sun goes out I'll never understand.

I never will.

And it never is his son that comes. I'm standing at the door with my hand on my forehead to keep the blue brightness from my eyes, and it's not the son at all but some man in a green-checked shirt trying to sell the farm some chemicals for spraying or some machinery that has no place here now – the animals are long gone and the parks are confusion. I send him away and turn and shut the heavy door, needing paint now, and lean against it and wonder what dropped me in this life, what led me here, this cleaning job that turned out to be an intertwining, like his fingers twisting on his scrawny chest as he tries to tell me what he means, or what things meant.

He says: 'I ran away to the sow – to the shed we called it – she had her piglets then – the runt pushing away at the edge – pushing at the milk he couldn't reach and I knew – even then I knew – he'd be dead in days – he'd never push down far enough through his brothers and his sisters – I hung over the wood – the wooden barrier – the straw and the warmth rising from the pushing bodies – and the sow looking up at me – the sow lying on her side – looking up at me with the piglets drawn to her – I watched them – pushing in. And then it was the horse – I had to see the horse – the horse and the foal – I ran from the shed and down the ruts in the lane to the paddock – and all the time feeling the heat – the heat and the sun and my mood rising up – rising up – and all this twenty years before my child did the same – running through the farm – that's what I see – what I see when the memory – the memory of my son comes – tell him I did this – I did this too – and how I did this before he ever came – the horse and the foal – the foal with its long legs – I held my hand out – I climbed the wall to see the foal – head-height hard stones stacked with moss and lichen – footholds that I knew – my son knew years after – until I pull myself up and swing over my legs – my legs hanging down – I sit on the rough top of the wall – the horse and the foal walk slowly over – their necks and heads rising and dipping as they walk – my clutched handful of grass held out – browsed and pulled – my son has done the same – tell him I know – I *know* that what he does I've done – that when I held out the grass for the pulling lips it meant that he – he would hold out the grass too – that all he's done must be because I have done these things – I *make* him – what he's done – it must have come from me.'

He pauses. I can see the teeth still white, the yellow white of his eyes, the dulled pink of his skin, but his words have no colour for me. I do not know what I should say, or do, or if I'll tell his son these words. Maybe the boy (who'll be a man now, of course) will not want to hear my versions of these tales in any case. He might just tell me to pack up my case and go and, well, I won't be sorry to walk down the track between the brown beeches and off home. I was scarcely more than a girl when I came here, knowing nothing. That seems so long ago now, I can scarcely remember my yellow hair and the smile on my lips and the way I thought I'd help the old man and his wife, alive then of course, and the two of them capably running the farm when I arrived, having heard they'd wanted a girl to clean. Knowing nothing. Not knowing what colour my life would turn out, and twelve years on I still don't know. I don't know why I've been here so long, or how things happened so that I am here at all, what made me be here, lying in this life without the strength to haul myself up from the ground and float away. I'd like to float while he talks.

'The sun – the sun pushing down – and all I can feel – I can feel a warmth – it's not just outside me – inside me – tell him about the warmth I felt then – that warmth that carried me on and the warmth that plunged me through my life – through my life I've fallen down – and on the way catching Amy – clutching her as she fell – she fell beside me – then we fell together – we caught my son – tell him that – and tell him this – this is what I'm talking about – how I turned from that hard grey wall to jump down and leave the mare and foal and run – run to help old Iain – I stood on top of the wall – on top of the wall and faced the sun – and face the sky and jump – the warmth and the air holding me up for a second – then falling and I look below – I look below to see the track of dirt and stone come closer – up towards my feet to meet my weight – my weight fading as the track comes up – and on the track – below my feet where I will land – where I will fall – a kitten from the barn – my weight upon it – I see its eyes.'

He stops now, tired by his talk, and his eyes close and I look out the window at the black sky with every now and then a white star point. I know the story is as complete as it will be; there is no more to come tonight. I do not know what I should do if ever I can tell this story to his son. Maybe when he comes I'll say his father never spoke these last ten months. Better that than try to tell all this, these stories which I cannot see through. Better to let it lie, to let these words all sink down below the soil and shovel the unlit earth on top, and ask my own questions about what has happened to *me* so far, and in the time to come. I look at him. There's just the final words to come now and I wait for them, patient, until he says:

'Tell him – tell him – unless he comes – unless he comes and *I* can tell him . . .'

So now he'll sleep, I know. I watch him for a few moments more and when I am sure that the breathing in his chest is there, and steady, I gently lift his old head and take out one of the pillows and lay it on the floor, pull the red curtains on the evening cold, the window an inch open, and, switching off the light, leave him and let myself sink downstairs to the kitchen, where the fire is just about out and the stone floor is as chill as the dark and I sit for a while, listening to the house.

So that was that story, and whether the son will come or not I don't know, nobody knows, but tomorrow I'll climb up to his father's room and listen once more, and the next day I'll hear another story, and the days will go by like a stone falling to the night-black ground, and so on.

# The Visit

## *M. S. Power*

I t was as if she was making a small, private ceremony of it.
She moved the high-backed chair closer to the window.
She plumped the cushion, and sat down. She reached out and
raised the net curtain, hitching it to a brass flower pot. Then
she folded her hands primly on her lap, and took to peering
out the window, waiting. To calm herself she had made tea,
but the cup remained untouched. A sort of skin had formed
on the liquid as it got cold and uninviting. Her face was gaunt
and expressionless, and black sleepless bags sagged under her
slightly bulging eyes. From time to time she wrang her hands,
letting her fingers intertwine, or she twisted the narrow gold
wedding band round and round. There was something about
the regularity of her actions that suggested she had done all
this before. Once she glanced over her shoulder and gazed
dully at the photographs on the mantleshelf, but she looked
away again almost at once, shaking her head in a small, angry
gesture. It would, she thought, be acceptable if this was a
proper war, but this – she closed her eyes and shuddered.

The street outside was shabby, and wet from the slow
unceasing rain. Dustbins had been overturned by dogs that
scavenged in the dead of night, their contents strewn long the
pathway. Opposite, and a little to the left, on the derelict site
they called a playground, two burnt-out cars stood like

monstrous sculptures, living art, perhaps, since one of them still smouldered. Rubble – bricks, slates, broken bottles, fragments of paving stone – was scattered about the whole area, and in the distance the wail of an ambulance gave the scene an added sense of melancholy. The clock in the hall chimed the quarter hour.

'Molly?'

'In here.'

'Just popped in to see – ach, would you look at you!'

'Don't.'

Sheila Lannigan understood, and stayed quiet for a moment. Like Molly she could not fully comprehend the terror that was taking place around her. It had, it seemed, just crept up upon them, sneaking up like a terrible plague, taking husbands and children away and killing them without reason, without a reason she could understand anyway. All in the name of something vague called freedom.

'It's Declan,' Molly explained finally.

'Oh.'

'He hasn't come home.'

'Oh.'

'He should have been home last night.'

'Maybe –,' Sheila Lannigan began, but stopped under the woe-filled gaze that answered her.

'A disco. That's where he said he was going. Just going to a disco, Mam, he said. Won't be late. That's what he told me, and went off all decked out and smiling as if he didn't have a care in the world.'

'He could be with friends.'

Molly shook her head. 'He'd have let me know. He knows how I worry. Every since his Da was killed he knows I worry when I'm not sure where he is.'

A car drove slowly up the street, a dark blue Sierra, and the two women froze. But the car drove past the house, gathered speed, and disappeared out of the estate. That was how the news was brought: a car would come and two policemen would announce that so and so had been killed. All the women in the area had come to regard those cars as sinister missiles directed willy-nilly at themselves, like the mortars that went off unexpectedly and slaughtered indiscriminately. They were always driven slowly and, as if in some daemonic game of spin the bottle, came to a halt outside a house, any house, and the dreadful news would be delivered, and the occupants would be left in desolation.

Sheila Lannigan moved across the room on tiptoe, and put a comforting arm about Molly's shoulder.

'Don't *do* that,' Molly snapped.

'I only—'

'I'm sorry, Sheila. I'm sorry.' Molly shook her head and shivered. 'I know you mean well. It's just – it's just as though you're tempting, fate, don't you see?'

'I see,' Sheila said, but clearly didn't. She felt hurt, rebuked. 'I'm sorry,' she said.

'Damn these people and their stupid fighting.'

'Yes, I'll make us some fresh tea, will I?'

Molly nodded vaguely. Curiously, although she would never have admitted it, she felt a resentment towards Sheila. *She* had never been married, never had a husband to lose, and in an odd way her sympathy and undoubted kindness had a condescending air to it. Or so Molly felt sometimes. Besides, Sheila was pert and still pretty enough despite her forty-five years, while Molly, three years her junior, was haggard by comparison, her thin, pinched face marred by the lines that tragedy etch, and by constant, secret weeping. 'Here we are,' Sheila now said, putting the tray on a small table near the window.

'Thank you, Sheila,' Molly said with a small, wan smile.

Outside, someone kicked a tin can along the road, a dog

barked, a woman with a shrill voice demanded that her child 'get in here this instant before I come out there and thrash you'. An armoured car went past, rattling the windows, and Molly tensed: usually an armoured car preceded the police on their terrible mission.

'It's not stopping,' Molly said, meaning only to think it.

'Of course not,' Sheila told her reassuringly.

'Not that one. Another will come. I know it.'

'You don't *know* any such thing, Molly.'

'I know,' Molly insisted.

'Here you are,' said Sheila, thrusting out a cup of tea.

'Why, Sheila – why is all this happening?'

'Things just happen in life,' Sheila told her, and oddly that seemed to satisfy Molly. 'And any way, I'm sure Declan will turn up right as rain.'

'He won't. He's dead.'

'You shouldn't say that. And you giving out to me for tempting fate.'

'I know he is.'

'You can't know.'

'Yes I can. There's many of us that can. When it's happened to you once you get a feel for it.'

'That's being silly.'

'You couldn't understand.'

'Of course I understand.'

'How could you? You've had no one taken from you. You've had no husband dragged from a ditch and him riddled with bullets when all he was doing was walking his stupid greyhound.'

'No,' agreed Sheila.

'Well then. Don't tell *me* you can understand,' Molly said. 'They even shot the dog,' she added as an afterthought, as if that was just as bad. She added a wisp of a smile. She knew she was being unkind, and felt genuinely bad about it. Yet she

wanted to hurt her friend. It just wasn't fair, was it, that some
had never been bereaved? Bereaved so senselessly, and left
alone, which was the worst thing of all. Suddenly, all she could
think about was the night her husband had been found
murdered. What had been most strange was that the death
of her own husband had moved her less than the deaths of
other men, young and old, from the street. She had wept
freely and unashamedly as she comforted other widows,
moaned with them and shared their dreadful plight. Yet,
standing over the corpse of Peadar she felt detached, somehow
uninvolved. It was as though, the thought struck her and
terrified her, her dead husband no longer had anything to do
with her precisely because he was dead; it was almost as if any
expression of grief or anguish would be seen as gross, un-
warranted and impertinent.

Now, to rid herself of these thoughts, she sipped her tea,
and gave Sheila another thin smile.

And she recalled how tea had been on offer that day also.
'Better get her home and fix her a cup of strong tea,' someone
had said, and she found herself being manoevred away from
the body, a neighbour on either side, holding her firmly by the
elbows. Oddly, through it all, through the dismal drive home,
through the flickering images of that white, pudgy, unmoving
face, she realised that a cup of tea was exactly what she needed,
remembering that she had been on the point of having
breakfast when they brought her the news, and it was as
though the intervening time had not existed. Meekly she
allowed herself to be steered away from the car and towards
the house. As she climbed the four steps that led to the front
door she made each step underline an incident in the se-
quence: the arrival of the police, the numbness, the identifica-
tion of the body, the advancing inevitable cup of tea. Then,
imperceptibly at first, she felt herself getting giddy. She
wanted to scream out that she didn't want any damn tea.

She wanted no part of this neighbourly kindness. She wanted no consolation, no holding hands, no patting of her hair, no promise of prayers, no sympathy whatever – nothing that might make her cry. But she remained silent, and sat in the armchair where they placed her, staring at the single bar of the electric fire that someone had thoughtfully switched on, perhaps in the hope that it would remove some of the chill from the awful event. And without a murmur she let them make tea and bring it to her, and she managed a smile as they encouraged her to drink it with little clucking noises of compassion.

And later, when they had all gone, feeling they had done all they could and that now was the time for the new widow to be on her own, she went upstairs and curled herself up on the bed, staring wide-eyed into the darkness, willing it to wrap itself round her and obliterate the wicked feeling of isolation. It was only now, alone and without Peadar beside her, without the snorts and coughs he always gave before he slept, without, too, the annoyance of him sprawling across the bed and accidently thumping her into wakefulness, that the full extent of her loss and loneliness dawned on her. What was most curious was that the love she had for him when they were first married, the love that had swept her off her feet and made her float wondrously into her one and only pregnancy, the love that had gradually dried up and become more a kind of affable tolerance, now came sweeping back over her. Yes, isolation was certainly the word. She was the widow of a murdered man – not at all the same thing as just a widow. Not in Belfast at any rate. She was now, she thought, one of the untouchables: on the one hand strangely revered and respected, on the other shied away from as though her loss would contaminate others. She knew other women who had gone through what lay ahead of her, had seen them age, and dry up, and withdraw into the isolation of their souls. It was the horror of this that quite unexpectedly made her cry, rocking herself into a fitful sleep.

'Another?' Sheila asked, stretching out her hand to grasp Molly's cup.

'Please. Thanks, Sheila.'

And 'please' she had pleaded to some phantom god, mutely begging him to make it all untrue. She knelt on the floor of the bedroom. About her, strewn haphazardly, were all that she had by which to remember her husband: his clothes. She reached out and picked up a pullover, dark green with a design of a brown deer prancing across the chest. She had knitted it herself. She held it close to her, biting it, weeping gently. Then, for a long time, she knelt very still, just hugging the garment, not crying now.

It was getting light, and the first birds were chattering when she heaved herself to her feet. In one sudden, violent action, she hurled the pullover from her, and started kicking the other clothes that were scattered about the floor, goaded by the painful awareness of how little she actually knew about her dead husband. It was little short of amazing that she had lived with him for twenty years, given him a son, watched him grow older and become a little more secretive in the way age seems to make people, noticed him adopt new foibles and irksome, petty little habits as he slowed down, and still managed to know nothing intimate about the man she had married.

'I'd better be making a move,' Sheila said, standing, and smoothing her skirt with both hands. 'Unless you want me to stay.'

'No, Sheila. Thanks. You go on. I'll be fine.'

'You're sure?'

'I'm sure.'

'Try not to worry.'

'I'll try.' Molly said in the tiny voice of an obedient child. Sheila was slipping her arms into her coat when the ar-

moured car came to a halt outside the house. Seconds later the
police car, unmarked, slid to a stop behind it. Two doors
slammed. The women remained motionless, waiting in the
frightening quiet. 'Oh, Molly,' Sheila said in a kind of wail,
looking as if she was about to add something to that but
changing her mind. Someone knocked on the door.

'I'll go.' Sheila volunteered.

'No, I'll go. It's me they've come to see.'

'I know, but—'

'I'll go.'

In the hall Molly stopped by the mirror and straightened
her hair. She ran a finger under each eye, removing imaginary
traces of tears. She moved defiantly to the door, and opened it.

'Mrs Rocks?' the older of the two policemen asked politely.

Molly nodded.

'I'm sorry—'

'No!' Molly shouted suddenly.

The policemen stared at her.

'No,' Molly said again, this time in a whisper. 'I'm sorry.
I'm not Mrs Rocks. That's Peg, Peg Rocks. She lives two
doors down.'


Sheila cuddled Molly. 'There, there,' she murmured, patting her gently on the back.

'They made a mistake,' Molly said, bewildered.

'Yes. Hush now.'

'They made a mistake.'

'Yes,' Sheila repeated. 'There's no need for you to cry like
this now, is there?'

Abruptly Molly pushed her friend roughly away, glaring at
her. 'No need to cry? No need to cry?' she screamed. 'God,
but you're great!'

'What have I—'

'Just go, Sheila. Please. Just go. Go and leave me in peace.'

Alone, Molly cleared away the dirty cups, putting them tidily by the sink in the kitchen, telling her self she'd wash them later. Then she returned to the sitting room and took up her place at the window, folding her hands on her lap again. Tears streamed down her face. Once she wiped them brutally away with her fists, but then she ignored them, and allowed them to flow. And through her tears she saw her son, Declan, come trotting up the street, looking a little rough, his hair tousled, but perky enough for all that. Oh God, Molly thought. Oh my God. Slowly the thought of poor Peg Rocks filled her consciousness, the thought of her suffering and her terrible isolation. And Molly felt overwhelmed with guilt. She buried her face in her hands, sobbing uncontrollably. That guilt, she knew, would be harder for her to live with than any sorrow.

# Dead of Winter

*Wayne Price*

He'd had to park in Union Crescent, two long streets away, and now as he hurried towards home on foot, soaked and cursing, carrying the two heavy pike in a straining plastic bag, the police loomed like sudden monuments out of the dark and swathes of rain. There were three of them and they stood around the street-level entrance to his tenement building, muttering and laughing, blocking the steps to his basement door. As he drew close he noticed that the ground floor flat above his own was cordoned off with red and white police tape. He stopped and waited for the figures in front of him to move. The three men were tall and still in the rain and the water spattered heavy on their flat hats and streamed in rivulets down their bulky black-nylon coats. Finally one took notice of him and shifted back towards the road, letting him by. He felt their sudden silence at his back as he made his way down the steps and across the basement yard. Under the arch of stone steps that connected the ground-floor entrance to the street he paused, out of sight of the police and shielded from the rain. He shook himself and loosened his clothes where the rain had plastered them to his skin. The yard smelled like old bread under the span of the arch, and the damp, sheltered air was filled with tiny grey gnats. He waved a hand in front of his face where the gnats had already begun to congregate. For a short time he stood still and strained

187

to hear what the police were talking about, but the spit and hiss of the rain drowned out everything other than one more low purl of laughter from above.

Inside, the kitchen strip light was already on. He kicked off his wet shoes and crossed the tiles to the cooker. It was off but there was a covered pan on the hob. Lifting the lid, he saw it was half full of cold baked beans. The smell that bloomed up from them carried a strong, almost caramel-like sweetness. He put the lid back on and hefted the bag of pike up on to the empty steel draining board next to the hob. Both fish, stiff and curved, slid under their own dead weight through the plastic neck of the bag on to the metal. They were each between four and five pounds. Good solid pike, though their colour was already spoiled. He considered cleaning them but decided it could wait until he'd dried and changed. Leaving the water and slime from the bag to drain, he opened the door to the living-room and looked in.

Rhona was slumped on the sofa, asleep in front of the TV. A thin downie covered her up to the chin and outside it her head was fallen to one side and her mouth was slack. The downie cover was patterned with big prints of washed-out blue roses. Malcolm looked at the way her mouth was, then at the way even the bunched, flowered folds of downie didn't hide her size. A hungry tiredness washed over him. He peeled off his sodden jumper and draped it over a kitchen chair, then went back to the living-room. The TV was still on, the volume turned low. He crossed the room and turned it off. With the TV off the sound of the rain washed in, whispering and spluttering. Rhona closed and opened her mouth, making a tacky chewing noise, then opened her eyes.

Malcolm, she said thickly, what time is it?

I'm not late, he said.

She yawned and thought for a moment. I left some food for you.

I know, he said. He scratched the back of his neck, staring at a point somewhere to the side of her. Thanks.

Did you catch anything? You didn't bring anything back, did you?

Only two.

She groaned. Why do you have to bring them back? They taste terrible. No one else I know ever had to eat a pike.

They taste fine. It's just the bones you don't like.

Oh Christ. Don't even talk about the bones.

He shrugged. I'll eat them myself. You don't have to eat them.

She grimaced. Why don't you just put them back, Mal, like everyone else? Just because you catch something doesn't mean you have to kill it. She sighed and lolled her head. What pleasure is it anyway, fishing that godforsaken loch in the dead of winter? More wakeful now, she looked him up and down. You're soaking, she said. It was so sunny this morning.

It came on with the dark. He tilted his head from side to side, stretching the tight muscles. What're the police doing out there?

God, yes, she said, sleeping made me forget! God, Mal, you won't believe it – the old woman above us got killed. They questioned me and everything.

Killed?

Murdered. I couldn't believe it. Right over this room. She stared wide-eyed at him. It really spooked me, Mal. What if—

Christ, they don't want you for a witness, do they?

No, no. I heard some banging and thumping but I didn't tell them. They'd already caught who did it – two kids broke in and they were still there when the police came. Someone in the block opposite saw them getting in and phoned the police.

Malcolm shook his head, looking at the blank screen on the TV. He could feel Ruth staring at him. He started cracking his fingers. So they beat her up? he said abruptly.

With bits of furniture, I think. It was horrible. Mal, don't crack your fingers, she said.

I doubt if they meant to kill her. Probably she started shouting.

Well they killed her alright. Anyway, Mal, don't be like that.
Like what?

She didn't answer.

I'll get changed and have something to eat, he said at last.

Not looking at the two cold pike curved and glazed at his elbow he heated the beans quickly, the sauce breaking into rapid, dull bubbles. He stirred them up and then left them on a low heat while he grilled and buttered some toast. The beans poured like slurry over the bread. He filled the pan with cold water and let it soak while he ate.

Once he'd finished eating he looked in the fridge and found a can of Guinness. Back in the living-room the TV was back on. Montel was reasoning with somebody.

Can you see if I've got any ciggies left – I'm hiding them in the cupboard so I don't get tempted too much.

He checked the sideboard cupboard and took out a half-full pack of Silk Cut. You shouldn't smoke at all, the way you are.

I know, she said, wounded. I've only had two all day.

That's pretty good, he admitted, surprised.

She smiled at him and held a hand out towards his drink. He passed the can over, closed the door behind him and sat on the sofa next to her. She took a few long, thirsty swallows. He took the can back.

It's been moving a lot today, she said, and smiled again at him.

He nodded. Good, he said. He handed her the cigarettes and she tucked them away before leaning over to kiss his cheek.

Feel, she said, settling back again and fixing him with a look.

No, no. I believe you. It's moving.

*Feel*, she insisted.

He slipped a hand between the buttons on her dress and laid the palm flat on her taut stomach. It felt hot. He waited.

Wait for it, she said.

He left his hand there, glancing over at the TV. The news was running – a war somewhere, some cold, crumbling city.

There! she said.

Something pressed, then seemed to writhe across the flat of his hand. He jerked his arm back.

Did you feel it?

A kick, he said.

She pulled the downie back up.

He took a long drink. He held the black, sour liquid in his mouth until it warmed into froth, then swallowed.

Give me your hand back, she said.

No. Leave it now.

Go on. Please, she murmured, put the can down.

He placed the can on the floor and let her take his hand. She warmed it between her palms then guided it under the downie to rest on her thighs. He felt her hitch her dress shorter, inch by inch, then felt her hand on his again, urging his fingers on to the heat between her open legs. She was damp through the cotton of her pants and for a while he pressed and circled gently there without slipping inside them. Then finally he eased his way under the gusset and between her slick, swollen lips, working his fingers quickly and bringing her almost immediately to a series of sharp, juddering orgasms, stopping only when she snatched his hand away, half shrieking, half laughing.

Oh Christ! she gasped, and laughed on almost soundlessly. It's so easy to come when I'm this big. She took a deep breath. It must be the hormones, or the pressure down there or something. I get so horny some days, too.

He smiled and drew his hand back.

God, she whispered, and rolled her head, her eyes shut.

He reached for the can again and watched the rest of the news. By now the local reports were on and suddenly he realised the pictures were of the street outside and the dead woman's flat. The sound was too low to hear the commentary, but they were interviewing someone half familiar, maybe a neighbour. The day had still been dry then, Malcolm noted. In the background the sun was flashing on the tenement windows.

Why does everyone love murders? Rhona mumbled.

I thought you were sleeping.

She shook her head. Every afternoon they put on *Columbo* and *Quincey*, and on the news it's always this kind of thing. And now it's our street. Why does everyone want to see it? Then she smirked at him. I'm still tingling though, she said drowsily. But I shouldn't have had that Guinness – it's repeating now. I feel like that fairy-tale wolf sewn up full of stones.

Guinness is good for you.

Uh huh. She belched loudly and they both laughed. Then she closed her eyes again.

Malcolm looked down at the can clasped on his lap. Rhona's scent was strong on his fingers: a heavy, bacterial perfume, much more pungent, he thought, than it had been before she fell pregnant. He closed his eyes, fighting back a familiar rolling black wave of unhappiness, and found himself thinking about the generations that must have lived out their time and died in the building around him, in the dark stone layers of tenement flats above, through centuries, layer on layer of births and lives and deaths. The stone steps to the dead woman's flat and to their own were worn smooth and cupped. How many lives to do that? How many dead, forgotten feet? Brooding, he remembered the two pike, cold and smooth as enamel, and then his mind went back to the small, deep, peat-blackened loch he'd fished through the day. As the dusk and first drops of rain had come on a third fish had run with his bait: two heavy, jarring knocks and then clean away. A big fish, he instinctively knew; as big or bigger maybe than anything he'd caught before. He knew the loch hid monsters. One autumn evening, fishing it in his brother's small, fibreglass dinghy, he'd hooked something on a deadbait that for five minutes or more towed the boat in a slow, deliberate circle round its anchor. He remembered like muscle-memory the feeling in his arms and shoulders as he'd tried to wear out its terrible, lazy strength. He'd been almost glad when the trace snapped, the wire shredded through.

The fish he'd hooked today was nowhere near as monstrous. Though there was no way of knowing for sure – it had thrown the bait so quickly. Just two sickening arm- and heart-wrenching thumps and then gone; back to the deep-black rot and weed forests of the bottom, lost to him forever, probably. It occurred to him that as a boy he'd taken the loss of such fish badly, as a kind of bereavement even, which could wake and torment him at night with frustration and sorrow; now, the thought of failing to draw such loaded, cold bodies out of the loch's deepest dark to himself brought him less a feeling of loss and more a morbid, premonitory sense of relief. What pleasure is it? she'd asked. And she was right – it was something, but not pleasure. Not that at all.

Mal, what's wrong?

He turned to her, startled. Nothing, he said. He got up and stretched, glad to move his tight chest. He picked up the remote and switched channels on the TV, finding what was left of a film and then watching it, still standing. Suddenly he looked up from the screen. Christ it's dark in here, he said. He reached over to the dimmer switch on the wall near the door and turned the lights right up.

193

Don't, Mal. You can see the lights on the screen. Turn it back.

He looked at the screen and saw it was true: the lights made ghost-lamps on the screen. He turned the switch back again and the reflections faded to pinpoints. He sat on the sofa again but leaning forward, ready to move.

Now I know where they are I can't take my eyes off them, she complained.

He didn't know the film but there were plenty of half-familiar faces in it. He started trying to remember what other parts he'd seen the actors playing. The film was some sort of detective story with a priest in it. Mainly he wondered what else he remembered the priest as. Something in uniform, he guessed.

We ought to get a dog, he said.

She looked at him, surprised. Not a dog. I'd rather a cat. I love cats.

Not for a pet, he said. He belched quietly, holding his chest. I mean for protection. To warn you.

Cats can warn you too, with sixth sense, she said.

He shook his head. A cat's no good, he said. What use is a fucking cat?

A cat could eat all the filthy fish you bring home. Anyway, I thought you'd like a cat. You're a bit of a tomcat yourself, aren't you? With your fish. Like a big daft cat dropping dead stuff on the doorstep. She reached out from under the downie to prod his ribs. Aren't you? she teased.

He realised he didn't want to talk anymore. He felt tired, and thought of the rain drumming on to his head and back, heavy and steady like it might never stop. He felt as if all his life's tiredness had been hammered down into his bones. I'm going to bed, he told her.

I'll come too, she said. I'm tired too.

He turned the TV off, then made his way through the kitchen to the bathroom.

She got up, pushing herself straight. She heard the bathroom door close and the bolt slot into place.

Lock up, he called out to her from behind the door. Both locks.

Carrying her cigarettes she walked into the dark kitchen and flicked on the light. Outside, the rain sounded heavier than ever. She opened the pack, took a cigarette and lit it from the hob. She turned to the pike resting on the steel drainer and inspected them, running a fingertip lightly over one of the smooth dry eyes. There was no sound of movement from the bathroom. She paused, then moved to the front door and opened it.

From the doorstep she looked up to the street above and saw the police cars had all gone. The night was quiet except for the rain. There was no traffic, no footsteps or voices. It was pleasant to stand there, listening and smoking. Beyond the step most of the yard was awash now, though nowhere near threatening the kitchen, she decided.

Suddenly her right eye pricked and blurred and when she blinked she felt something give under the wet lid. She cleared her eye and looked up again and noticed the gnats, a cloud of them lifting and falling in the brightness streaming out from the kitchen at her back. She watched them and up above, through the downpour; a car sped past, its wet tyres making a sound like leaves soughing in the wind. For a little while she tried to remember the last time she'd seen the old woman from the flat above. Maybe crossing the road with a small dog. Did she have a dog, though? She couldn't remember. She swept something, another gnat, out of the hair above her eyes, then brushed at her face as it fell. She wondered at them coming so near – in the day her cigarettes always kept them at a distance. They were certainly getting close now though, drawn to the light, she guessed. In the yard itself, she noticed then, her old fag ends were swimming around the flooded slabs close to her feet. The rainwater had welled them up from the drain where she'd dropped them and there were four of them butting against the raised grill. Others drifted in the opposite corner of the yard, just under the surface, making big, lazy circles. Disconcerted, she took a long, deep draw, then let the smoke go slowly. Another gnat whined in her ear, making her flinch, and in disgust she dropped her cigarette and lashed at them, one arm cradling her stomach. She felt tiny forms hit and stick to her palm, then crumple as she curled a fist. She reached out again, further, straining forward into space.

# A Little Bit of Trust

*Dilys Rose*

I t was almost dark. The heat had gone out of the day and Malek had sold no carpets. He pushed his hands deep into the pockets of his Italian coat, savouring its warmth, its style. Maybe he'd have to sell it. His fingers rubbed against the flaccid, greasy banknotes. Twenty dirham. Enough for something to eat but not enough for wine and wine was what he wanted, needed. Tourists were thin on the ground now and the few backpackers who drifted round town day after day were a waste of time, spinning out their cash and days like threads, eating bad food which made them sick, so they could hang out in the sun a bit longer.

Malek had sold no carpets though he'd been pacing the alley since early morning. Now it was almost dark and there was nothing to be done but wait and see if tomorrow brought in a busload of Germans. The way things were, the bad situation getting worse from one newsflash to another, the world rushing towards war, it was not at all likely that tomorrow would bring anything better than today.

Maybe he'd visit his mother after he closed up. She'd feed him. He'd get an earful of her worries about his bad ways but he'd still have money in his pocket. Yesterday, Yousseff had sold a carpet, everybody knew it. It had taken him two hours, several pots of tea and a mountain of patience but he'd done it, he'd got rid of a carpet. Maybe Yousseff could spare enough to make up the difference on a bottle.

Jane had been wandering the town for hours, trying to acquaint herself with the medina, to fix in her mind the maze of twisting alleys within the walls of the old town. In spite of assuming an air of determined confidence (as recommended in her guide book), in spite of having done this kind of thing before – in places where more overt hostility had greeted her, where the stares had been more accusing than curious, the swearing more vehement, the spitting more accurate, where worse horrors had swarmed in the shadows – still the place evaded her.

Every alley seemed the same, crammed with people and produce, the air heavy with smells – spice, petrol, perfume, drains, everywhere the jangle of horns, bells, cart wheels and radios blasting out a jarring mix of eastern and western music. So many people extended a hand – a beseeching, scabrous hand or firm insistent trader's hand – everyone saw her coming, her skin pale as a mushroom, her hair an ashy blonde. She stood out from these dark, forbidding people like an aberration.

Turning a corner and finding herself out of the medina at last, back on the main street not far from her hotel, looking up and seeing the clocktower black and solid against the last dregs of sunlight, Jane's eyes began to water. Perhaps it was the dust. There was a great deal of dust, of course, dry red dust, like the paprika and harisa which the spice merchants piled into fiery pyramids, the sky was thick with dust, the light a colloidal orange as the sun dropped behind the ramparts.

Jane's eyes hurt. They were tight, stinging around the rims, contracting in on themselves, shrinking into pinpoints. For several nights she had barely slept. She had gone beyond normal weariness into a fatigue which brought with it a superawareness, an ultrasensitivity like that induced by hallucinogenics. Everything ached and clenched, from her bones to her guts to the pores of her skin. Her teeth ground together as she held a tense, pained smile. In addition to fatigue an indefinable sadness.

The muezzin's sunset call from the clocktower reminded Malek that drinking was bad for body and soul but Allah says everyone is free and drink he would if he got the chance. Others did. Tourists came to town, ate in restaurants every night and drank in the waterfront bars until they couldn't walk and had a taxi take them a hundred metres to their hotel. Tourists could do what they wanted, no problem. All they had to do was pay, tourists in their designer clothes, haggling over the price of a carpet, happy only when they came away with a bargain, settling only for the cheapest price, never believing that when the vendor got down to his last price, he'd sold for no profit, only for ready cash – because you can't eat carpets – tourists hiding their money as they counted it, as if the very walls of the medina were out to cheat them, tourists excited and happy, making a transaction, rolling up a carpet, imagining going home to their cold grey country with the bright beautiful thing, spreading it on the floor, pointing out aspects of the handiwork, urging friends to feel the quality. Later they would walk all over it in their dirty outdoor shoes until it was dull and threadbare, by which time they'd be thinking about another holiday in the sun, about living it up in a place where for them everything was cheap, dirt cheap, thinking about buying another carpet. Tourists – he wanted to piss on them all.

She had come for a rest and here she was, walking down the street with tears springing from her eyes, keeping on walking because if she stopped she would crack, right there in the middle of the street, amongst dark, forbidding strangers. And if she cracked, would she mend? She put on her sunglasses. Here women hid their entire bodies beneath wraps and veils:

all she could hide was her eyes. But it was too dark for sunglasses. She could barely see. She was bumping into people. The tears were already trickling below the black plastic frames and spreading over her cheeks so she removed the sunglasses, wiped her eyes and – seeing a pretty courtyard draped with carpets – left the main street again.

He was just about to lift the carpets off the wall and take them inside for the night when the woman came by. It was her jacket he noticed first, a loose, shimmery black thing which picked up the reflections from the coloured lights in the rubber tree. New to town, he could tell. She walked slowly, only the blue eyes raced, scanning walls and shop windows. Nervous, he could tell. Clutching her purse so hard her knuckles shone through her white skin. She held herself straight, stiff but when she turned to watch as he unhooked a handsome silk kilim, her jacket rippled, softening the angles of her body. Not French. Not German.

Hello! How are you? Welcome! She looked at him, straight at him.

I like your jacket, he said, and – knowing the answer – added: Did you buy it here, in Morocco?

Of course she shook her head and at that moment he should have asked her into the shop, offered tea, pulled out the carpets but she was already past the door, he had been too slow, too taken up with admiring her jacket, wondering what it cost, too busy looking at her eyes, mouth, breasts, legs and trying to think of something else to say in English. But his English was not so good, he was out of practice, so when he finally called.

Come please. Only for look, no for buy, it was too late.

The moment to embark on a sale had passed, the moment when their eyes had met. Now her back was to him, her long shimmering back and she had to look over her shoulder, to reply, in English.

Another time perhaps. I need to eat.

That's when he should have let her go and find the ugly overpriced hole she'd circled in her guide book but no, he'd taken hold of her arm – and she had put up only a little resistance – and guided her to Restaurant Yasmine.

A clean place, not expensive, very near.

Your brother's place, is it? she said, but not nastily, not like a smartass tourist, not that hard, knowing tone he had endured day after day before all this talk of war killed off business. He denied any connection to the patron of Yasmine though, of course, Amal would slip him a couple of coins for bringing in a customer. With weary amusement she let him settle her at a table, summon the waiter, shake her hand as if being led around was all a harmless little game, no big rip-off.

*Bon appétit* he said, and went back to close up the shop.

She had gone past hunger. Eating was an effort. Her hand shook as she lifted forkfuls of spicy stew to her mouth. Though the restaurant was deserted, though there was no one to notice her except the waiter she felt too visible, too conscious of every movement, as if she had lost the habit of eating. Food fell off her fork, stringy bits of meat and vegetables lodged between her teeth, her cutlery rattled against the hot clay bowl.

The commotion outside was a convenient distraction from the gravy spattered tablecloth and the embossed wallpaper. A procession of some sort, announced by drums and demented pipes, passed the open door of the restaurant. From her seat she could see a long table being carried through the narrow alley, a table set with cloth, candlesticks, flowers and utensils, held aloft, rocking by on the swell of the crowd. A table and then a calf, skittering behind.

The wedding feast, on spindly legs, pissed with abandon as it was nudged towards its own slaughter. Malek hammered home the lock on the shop door. When he recognised the wedding party he spat loudly into the dust. The husband, an English with wispy hair and a belly like a woman with child, a 40-years-old English marrying a local girl, a virgin of 16 years. He'd come here for that, lived half his life doing whatever with women and now he wanted to buy himself a child bride – and of course these poor people had given him their daughter – he wanted feasting and dancing, the *marriage typique*, the big ritual; he wanted his guests waiting outside the door so he could go to them with his bride's bikini briefs and say,

See? I have made a woman from this girl. See, the blood of my wife.

Jane put the change from the large bill into her wallet, left the restaurant and walked straight into the path of the man from the carpet shop, who was approaching her. He was walking between a young man and woman. Their arms were linked. They were laughing. When he saw her he broke away from his friends.

Did you enjoy your meal? You want to drink something? Where?

Where you like.

He felt for the money in his pocket. A crisp fifty – thanks to his good luck of running into Youseff and Fatima – and twenty of his own.

Without thinking she had responded, without making any decisions Jane had begun to walk in step with Malek. His friends had gone.

Not far, she said. I don't want to go far.

Of course. You want to be near your hotel. I know this. No problem.

When the first bottle was empty he wanted to order another but she said,

I'm tired. I should go now. Back to my hotel.

No please. Stay longer, just a little longer, he said, reaching for her hand which she withdrew.

Please, he said, I like you, you understand? We drink one more bottle, then I take you to your hotel, no problem. Please, he said and when he spoke he seemed so sad, so hurt by her refusal, as if all he wanted was a little bit of trust, a little more time together, nothing else, no sex adventures, he knew her situation, knew she was not free, she had made her situation clear before they reached the bar. And it was better sitting there, drinking wine and looking out at the sea, better than huddling under too few blankets in the gloomy hotel room with its maroon curtains and dirty yellow walls.

Please, because for me . . . you know what is *coup de foudre?* She didn't. And she had left her dictionary in her hotel room. And his explanations involving a flash in the sky did not clarify anything. But when the waiter appeared with another bottle she remained seated and let her glass be refilled. When the wine ran low, so did his English and her French, and Arabic was out of the question. She took to looking out at the boats in the harbour, he to watching her. He could tell that in her mind she was far away from this place, this man she didn't know, in her mind she was on another shore, in another bar, with another man, her husband, an English, maybe like the one in town who'd be at that moment dancing with his Moroccan bride, preparing to penetrate her body and no questions asked. The family and the nation had given their permission, opened their arms and said,

Come in. Welcome. Take what we offer. You can pay the price. It is a good price, special price for special person. Nothing to you.

She was looking out to sea and he was looking at her elegant jacket and the fat purse at her fingertips. How much did she have in there? And at home? A car, a video, hot water day and night, a wardrobe full of good clothes? The Italian coat was all he had and maybe he'd have to sell it. And what would she take home? What would she take from his country? It was always take with tourists. Souvenirs, photos, memories.

A carpet would look good in her house. Maybe she had a big house, maybe she'd take home two, three, four carpets, maybe he could really make a sale. If everything was nice for her tonight, maybe tomorrow she'd come to the shop, he'd serve her with tea and they'd made some good business, enough to keep him going for a bit. But she hadn't said anything about buying a carpet. In fact, she'd said many times already that she had not come here to buy, that she did not want to buy, she hated bargaining, it was not her way. She was clear about that, about her way, definite, as if at other times – when she was not so tired and so far from home – her life was a neat and intricate pattern, one she had chosen from a whole range, the way she might choose a carpet.

Your jacket is like the sea in moonlight, he said, touching her sleeve, but his pretty phrase didn't bring her eyes back to his and now that the wine had been drunk and paid for – he had offered to contribute Yousseff's fifty but she refused it – now he should take her to her hotel.

The night air bites as they walk across the uneven cobbles of the harbour. Her jacket is thin. She is cold. Though she protests, he takes off his coat and drapes it over her shoulders. The waves can be heard smashing against the sea wall. The boats creak and scrape together. Away from the bar the harbour is badly lit. No one is about.

Come and hear the sea, he says, as they veer away from the exit towards the far side of the harbour.

I can hear it, she says, and stops, but he is pressing her to go further, to give him just a little bit of trust, and just as she is thinking that it would be good to feel the spray on her face, that had she been in her own country she would have gone – accompanied or alone – past the dark huddle of boats to the sea wall, just as she is beginning to feel sick of her own fear and suspicion – she has been saying No, No thank you, Another time perhaps, since she arrived – just as all this denial is getting to her, he grips her arms.

Come please. You come now, please, he is saying but the tone has changed, the 'please' is no longer a polite request, he is pressing her towards the dark and she knows she has already taken a step too far, such a short step and yet everything has changed, the bar is already too far away, her hotel also . . .

. . . but how can she push him away now, she who'd sat all night asking questions about the crafts, the spices, the economy, the lives of girls and women, the *mariage typique*, the war, and he had told her everything he knew. It had not been easy for him to say so much in English and she had wanted details, wanted to take from him so many details, he had given and she had taken and now – He lets go of her. He needs to piss.

Moving away to the sound of his urine hissing over the cobbles, walking fast, she puts a distance between them. When she reaches the exit to the harbour, she begins to run across the lorry park. She remembers that she is still wearing his coat, she throws it off her shoulders, the ground is muddy, her shoes become caked in mud, the mud slows her down, her feet drag but she doesn't stop, with each step she is nearer her hotel. He picks up the coat. He continues to follow her but is too far behind to catch up, close enough only to wave his muddy coat in the air, to wave his coat like a flag and roar at her shimmering back:

I hate you! You and your filthy rich nation! You understand!

# At the Edge of the Country

*Alexander McCall Smith*

'Little things,' once he said to his son. 'Little things change your life. Something that somebody just happens to say to you. Everything can be different after that.'

Fraser had left Scotland in 1946, as a young man of eighteen. He had been promised a job in a jute firm in Calcutta, but had left ship on the coast of Africa, at Durban, and made his way to the Basutoland Protectorate. He chose to do so because of a chance conversation with a man on board, who had told him that if he followed him up to the Protectorate he would arrange a job which would pay twice what he had been offered in the jute office.

'Very demanding place, India,' the other man had said. 'I've lost friends out there. River sickness. Heat. Now all those politics too. Congress and so on. The Protectorate is much healthier. Altitude. Good mountain air.'

He had needed little persuading. It was poverty, rather than any desire to leave home, which had driven him from Dundee, and Africa seemed not so far away, just one wide, dotted loop on the map of sea-routes, rather than a long series of attenuated strings that implied great distances and long separations. So he made his way up to the Protectorate, half-expecting that the job might not actually materialise, but it did. After a few years, he set out on his own, establishing a trading store on the edge of a small town on the border. There was house behind the store, three rooms and a verandah, and a lean-to kitchen at the back. The kitchen had a boiler in it – an old petrol drum heated by a wood fire, and this provided a supply of scalding-hot water for the shower that he had rigged up at the side of the house. In the mornings, with the smell of wood-smoke in his nostrils, he would stand under his steaming shower and look down the hillside to the scruffy stand of trees that marked the very edge of the country. Then he would smoke a cigarette on the verandah and contemplate the day ahead, which would almost inevitably be exactly the same as the day before, and the day before that. The only variation in his life was the hot season, when the temperature soared into the nineties, and the cold season, when the crisp, dry air cut into your lungs in the morning and the Basotho people wrapped themselves in their brightly coloured blankets, like cloaks. Sometimes a group of men would go riding past on their mountain ponies, all of them attired in blankets of the same pattern, a clan outing, clutching the hide whips which they would crack over the heads of their thin hunting dogs.

Like all colonial societies, it was full of small cruelties, and he found himself despising the narrow ways of the British administrators and their wives. He was a Scot, after all, and one of the few things that he remembered from his education was the Burns that he had been obliged to learn by heart. The egalitarian ethos of the poems had touched a chord within him, and, translated into the circumstances in which he now found himself, meant that he recognised his common humanity with the people among whom he lived. At the age of twenty-one he took an African wife, in an informal sense, although he paid the full bride-price which her father would have expected under the customary law of the Basotho. She was a fat woman who oiled her skin with palm oil and who laughed bashfully whenever he looked in her direction. He did not mind this. He was a man of few words and he had no desire to share what inner life he had with another.

There was only one child, the boy. He looked more like his mother than his father, with her almond-shaped eyes and brown skin, like dark honey. He took the father's name, though, and the father said to him: 'You're a Scotsman. Just remember that. You may never see Scotland, but you're a Scotsman all the same. Dundee.' What the father did not tell him, though, was that he would belong nowhere; that he was caught between two worlds. He would discover this, he knew, later on; there would be tears, and bitterness, and that, he knew, was absolutely inevitable.

The boy never went anywhere. He put in a few years at school, but his education did not amount to much, although his father insisted that he learned Burns, as he had done.

'There's all the philosophy you need in those poems,' he said. 'That's all you need. Learn them.'

The woman died shortly after the boy's sixteenth birthday. She developed an infection, which had been made worse by her consulting a traditional healer. By the time they took her to the clinic, which was over fifty miles away, she had gone into a state of shock and it was too late for anything to be done. Fraser survived her by three years, and then one morning the boy discovered him on the rough concrete floor of the makeshift shower, the water still pouring down upon him, but his heart quiet within him. The boy felt ashamed that his father should be naked, even in death, and he turned off the tap and covered him gently with some old sacking.

The boy was now alone. There had been changes. The Protectorate had been given its independence and there were pictures of the Paramount Chief on the stamps. People said: everything will change now, because we are free. But it did not, as the country was still poor.

An attorney in Maseru came out to the store and told the boy that he had inherited everything.

'Your father was mean . . . I'm sorry, I mean to say that he was canny. That's the word, isn't it? He made quite a bit of money, you know, and that's all yours now.'

The boy looked at the lawyer. 'I don't need much money,' he said. 'I haven't got much to spend it on. What is there to do up here?'

'You could go away,' said the lawyer. 'You could come down to Maseru.'

'What is there to do there?' asked the boy.

The lawyer smiled. 'Nothing, I suppose. Maybe you should just stay up here.'

'Yes,' said the boy.

On Friday and Saturday evenings, the boy went to a café attached to a nearby garage. This was a small room, with a fridge on one side, and four of five tables with gingham tablecloths. Behind a bar, the woman who owned the garage served large, icing-covered buns and rolls filled with bacon and fried eggs. The fat oozed off the bacon and became encrusted around the edge of the rolls. The boy liked to lick this off before he bit into the bacon.

This woman, who was in her late thirties, was called Mimi, and when not behind the bar or cooking the egg and bacon rolls, she would sit at one of the tables and play cards with the sister of the local Roman Catholic priest. They played a game which the boy never quite understood, although he often watched them. Every now and then they would accuse one another of cheating, and the sister of the Roman Catholic priest would look to the boy for support.

'She's cheating, isn't she?' the priest's sister would say. 'You saw, didn't you? She's a cheat.'

The boy shrugged his shoulders. 'Maybe. Maybe not. How can I tell?'

'Leave him out of this,' said Mimi. 'He's just a boy. He doesn't know anything.'

On the first occasion that he went into the café after the death of his father, the two women fell silent.

'Ah, shame,' said Mimi. 'You poor boy. I'm really sorry that your father died. I really am.'

'He was a great man,' said the priest's sister. 'He was a great man, your dad.'

'Why?' asked the boy. 'How was he a great man?'

The priest's sister thought for a moment. 'He came all the way from Scotland,' she said at last. 'That's a long way. He was a Scotsman, you see.'

Mimi nodded. She was about to say something, but stopped. Her cheeks were wet.

The boy stared at them with his almond eyes almost black, opaque.

'But now he's gone,' said the priest's sister. 'And you're going to have do something. Why don't you build a house? Build a big house with a proper bathroom.'

They were now joined by the mechanic, who was wiping his hands on a piece of lint.

'If you want to build a house,' he said. 'I know a builder. He's my brother. He could build you a really good house. Much better than that shack your old man built. Beg pardon. Much better.'

The priest's sister reached over to touch the boy's arm.

'They've got your best interests at heart,' she said. 'Get Tommy's brother to build you a house.'

They found a spot about five miles away, on the banks of a small river that ran deep in the rainy season and which was no more than a trickle in the dry months. The builder, who came up from Maseru for the weekend to examine the site, pronounced it ideal.

'It's good firm ground,' he said. 'You can build a good strong house here. Remember the story of the three little pigs? Remember it?'

'No,' said the boy.

The builder glanced at him. 'Two of them built damn useless houses and the wolf knocked them over. The other built a house made of brick and the wolf couldn't do a thing. Boy, was he cross! Hopping mad.'

'Where did these pigs live?' asked the boy.

The builder said nothing, and the boy looked at him while he extracted a packet of cigarettes from his breast pocket and offered the boy one.

'Your father was the Scotsman, wasn't he?' he asked.

The boy nodded.

'He was quite a man, your father,' said the builder. 'A great man.'

'Why?' asked the boy.

'He just was,' said the builder. 'Great man.'

Mimi and the priest's sister designed the house for the boy, sketching it out on two sheets of paper which they had taped together. On the one side were the front and rear elevations, and on the other was the internal lay-out of the rooms, all drawn to scale, with a six-inch wooden ruler.

The mechanic, who watched this procedure, was doubtful, and took the boy aside.

'Don't let those bloody women design your house for you,' he muttered. 'They're bloody useless.'

The boy spread his hands out, palms upward; it was a gesture he had inherited from his father, who did it to express the hopelessness that he saw all around him. 'I can't tell them to stop now,' he said. 'They've already spoken to your brother.'

The mechanic shook his head. 'They don't know the first

thing,' he said. 'You're only lucky that you've got my brother to stop the whole thing turning into a disaster. True as God.'

'You must have a house-warming party,' said Mimi, when the house was finished. 'We can invite the fathers from the mission. They like to drink when they get the chance. Irishmen, you know.'

The boy agreed, and the party was planned for the evening of the day that he took possession of the house. He closed the store on that day, putting up a sign which told his customers that he would be back the following day. Then he packed all his belongings in the back of his truck and drove off to the new house to install himself.

He noticed that there was something wrong the moment he stepped into the house. The walls seemed straight enough, but the floor was definitely uneven. In fact, the whole house sloped towards the river, at a sufficient angle to make one feel slightly disorientated as one crossed a room or walked along a corridor. The boy sat down, and then stood up again, to test the impression. It was confirmed.

The guests arrived at half past five, when the last rays of the sun were still visible on the tops of the mountains behind them.

'Great house,' said the mechanic, his cigarette between his lips as he talked. 'Tommy's brother's done another good job. I told you he was good.'

'It's a nice place,' said the boy. 'It's a big house. I wish my dad could have seen it.'

'Oh you poor boy,' said the priest's sister. 'And him being dead and all that.'

There was a silence. A car was approaching, with some people from the town, and once these new guests arrived drinks were poured – bottles of cold beer from a zinc tub which had been half filled with ice by Mimi. Then the fathers arrived from the mission – five of them – and they all went out on to the verandah to admire the view of the river.

'I hope that the river doesn't flood,' said one of the fathers. 'You're a bit close to the banks here. That river gets nasty when there's run-off from the mountains. You wouldn't want your house washed away. That would be a terrible shame.'

'Terrible,' said one of the other fathers. 'But, forgive me, I'm no judge of these things, but is there a bit of a slope here? I get the impression that the house goes down in that direction. East to west, so to speak. Lovely place though.'

There was a silence. One of the fathers lifted his glass of beer to his mouth and glanced at one of the others.

'Slope?' said Mimi 'Slope?'

'Well, yes,' said the father. 'Look, I'll put one of these oranges down on the ground, like this. There. Now watch.'

He gave the orange the tiniest of pushes, and it rolled convincingly across the floor, gathering speed as it did.

'See?' said the father. 'That's a slope for you.'

The mechanic bit his lip. 'My brother built it,' he said. 'All right. But he built it from plans drawn up by those two women. I told the boy that he shouldn't let a couple of women design a house for him. It's their fault.'

Mimi put down her drink and stared at the mechanic.

'There you go again,' she said angrily. 'You're always blaming us for everything. Your trouble is that you don't like women, do you? Don't think we can't tell.'

'Shut your face,' snapped the mechanic. 'The fact is: you shouldn't have tried to design a house, should you? Who taught you? Where did you learn?'

She glowered at the mechanic, before retorting: 'You try and do better yourself. The point is that the house doesn't slope: it's the country. Look at the map. The whole country slopes to the west. So it's not surprising if there's a little slope in this house.'

'Some architect!' said the mechanic. 'Anyway, let's not talk about it. This is meant to be a house-warming party, for God's sake.'

The priest's sister laughed nervously. 'You two are always bickering,' she said. 'Even in front of the fathers here. What do you imagine they think?'

They returned to their drinks. Later, when people began to drift away, Mimi came to the boy's side. He was standing in the kitchen, gazing at the floor.

'Did you enjoy your party?' she said. 'It's been an important day for you, hasn't it?'

'Yes,' he said. 'It has.'

She looked at him.

'Your daddy would have wanted me to take care of you,' she said. 'He often said to me: If I kick the bucket, Mimi, please look after that boy of mine. That's what he said.'

'So, what now?' asked the boy.

'So I'll move in and look after this place for you,' she said. 'We'll be happy enough. You run the store and I'll run the café. How about that.'

The boy looked down at his shoes. He was no match for these women, he thought, which is just what his father had told him. We're no match for them, son. That's just the way it is.

'So,' said Mimi. 'I'll get my stuff tomorrow.'

'I'll bring it over for you.'

She smiled. 'Just like your daddy,' she said. 'A great man. He really was. And you are too.'

The following week, in the bar, the mechanic said to the priest's sister: 'Your friend has got what she wants, hasn't she? She always wanted the father, and didn't get him, and now she's got the son.'

The priest's sister pursed her lips. 'You wouldn't tell him that, would you? Even you must have some feelings.'

The mechanic reached for his glass. 'No, I won't. I won't be like that missionary who told him his house slopes.'

'You're a good man,' said the priest's sister.

The mechanic smiled. 'I like you too,' he said.

They lifted their glasses to one another and for a moment, through the liquid, they saw one another in a different light.

# Text for the Day

*Ali Smith*

I magine Melissa's collection of books, spread between her bedroom and her living-room, when Melissa was in bed at night asleep or out at work all day or away for the night or weekend. Hundreds sitting silent on their shelves from Agee to Yevtushenko (she had no Zs). A substantial set of English and Scottish literature course Canon Classics – Melissa studied English at university ten years ago. A large collection of recent American, English and European literature; Melissa's friend Austen works in a bookshop and often lets her buy books at one-third discount. Books and books, blocks of books shifting infinitesimally in the night as the renovated tenement foundations sent shivers through the building. Books pressing together, so close that the covers of several of them stuck together; for instance if Melissa had tried to remove Charlotte Brontë's *Villette* (Penguin) to read again she would have found it attached on one side to *Shirley* (Penguin) and on the other to a 1933 copy of *Testament of Youth* by Vera Brittain (Gollancz), signed by the author and found for 50p in a public library sale.

Imagine the silent books in the silent flat at night, unmoving in the dark, Melissa's name, the place she bought them and the date shut in each between the first page and the outer cover; imagine the spines of the books by day in the still flat, yellowing, losing their colours, fading with the light moving round the room.

First of all Melissa told her boyfriend Frank to piss off and get out, she was fed up of him calling her Honey; it wasn't funny any more. And the next day instead of going to work she stayed in bed, pulling the covers up to her neck and, when the heating had gone off and it got cold, using her hairdryer to warm herself between the duvet and the mattress, something she had always refused to let herself do before because of global warming and the electricity bill. After that she got up and threw her hairdryer out of the window; it smashed on the pavement just missing the next door neighbour's car. She threw all the windows open in the freezing cold. Then she threw her books all over her flat. That was then. Now she was fast disappearing; she was almost gone.

Later, when she had been gone for quite a long time, those who were less imaginative among the friends who noticed she wasn't there anymore thought she was probably off doing something like taking time out, backpacking across the USA or something like that. Someone else, someone at work, thought that maybe she'd landed some hot new job better than Information Transference and had taken it without telling her old boss so she wouldn't have to work notice. Though neither of these was really like her, like what you'd expect. Other friends and acquaintances didn't notice or know; most didn't think of her at all and those who did assumed on the whole that she was still where they'd last seen her, doing what they'd last known she was doing, rather like you assume someone you know is doing the usual things, breathing, walking, going to the shops, eating biscuits, before you discover that he or she is dead, died a long time ago and you never knew it.

Austen knew something was wrong though because she had

a key to Melissa's flat and the books, the books, the pride and joy, were so peculiar in both rooms, in such a mess, all over the floor or piled in haphazard order, great gaping holes in the bookcases all up the walls and books fallen on their sides askew, even a scatter of books in the bath. Like the advert on television showing a burgled house to warn you against thieves and suggest you leave your light on at night to pretend someone's always in, Austen thought. The light in Melissa's flat had been left on, baleful with the curtains and windows still open. Nobody there and nothing taken, everything smugly intact except the books.

She shut the windows in the cold and turned the heating on in the kitchen cupboard. On the table some loose-torn pages lay beyond a milk bottle; from where Austen stood she could see, distorted through the glass of the bottle, the word *Introduction*. By her foot, the cover of a Kafka paperback (Penguin Modern Classics). She made herself a cup of tea – sour milk – opened the pedal bin to drop the teabag in and found the bin was full of the ripped-out pages and the empty shell covers of several books. Down the back of the bin, more loose pages on the floor. She went through, sat on the couch and found her feet resting unavoidably on books. Beside her on the cushion, as if it had landed there clumsily after flight with its wings still fanned out, lay an upside-down copy of Seamus Heaney's *Seeing Things* (Faber and Faber).

Right then, as Austen dipped her finger into the tea to squash a lump of milk against the side of the cup, Melissa was leaving an eight-till-late supermarket in the rain, gnawing something out of a packet, a paperback in her other hand, and an elderly lady wearing a rainmate was shouting after her in a rare kind of anger, her arms in the air, calling to the boys collecting the trollies in the wet carpark to look, look what the girl had done, never in all her life.

\*      \*      \*

219

Frank phoned Austen the next evening. He didn't particularly like Austen; she was Melissa's friend.

She told me to get out, Austen, so, well, ha ha, I did. She went a bit mad. I'm a bit worried about her, said Frank. He was still pleased with himself for having demonstrated to Melissa how absurd her demand was by actually doing what she asked.

– Mm. Funny, I'm not, I don't think.

– Not what?

– Worried. At least I don't think so. Mad like what? Like when you spilt the hot chocolate on the Keats and all over the couch? said Austen.

– Well, no, not really, it wasn't mad-angry. It was because she was so calm, it was weird.

– Right, weird, said Austen.

– But that made it, you know, *more* mad. She said these really weird things. Just sitting on the floor, cool as a cucumber talking this stuff.

– Mm, said Austen. She didn't like Frank much, hadn't liked him since the first moment they met, when he had told her she had a weird name.

– She's not at the flat, you know, said Frank.

– I know. Look, Frank, I've got to go.

– Do you know where she is?

– No, I don't, but how about if she calls I'll tell her to call you. Look, I've got something frying on the cooker.

– I can't get an answer and I can't get into the flat any more. Nobody knows where she is at the office, she hasn't phoned in sick, I called to ask. Do you think I should tell the police?

– Well, no, not really, but if it'll make you feel any better, said Austen absent-mindedly.

Later that evening Melissa phoned Austen and Frank from a call-box. It was a bad line and her voice was faint, from the middle of a sea of white noise.

– Austen, you shouldn't have tidied up. No, it was good of you, but – yes, I went to pick up some things. No, listen, I can't stop, I've only got twenty pence – listen – use the flat if you like. *Have* the flat if you like, enjoy it, and Austen, use the car. I'll send you – I don't know – a postcard, (her voice grew fainter) must go —

– Hello Frank? It's me, Melissa. Oh Christ DON'T call me that – yes – no, can you hear? I am, as loud as I – No, there's no need, I'm obviously not missing. I said I'm obviously – Look, I just phoned to say, no, I just phoned to say goodbye. *Goodbye*. Got that? okay? No, no need – goodbye—

Frank put the phone down, then picked it up again and called the police. Austen realised that she'd been staring into space and put the receiver down. She imagined the call-box door swinging shut, Melissa coming out of the smell of urine into a clear frost.

Melissa sat in the weak moonlight, curled like an animal. She had scaled the locked gate, swung over the spikes at the top, letting her rucksack thud onto the grass beyond the gravel, and she had landed more or less noiselessly on the other side. Condensation blanked out the windows in the gatehouse. Invisible, silent in the dark, the cold, she made her way to the other side of the graveyard and dropped by a random grave. She leaned back against the stone. Below the silhouette of a stone angel she took the books out of her rucksack. Already today she had ripped the pages out of *Tender is the Night* by F Scott Fitzgerald (Penguin), *Bliss* by Peter Carey (Faber and Faber), *The Novel Today* edited by Malcolm Bradbury (Fontana), *Madame Bovary* by Gustave Flaubert (Penguin), *Selected Dramas and Lyrics of Ben Jonson* (publisher Walter Scott, 24 Warwick Lane, Paternoster Row, London in 1886, a favourite), *Memoirs of a Dutiful Daughter* by Simone de Beauvoir (Penguin, another favourite, and after an initial moment of nostalgia, nothing but relief), and finally Joyce's *Dubliners* (Penguin). *Dubliners* she had read again, enjoying it immensely, removing each page as she finished it and leaving it where it fell as she walked or sat. She had never enjoyed reading 'The Dead' so much, she realised, as near to tears she tore the last page, the page about the snow, and let it fall.

Here was a place where no one would stare or comment or shout angrily. She took the first book off the pile, *The Sunday Missal and Prayer Book* (Collins). Out came the table of movable feasts, the prefaces, the order of Mass; she didn't need light to know she was tearing out first Sunday in Advent, second Sunday in Advent, third Sunday in Advent, fourth Sunday in Advent, Christmas, Easter, the whole of the year. Thin leaves fell round her, turned in the grass between the gravestones, rustled across the gravel.

The police were worried. The missing woman or someone pretending to be her had emptied her bank account. They called on Austen and Frank and at the insurance company where Melissa worked. They found Melissa's address book under her bed and contacted everybody in it. Austen told them how she had found the flat and what Melissa had said on the phone, and they took away the car and several ripped-up books for forensic examination, opened a file on Austen and tapped her phone. They did the same to Frank, who also told them about his phone call, about his call to Austen, about the weird way Melissa had been acting anyway, and what she'd said the night he left.

They opened a file on each of the employees at the company where Melissa was Information Transferer, which meant she spent the day typing the numbers of accounts from letters and applications into a computer so that people could be traced and monitored by number rather than name.

Meanwhile, Melissa disappeared. Sightings of her filtered

back to Austen now and then via Frank, via mutual friends, even via people standing chatting in the bookshop where she worked. Sightings took on an almost mythological quality. Austen told Melissa this in the letter she packed in the box of books she sent to a postal collection point near the American border. The postcard Melissa had sent was a colour photograph, a long American car upside down in a crevass, above on the edge of the crevass a house and garden, intact. Melissa's spidery handwriting on the back, in ink that looked faded from the sun, said that she was fine, that where she was writing the card she could smell carnations and coffee, just like in Lawrence's *Mornings in Mexico and Etruscan Places* which she was reading, and please to send the books, whichever Austen chose, from the flat. And to send if possible a similar boxload at the same time annually until there were none left. *I'm rereading almost everything now*, she wrote. *I'm rereading Emily Dickinson in the desert here. It's great. Love, M.* Austen passed the card on to the police, packed the books. *I can't help wondering*, she wrote in the letter, *what you'll do when you run out of books.* There was no reply.

A girl leaning against the poultry section in the supermarket reading a book ripped out the page and dropped it where she stood. A shocked elderly lady watched her tearing her book near the freezer compartment; speechless she watched her drop poems in several different aisles, near the bakery, by the household goods, in the check-out queue. The woman, pale with rage, followed the girl picking up the poems she dropped. Outside the automatic doors she stood in the rain and watched the girl leave. Look what the girl's doing! she called to the people going in. Never in all my life have I seen something so wanton, so disgusting, so wilfully destructive. When I was young we knew the value of things. She turned, caught the eye of one of the people coming out of the doors, she waved the fistful of torn poetry. Look, she pleaded; her eyes were desperate.

On an overnight bus to London a man watched, curious, as a young woman sitting across the aisle reading a book removed each page carefully after she read it. Her clothes were dishevelled; her hair looked like it could do with a good wash; she placed each finished page neatly beside her on the empty seat. At the end of the journey the man let the woman get off the bus before him, picked up the pages, took them to his hotel room and read them. He wondered who she was, where she stayed, how he could contact her so he could read the rest.

A woman standing at a bus stop in a large city found a fragment of paper stuck to her heel. It said on one side something about oaths and resurrections, something she couldn't make sense of. But on the other, words were spaced like poems had been at school, and she read:

*Celestial recurrences.*
*The day the flowers come*
*And when the birds go.*

The woman looked up the word *celestial* in her husband's dictionary when she got home. She thought the words she'd spiked her heel through were beautiful and she folded up the piece of paper and hid it in the secret place inside the lining of her make-up drawer. She didn't tell anyone about finding them.

Austen stands in the bookshop and sells books to people, pressing the buttons on the till with the blank knowledge of an automaton as the multicoloured covers of books, hundreds of books each day, shiny exciting new books, flash past her eyes and into little plastic carrier bags. She tucks the money into the correct compartments. Barnes and Byatt are selling well at the moment, and a new biography of the Kennedys, out for Christmas.

The shop she works in is pleasant, airy, tasteful, stays open late. They play classical music by day and jazzier music in the evenings; the public likes it; people tell Austen all the time what a pleasure it is to shop there. There's a Canadian writers' dumpbin of Atwood and Munro on one side of the doors, on the other there's a special display of new hardback fiction about Eastern Europe, this month's special interest. The shelves are open and well organised, well stocked. From where Austen stands she can see the whole range of the fiction department stretch down one long wall of the store, hundreds and hundreds of books, a mere echo of the hundreds of others before them. Austen knows it's insufficient, it's all not enough, but she doesn't know what to do. When people want poetry she sends them downstairs. In Melissa's now musty-smelling flat the shelves are gradually emptying; sightings of Austen's friend are rare now. Austen scans the shop, looks at her watch, sighs.

All the Margaret Atwood, gone, all the James Joyce, the Virginia Woolf, the Hardy, Lawrence, Forster. All the Carter and Rushdie, the Puig and Marquez, the Klima and Levi and Calvino and Milosz, all the Spark and the Gunn and the MacDiarmid, all the Shakespeare, all the Coleridge and Keats, the Whitman and Ginsberg, the Proust, the Eliot, the Scott, the thick books, the thin books, all the one-volume obscure poets and novelists, all the known names and the lesser or unknown lost or forgotten names flying immeasurable in the air, settling on the ground like seeds or leaves dropped from the trees, rotting into pieces, blown into the smithereens of meaning. Pages flutter across motorways or farmland, pages break apart, dissolve in rivers or seas, snag on hedges in suburban areas, cling round their roots. Fragments litter a trail that blows in every direction, skidding across roads in foreign cities, mulching in the wet doorways of small shops, tossed by the weather across grassland and prairies.

There are poems in gutters and drains, under the rails laid for trains, pages of novels on the pavements, in the super-markets, stuck to people's feet or the wheels of their bikes or cars; there are poems in the desert. Somewhere where there are no houses, no people, only sky, wind, a wide-open world, a poem about a dormant grass-covered volcano lies held down half-buried in sand, bleaching in the light and heat like the small skull of a bird.

# Nessun Dorma

## *Alan Spence*

I t's the first thing I hear when I step put into the street, Pavarotti at full volume, belting out *Nessua Dorma*. Half past six in the morning, the streetlights on, the sky above the tenements just starting to get light. Three closes along, on the other side, the groundfloor window is wide open, pushed up as far as it can go. That's where the music is coming from. It builds to its crescendo, *Vincero*. It stops. There's a brief silence. Then it starts all over again.

I peer across as I pass by, but I can't really see in. The lights are off in the house. All I can make out is a faint glow that might be from a TV in the corner. The curtains are flapping, whipped about by that freezing Edinburgh breeze, straight off the North Sea.

In the papershop at the corner, Kenny from upstairs is buying his *Daily Record*, his cigarettes.

'Early shift this week?' I ask him.

'That's right. It's a bugger,' he says. 'Wife still away?'

'She'll be back at the weekend. Hey, did you hear that racket in the street?'

'The music,' he says. 'That World Cup thing?'

'Pavarotti.'

'I think it's been on all night. I got in the back of ten and it was going full blast then.'

'Weird.'

'The thing is.' He has pulled open the door, set the bell above it jangling. He stands half in half out of the shop. 'I couldn't help wondering if she was okay. The wifie in the house like. I mean, I looked in the window when I was passing and she was just sitting there in the dark wi the TV on and that music blaring out. Over and over.'

'Could be a video and she's rewinding it.'

'Aye.' He looks uncomfortable. 'Anyway. Maybe somebody should make sure she's all right. I'd do it myself but I've got my work to go to.'

'Sure.'

'So.'

'Right.'

He lets the door go and it closes behind him.

'Thanks, Kenny.'

'Christ.'

Back along the street with my milk and rolls, the paper. I have to look in and see for myself. The music is still playing, louder the nearer I get. Right outside the window it's deafening. The curtains are still being tugged about by the wind, white net gone grubby. They flap out and I catch their dusty smell.

Inside, the TV flickers bright and harsh. Pavarotti is in close-up, the colours lurid and wrong, his face orange. Silhouetted in the blue light from the screen, I can make out the woman, sitting in an armchair, her back to the window. I lean right in and call out hello, above the music. My eyes adjust to the light and a few things take shape. A stack of newspapers on the table, an empty whisky bottle, ashtray full to overflowing, a carton of longlife milk. And the smell hits me, reek of drink and stale tobacco and somewhere in at the back of it a pervading sourness like old matted clothes in a jumble sale. The room stinks of misery. It's a smell I remember.

I call out hello again, hello there, and this time her head turns, she makes some kind of noise.

'Are you all right?'

She heaves herself up in the chair. She's a big woman, heavy. I recognise her, I've seen her in the street. Not old, maybe late forties, fifty. She steadies herself, peers at me blankly, takes a careful step or two towards the window. She looks terrible, her face blotched and puffy. Her hair is flattened, sticks up at the back, the way she's been leaning on it. She wears a thick wool cardigan, buttoned up, on top of what looks like a nightdress.

'What's that?' she says, bleary, looking out.

'Just making sure you're all right.'

'All right?' She has no idea who I am, what's going on. 'Yes,' she says. 'It's all right. Each one that has wronged me will come undone. Nice of you to take an interest, I would offer you a drink but it's not on. They sent for the police you know. But I told them. No uncertain terms. So now they're looking into it. Full investigation. I'll show them. Would you like a drink? No, of course. It's not on.'

She suddenly stops and looks confused, stranded in midstream. The voice of Pavarotti swells, fills the room, she lets herself be caught up in it again, lost in it. Her face crumples, folds in a grimace, a tortured smile as she stands there swaying in her stinking kitchen. The aria builds to its climax again. *Vincero.*

She finds the remote control and winds back the tape.

The Chinese dragon I painted on the wall of my room, in Glasgow, all those years ago. Eight feet long in bright, primary colours, straight on to the blank white wall.

No reason why it should come to me now, but it does. I see it floating in its swirl of cloud, fire flaring from its nostrils, its long tail curled and looped round on itself like a Celtic serpent.

The room was the first one I'd ever had completely to myself. The twenty-third floor of a highrise block. My father and I had been moved from the room and kitchen where I'd grown up, where I was born. The room and kitchen that had come to have that stink of misery I recognised just now. The smell of hopelessness, my father not coping, myself useless in the face of it.

But all that was past. The tenements were rubble and dust. We had been transported to this bright, empty space high in the sky. I remember us laughing as we walked through it, shouted to each other from room to room, intoxicated by the cleanness and newness. It still smelled of fresh putty and paint. And the view from the windows had us stand there just staring. Instead of blackened tenements, the back of a factory, we could see for miles, clear down the Clyde.

I kept my room simple and uncluttered, a mattress in the corner, straw matting on the floor. And I started right away on painting that dragon. I copied it from a magazine, divided it up with a grid of squares, pencilled a bigger grid on the wall and scaled the whole thing up. That way the proportions would be right, exact. And when I'd drawn in all the lines, traced every delicate curve, I set to colouring it in, with poster-paint and a fine-tip brush.

I worked on it meticulously, a little every day, with total concentration and absolute care. After a week it was finished, except for one small section – the last few inches, the very tip of the tail. I decided to take a break over the weekend, finish it the following week. But I never did. I lived in that house for four years and never completed it. That section of tail stayed blank. When anyone asked me why, I had no idea. I just couldn't make myself pick up the brush. The dragon remained unfinished.

When I head out later along the street, Pavarotti's *bel canto* is still ringing out. *Tu pure, o Principessa nella tua fredda stanza.*

Princess you too are waking in your cold room. Again that smell wafts out as I pass by.

My father had a record of *Nessun Dorma* – an old scratched 78 – sung by Jussi Bjorling. So I know the song from way back. He used to play it loud when the drink had made him maudlin, sometimes alternating it with records of mine he liked in the same way, records that moved him to tears, Edith Piaf's *Je ne regrette rien*, Joan Baez singing *Plaisir d'amour*.

In the years after my mother died, I grew to dread hearing those songs. I would stop and listen on the stair, halfway up the dank close, knowing the state I would find him in, guttered into oblivion.

It must have been those songs that made him want to learn French.

'Got to do something about myself,' he said. 'Haul myself up by my bootstraps.'

So he'd signed up for an evening class at the University, gone along once a week.

'Give me something to look forward to,' he said.

He made lists of vocabulary in a little lined notebook.

'That tutor's some boy,' he said. 'Really knows his stuff.'

He had told the tutor he was hoping to go to France on holiday, someday.

The night I came home late and that smell hit me as soon as I opened the door. No music playing, but in the quietness the hiss and steady click of the recordplayer, the disc played out, the needle arm bobbing up and down in place. And behind that, my father breathing heavy in a deep drunk stupor. He slept in the set-in bed in the recess. I didn't want to disturb him but I wanted to turn off the recordplayer, I switched on the light, turned and saw him.

Sprawled across the bed, still dressed, shoes on, his clothes and the bedding covered in blood, a bloodsoaked hanky wrapped round his hand.

I managed to wake him but couldn't get him up on his feet. He had drunk himself senseless, beyond all comprehension and pain, anaesthetised and numb.

I sat up all night, dozed in the chair. A couple of times he shouted out, nothing that made any sense. At first light I shook him awake, took him down to casualty at the hospital. He had lost the tip of a finger, had no recollection where or how. The doctors stitched him up, gave him injections.

'I was on my way to the French class,' he said. 'Met a guy I used to work with, in the yards. Drinking his redundancy money. Just the one, I said. Got somewhere to go. That was it. The rest's a blur.'

'What about your hand?'

'No idea,' he said. 'Except maybe.' He stopped. 'Just a vague memory. Getting it jammed in a taxi door.'

'Where in God's name were you going in a taxi?'

'I haven't a clue, son. Haven't a clue.'

For a while after that he was ill. A low ebb. He never went back to his evening class, never finished the course. He was giving up on everything, until this move to the new place, the high rise. A fresh start.

I like to get settled in the library early, get a good stint of work done in the morning. But today I just can't seem to focus. So I'm glad of the distraction when Neil comes in, sits down at the table next to me.

'How's the mature student,' he asks. 'Working on something?'

'Dissertation,' I tell him. 'Zen in Scottish literature.'

'Wild!'

'Of all the people on the planet, you're the one most likely to appreciate it.'

'Hey thanks!'

His beard and long hair are grizzled these days. The archetypal Old Hippy.

'Passed these young guys in the street the other day,' he says. 'And they're looking me up and down. And one of them says Hey, man, tell it like it was!' He shrugs, speads his hands. 'Thing is, I'd have been glad to.'

I hand over one of my sheets of paper to him, point to the passage at the top. It's a story from the legend of Fionn.

Fionn asks his followers. 'What is the finest music in the world?' And they give their various answers. The call of a cuckoo. The laughter of a girl. Then they ask Fionn what he thinks. And he answers The music of what happens. 'Beautiful!' says Neil, handing me back the page.

'I'm writing about MacCaig at the minute,' I tell him. 'He once described himself as a Zen Calvinist!'

'Ha! He won't thank you for that.'

'Listen. Do you fancy a cup of tea?'

'Hey!' he says. 'Is the Pope a Catholic?'

In the tearoom he says, 'Stevenson's your man.'

'Stevenson?'

'Have a look at his *Child's Garden*. Then check out a wee book called *Fables*. It's the two sides, you see. Innocence and Experience. Here, I'll tell you my favourite one of the fables. This man meets a young lad weeping. And he asks him. What are you weeping for? And the lad says, I'm weeping for my sins. And the man says. You must have little to do. The next day they meet again. And the lad's weeping. And the man asks him. Why are you weeping now? And the lad says, Because I have nothing to eat. And the man says, I thought it would come to that.'

Neil throws back his head and laughs. 'There's Zen Calvinism for you!'

'The Ken Noo school!'

'Lord, Lord, we didna ken!'

'Aye, weel, ye ken noo!'

He thumps the table, laughs again.

Over more tea, I find myself telling him about the woman this morning, listening endlessly to *Nessun Dorma*.

'Sad,' he says.

Then I tell him about that dragon I once painted on the wall. And he stares at me.

'Now that is something.'

'How do you mean?'

'There's this Chinese story,' he says, 'about an artist that paints a dragon. And his master tells him he mustn't complete it. He has to leave a wee bit unfinished. The artist says fine, no problem, but sooner or later his curiosity gets the better of him. And he finishes it off. And the dragon comes to life and devours him!'

I stare at him.

'I've never heard that story in my life. How could I have known?'

'We know more than we think,' says Neil. 'I mean everything's telling us, all the time. Only we don't listen.'

'Sure!' For some reason, his story's disturbed me. 'Better get back to my work.'

'The dissertation!' He looks amused.

Outside in the High Street he asks, by the way, how's Mary? And I tell him she's fine; she's away in the States; she'll be back at the end of the week.

'Good,' he says.

We stop at the corner.

'Right.'

'One last thing,' he says. 'Do you know the story of *Turandot*, where your *Nessun Dorma* comes from?'

'Just that it's set in China.'

'Aye.' He nods, grins. 'Check it out sometime. I think you'll find it interesting.'

Back at the library, I find myself looking in the music section, finding the libretto.

An unknown prince arrives at the great Violet City, its gates carved with dragons. In the course of the story, he finds his long-lost father. He solves three riddles which grant him the hand of the Princess Turandot. The answer to one riddle is the name of the princess. The answers to the others are hope and blood.

The word Tao catches my eye as I flick through the pages. The prince is told, *Non esiste che il niente nel quale ti annulli.* There exists only the nothingness in which you annihilate yourself. *Non esiste che il Tao.* There exists only the Tao.

One last passage jumps out at me, a paragraph in the introduction, explaining that Puccini never completed the opera, it was left unfinished when he died.

I see Neil's grin. Everything is telling us. All the time.

I close the book, put it back on the shelf.


When I'd lived four years in that white room with a view, the painted dragon unfinished on the wall, I met Mary and moved out. We travelled a bit, in France then Italy. We got work teaching English, enough to get by. I sent my father postcards from every new place. When we came back home I went to see him. The flat had come to have the old familiar smell, staleness of booze and fags and no hope. He was listening again to his sad songs. He had lost his job, been laid off. He was months behind with his rent, and we were too broke to bail him out.

In the end he had to give up the flat. I helped him find a bedsit near the University. He liked it well enough, liked the neighbourhood. The bedsit was his home for five years, till he died.


Ten o'clock at night and *Nessun Dorma* still going strong. She's been playing it for 24 hours at least.

## Nessun Dorma

At the World Cup, Italia 90, in one of the games Scotland lost, the song was played at half-time, the video shown on a giant screen in the stadium. Someone shouted, 'Easy the big man!' And the whole Scottish crowd started chanting.

*One Pavarotti*

*There's only one Pavarotti.*

Scotland in Europe.

Wha's like us?

My old neighbour Archie next door has started up on his accordion. He plays it most nights, runs through his repertoire. *Moonlight and Roses, Bridges of Paris, Spanish Eyes.* A taste for the exotic. He plays with gusto, undaunted by the odd bum note. I find it unutterably melancholy.

The long dark night. This wee cold country.

Ach.


I know the noise has something to do with me as it batters into my awareness, harasses me awake. The phone ringing at 3am. So it must be Mary calling from the States. Still groggy, I pick it up, hear that transatlantic click and hiss, then her voice warm.

*Hello?*

'Hi.'

*I know it's late, sorry.*

It's one of those lines. The person speaking drowns out the other. When you talk you hear a faint, delayed echo of your own voice. Not great for communication. Those little phatic responses keep getting lost. So I just listen as she tells me the story. New York's been hit by a hurricane. Roads are flooded, bridges closed, subways off. The airports are shut down, all flights cancelled, no way she can get out.

*Sorry.*

'So it'll be, what a few more days?'

*Whenever.*

I listen to the wash of noise down the line, feel the distance. Then she's telling me about a call she made to the airline, and the woman she spoke to knew nothing about the situation.

*So I says, Haven't you been watching the news on TV? And she says, You think I'm sitting here watching TV? I'm working!*

I laugh at that, miss the next bit.

*and I ask her what I should do, and she says Stay tuned!*

'Nice!'

*What?*

'I said, Nice!'

*Yeah, right.*

'So!'

*So this is costing.*

'Who cares?'

*What?*

'Never mind!'

*I'll call when I know what's happening.*

'See you soon.'

*Take care.*

I put down the phone, stare at it. I shiver and realise I'm chilled from sitting. I know I won't get back to sleep so I pad through to the kitchen, put on the kettle, light the gas fire. Then I hear the commotion out in the street, voices raised, an argument, crackle of an intercom. I pull back the curtain and peer out, see the flashing light on top of the police car.

Two young policemen are at the groundfloor window, trying to reason with the woman, and she's screaming out at them. 'I know the score here! I know what's going on!'

Finally she bangs the window shut. Then the music stops, cuts off.

A man's voice shouts out from an upstairs window. 'Nessun bloody dorma right enough!

'How's anybody supposed to sleep through this lot?' And he too slams his window.

The car drives off, and everything is quiet again, so quiet. For no reason I get dressed and go out, walk to the end of the street. I stand there a while, looking up at the night sky. The winds are high. The way it looks, the clouds stand still, the stars go scudding past. Somewhere a dog barks. A taxi prowls by.

The music of what happens.

Stay tuned.

That groundfloor window is open again, just a fraction. Smell of my father's house. Things left unfinished. The music is playing, one more time, but quietly now, so I have to strain to hear it. I stand there and listen, right to the end.

*Vincero.*

# Distances

## *David Strachan*

I am listening with Kate to the CD my mother sent me for Christmas and it makes me want to cry. The songs are all in German and I wonder why she sent me them; I don't know any German and there's no tune to them and the only accompaniment is a rumptitumpty piano. I switch from track to track but they all sound just the same.

My father opens the door and stands there, listening, with a shoe on one hand and a polisher in the other. He looks like an actor in his evening suit. Très elegant.

I switch the player off. He doesn't look at me; he is busy polishing the toecap of that shoe of his as if it were a precious ornament, breathing on it then rubbing. 'You're sure you don't want to come with us? You'd enjoy it.'

My father has a habit of suggesting things for me to do. 'We'll see,' he says if I suggest something.

He works his foot into the shoe and stoops to fastens the lace. Kate goes across to him and tries to take the polisher from him.

'It would be good for you. Take you out of yourself . . . Kate!' Kate has the polisher in her jaws, twisting her head from side to side, growling, eyes rolling. 'Kate!' She lets go of the polisher, jumps back and waits for him to make the next move.

He picks a hair from his jacket sleeve.

'Take Fatso here for a walk if you're stuck for something to do. She could do with the exercise.' He glances at his watch. 'You're sure now? Very well. Jennie says there are sandwiches for you in the fridge. We won't be long.'

He shuts the door firmly behind him. Disappointed, Kate slumps to the floor and looks at me dully over her paws. She should know by now my father won't play. He's not that kind of person.

Last Christmas was different. Since then everything has changed I think as I take off the CD and listen to the car start up. Since then my mother has moved back to Nairobi and my father has remarried and I have stopped eating. My father peeps the horn and Jennie shouts 'Coming!' but of course he can't hear her and peeps the horn again several times. Jennie is my stepmother; she was one of his students, and when we go out together, people take her for my sister. I hear her running down the stairs then she pops her head in the door. 'Will you be all right?' she asks. I nod. 'Sure?' My father peeps. She rolls her eyes. I smile. She goes.

Last Christmas my mother said it was time for a change and that instead of turkey we were going to have a goose for dinner which no one objected to but when my father took off the first slice of breast you could see how pink it was. I was the only one who ate up all my portion, chewing each rubbery mouthful over and over again and swallowing it all down and wiping the blood off my lips with my napkin. My mother said it was the oven's fault, that she had gone by Delia Smith's timings. Somehow we never recovered from that under-cooked goose.

Perhaps that's why I have stopped eating, I don't know. It's a recent thing and no one seems to have noticed; I hide the uneaten food in my napkin or slip it to Kate under the table.

Out in the garden Kate grubs about under the rhododendron and comes back with a chewed rubber ball. She drops it at my feet, wagging her tail and making little bounding turns in her eagerness to get the game under way. But it is Mandy's ball she has brought.

I stand there with the red ball in my hand.

Mandy, our first dog, a Shetland collie, just disappeared. She was in the garden; she was in the house; no one could remember exactly where they had seen her last; and then she wasn't anywhere. Each day for months we expected her to come limping home, put ads in shop windows and the local paper, went calling her name in the woods outside the village, but we never saw Mandy again.

I throw the ball across the lawn for Kate to scamper after. Father is right. You can't spend your precious days grieving over the past. I run into the house with Kate getting in the way when I hear the phone because I know it will be Stevie.

'Yes, just me,' I say. 'And Kate. They've gone to the theatre. Is that the sea I can hear?'

'No,' he says. 'It's Mom vacuuming. I've got something to show you.'

'Come round and show me then,' I say.

'Why don't you come round here?' he says. 'I'll pick you up.'

'We've been through all that.'

'So Mom's hoovering's been a waste of time? Okay. See you in half-an-hour then. Be prepared for a shock.'

'Ciao.'

My father can't stand being in the same house as Stevie, which is why I have to give him a time to call and a time to visit. A month ago he started talking American and now he's wearing make-up. I'm going to miss him more than I care to think about, not that I love him or anything like that but he's fun to be with. Most of the time. I go to the bathroom and brush my teeth. I once used my father's toothpaste and the next day he said, 'Have you been using my toothpaste?' I couldn't work out how he knew. Or why it mattered. I have a shower. I love showers. A bath takes all the goodness out of me. I think of wearing my jeans and the blue turtleneck, then try on the dress I had worn at my father's wedding, but in the mirror I look like Cinderella.

'Hi!' Stevie says when I open the door. 'Taaraa! What do you think?' He has dyed his hair black. Kate is barking like mad.

'Jesus! You look like Dracula. What does your father think?'

'Woof Woof! Hi Kate! He thinks it's ridiculous.' He is speaking very rapidly, high on something. 'Is that Chinese or what? Wow!' I am wearing Jennie's Christmas present, a silk tunic, white with embroidered green and orange birds. 'I'm going to get a tattoo next. A pair of butterflies.' He lifts up his T-shirt with TOMORROW IS ANOTHER DAY printed on it and nods towards each nipple. 'One here and one there. What do you think? Wicked eh?' He gives me a hug and moves his fingers up and down my spine as if I was a cello. He puts his hands on my shoulders and frowns. 'You'll soon be just a skeleton,' he says.

'So will you,' I tell him. 'So will everyone.'

He moves past me and heads for the kitchen. 'Anything to eat? I'm starving. A man with no legs goes to the railway station and asks for a ticket to Lourdes. Single or return? the ticket-seller asks. Just a single, the man says. I'll be walking back. Something that's not turkey.'

He crouches to examine the illuminated contents of the fridge, whistling tunelessly between his teeth probably because he knows it gets on my nerves, helps himself to Jennie's non-turkey sandwiches and a can of beer and entertains me while I make the coffee.

'Knock knock,' he says through a mouthful of sandwich. 'Who's there?'

'Biggish.'

'Biggish who?'

'Sorry, haven't any change. Mmm. Great sandwich. Have you heard the latest? We've sold the house.'

The living-room settee is made of black leather and if anything gets lost you're sure to find it by jamming your hand into the crack where the back meets the base. It has little metal nubs stuck all over it and is impossible to sleep on. I sit there fondling Kate's silky ears while Stevie goes on and on about New Zealand. His father's a dentist and his mother's his receptionist; they've been here for fifteen years, and seemingly New Zealand is crying out for dentists. Stevie pretends to be unenchanted by it all. I don't think the fact that he'll never see me again comes into the equation.

He puts on a CD and holds out a hand for me. 'Come on. Me John, you Uma,' he says, tossing his head from side to side, snapping his fingers, and I dance with him, forgetting everything outside the room, for a while anyway. 'I never thought –' he says but gets involved in some fancy footwork. He throws me from hand to hand, does that thing with the two fingers across the face. I follow what he does or he follows me: I'm not sure which.

The music speeds up. He raises his arms above his head and rotating his hips in time to the music moves in small circles in the middle of the room then throwing his head back as the music ends, drops on one knee to the floor.

'You never thought what?' I ask him.

'Oh yeah. I never thought of people actually going to New Zealand,' he tells me from his knees. 'Australia yes, everybody goes to Australia, but I had the feeling that people in New Zealand just got born there. Like the sheep.' He gets to his feet. 'I'll hate it and it'll hate me. I mean, what do you do in New Zealand if you don't play rugby?'

'Don't be silly,' I tell him. 'You'll –'

He jumps up on the settee, waving his arms.

'Silly? I'll show you silly!' and he jumps back on to the floor rolling over and over with Kate barking excitedly at each turn. He stops against the settee with Kate clasped to his chest and looks up at me.

'I'll come back and marry you,' he says.

'No, you won't.'

'Yes, I will. I'll fly back and we'll have a big white wedding.'

'No, you won't.'

Kate licks his chin and he stares at the ceiling, frowning. 'Dad says the skiing's good,' he says. 'And trout fishing.' He turns his head towards me. 'Big deal, eh?'

'Think of me stuck here while you're exploring the other side of the world,' I tell him. 'Stop feeling so sorry for yourself.'

He gets to his feet and brushes Kate's hairs off his T-shirt. 'Be positive, is that it?'

'Exactamundo.'

'Always look on the bright side.'

'That's it.'

'See it all as a . . . as a . . . CHALLENGE.'

'You've got it. Grow up a bit.'

'You're pathetic.'

'You're ridiculous.'

'So my father keeps telling me.'

'He knows what he's talking about.'

'You can be a real pain in the ass at times, know that?'

'So my father keeps telling me.'

He laughs and in spite of the cold we go into the garden so that he can have a cigarette.

'A horse goes into a bar and says, Drinks all round! I've just won the Derby! and the barman says, You've just won the Derby? Why the long face? These things are supposed to kill you,' he says.

'They do. Eventually.'

'Everything kills you eventually. Look at that moon!'

'What about it?'

'It's full.'

'So?'

'It's making me feel . . . FUNNY,' and he grabs hold of me and I can feel his mouth and his teeth against my throat horrible and wet and hard and nice and warm and soft all at the same time.

We lie back on the lawn and hold hands and look up at the distant stars. Some of them really do twinkle. Millions and millions of miles away.

Stevie's cigarette glows red as he points up. 'The Plough,' he says. 'Venus. Mars. Sirius. Someone's belt.'

'Orion's,' I say.

'I knew it was somebody Irish.'

'Orion was a hunter. He fell in love with Diana so Apollo had him killed. Or changed into a swan or something.'

'That Diana!' he says and shakes his head. 'It's time they renamed all these constellations anyway, brought them up to date.'

Millions and millions of earths spinning away in space without end. Time without end.

I think about the strangeness of it all.

Stevie points up again. 'Look. The Great Dome. Beckham's Boot. And that big blobby one with all the little ones round it? That's the Pop Star . . .' and on and on he goes but I'm not listening to him anymore until he suddenly sits up.

'I'm thinking about getting my ear pierced,' he says.

'Why?'

'What else is there to do in this crappy universe?'

*    *    *

When he leaves I say, 'Give me a ring.'

'With a big diamond on it,' he says. 'Then the big white wedding. We'll go to the West Indies for our honeymoon.'

'In your dreams,' I say. 'Give me a ring tomorrow. Same time.'

'We could take in a movie. *American Beauty*'s on at the Odeon.'

'Give me a ring tomorrow.'

'*Muppets from Space?*'

'Give me a ring. Tomorrow. Ciao.'

He puts his hands on my shoulders and I think he's going to say something but he just brushes my hair with his lips and off he goes.


My father and stepmother come back with some friends after Stevie has been gone for more than an hour. It is almost midnight, and I am propped up in bed with the electric blanket turned up to number 5, reading and listening to my mother's CD, which I'm beginning to almost like, when the door opens. My father is standing in the doorway with a glass in his hand. I zap off the CD player and lower my book. He comes over to the bed and picks up the CD case from the floor, reads the back of it. 'You missed yourself,' he says. 'You would have enjoyed it. A comedy. Very clever. Very funny.' He puts the CD case carefully with the others on the bedside table.

'Dad,' I say in my little girl voice, 'you remember the time you and me and Mum drove to that old farm place to pick up Mandy when she was a pup? We were on this farm track and it was hot and dusty? And we came to this old house and Mum got out to ask for directions and the man asked us in for cake and lemonade? And at the back of the house they had this pond with a wooden fence round it and the man said one day he had come back and there were two swans in the pond and they stayed there for the whole of the summer? Can we go back there? Can we go back tomorrow? Can we, Dad?'

'We'll see,' my father says. 'We'll see. Sleep tight.'

He switches off the bedside light and pauses in the doorway, still not looking at me. 'So. What did the Smith boy have to say for himself?'

After he has gone, the voices drift up to me like sounds from another planet.

There is a soft knock on the door. Jennie tiptoes in with a tray. 'Some hot chocolate and biscuits,' she whispers as though someone else is asleep in the room. I can hear my father's voice and then laughter. 'I'm sorry they're so noisy,' she says, still in a whisper. 'They've all been knocking it back a bit.'

She lays the tray down carefully on the bedside table and sits down on the edge of the bed. For a while she says nothing then she reaches for my hand and says, 'You found the sandwiches. I'm so glad. You were breaking our hearts, did you know that?' I hold her hand like I had held Mandy's ball. Then I let her hand go to pick up a biscuit but wait till she has gone before replacing it on the plate.

With the light out, I listen to the distant voices, feeling in the dark the immense distance between me and everyone else in the universe, then I think TOMORROW IS ANOTHER DAY, then I don't have any more thoughts except the thought that I have to hurry up and sleep.

# The Gift

*Robert Marsden*

T he railings are set in the top of a low stone wall, and by clinging to them with her hands she can stay off the ground. She works her way round the wall; hand over hand and foot over foot. It's a tricky operation; if she falls off she'll be swallowed up by the swamp, sucked down into dark oblivion. Her hands are cold and her coat is undone. She has conversations with herself, partly out loud and partly locked up tight inside herself. There are various gaps in the wall; at the school gates for instance, where she becomes cocooned in a protective membrane, and floats like a bubble to the next section. A group of other children are chanting something at her, but she doesn't hear them. The school bell goes and everyone disappears. Miss Clark crosses the play-ground and comes up to her with her hand outstretched. Come on, Becky, the bell's gone. Oh dear, have you had an accident? Never mind, come on, let's go and sort you out. They head off for the toilets together.

## Janice

We always wanted to be foster parents. Foster carers they call us these days. I don't know why exactly; we just wanted to look after kids, needed to maybe, though the social workers don't like you to say that. It's the most important thing you can do, isn't it, bringing up kids, and you get such a kick out of it when things go well, you know, when they begin to really talk to you, or stop wetting the bed or whatever. But we never imagined anyone like Becky. We'd had a couple of placements before, but nothing really testing. That's another word they like to use. When the social worker phoned us she was desperate; Becky was in the office with her things in one of those black bin liners. I can picture her now with her head down, not speaking to anyone. Her foster placement had broken down and they needed somewhere that night. You know what they're like: if you could even take her for the night, Janice, just to give us a breathing space . . . What can you say? She soils a bit they said. A touch of understatement there, I'd say. Some days Becky has to change her pants twenty times. She smears it on the bedroom wall; she shits in bed ('scuse my language, you become kind of immune after a while) and doesn't tell anyone; she shits on the landing and on the floor of the bathroom; and you stand in it and spread it about before you know what's happening. She hides her soiled pants in drawers and under pillows, even in the cystern. It can take a while to track down the smell. We've had five months of this so far.

Who knows what Becky thinks. Not that she's a quiet girl; she chatters away and on some days can seem like any other child, except that it can be difficult to follow the thread. And when you ask her why she has hidden her pants in the cystern she puts her head down and won't speak. Maybe she doesn't know, though it can seem a bit hard to believe. She's ten years old and this is her eighth foster placement. She's been home once or twice in between times, but it hasn't worked out. She's desperate to be with her mother, but her mother doesn't believe the allegations, so there's not much chance of that.

She could be quite pretty if she took more care of herself, but she doesn't seem to care. It's as if she wants to repel people. Her long black hair had to be cut off because she wouldn't brush it, and kept pulling it over her eyes. And of course she smells. The walking toilet, the children call her at school, and she's got no friends. She gets really upset about it at times, but doesn't do anything about it. If she'd just go to the toilet and keep herself clean.

## *John*

Becky's okay. It's quite funny at times. Our toilet is at the top of the stairs, and when she first came here she'd sit on the bog with her legs apart and the door open; she seemed to be waiting for me to find her like that, with a great smile on her face. At first I'd shout for Mum. Mum, she's doing it again. And Mum would come running up the stairs and say, Now, Becky, we've said before, in this house the rule is that we close the door. We've all become very matter of fact about it now. Becky, you've forgotten to close the door again. And she is getting a bit better, but it's a slow business. Mind, the word business has a new meaning round here. I don't know where they all come from. It's the ones you come across on the floor that are the worst; she seems to produce them in camouflaged colours, so that even when you're on the lookout you can easy miss them and end up standing in one. Mind even that can have it's funny side.

Michelle had a new boyfriend a few weeks ago. A stuck-up sort with a stripy tie and a personalised number plate. He said he worked in finance; probably on a supermarket checkout if you ask me. None of us took to him much, and of course that made Michelle all the more keen on him. She brought him back one night after they'd been out. Course he flies upstairs to the bog, straight into one of Becky's strategically placed deposits. He's gone for ages, till Michelle goes looking for him and finds him trying to clean the stuff off his shoes and off the carpet with a bit of bog roll. She tells him it's the cat and not to worry. Not that we've got a cat of course. But then he comes downstairs, you know for a coffee and a snog, and his hand strays under the cushion straight into one of Becky's little parcels of jobby. He was out of it after that; a house of nutters who wrap up cat shit and hide it under the cushions. Michelle was furious. The rest of us had been in bed, but we were soon awake when we heard her screaming at Becky that she'd ruined her life. Becky just sat there on the bed, saying it wasn't me, it wasn't me. Then Mum made Michelle apologise to Becky. I told Becky afterwards that we were all well rid of him.

## Doug

It's like living with a time bomb. I mean what if she makes some allegations about me? Her last foster parents are suspended, but we don't know the full story. She's made allegations about a whole string of folk; you just don't know what to believe. She calls me Uncle Doug. She's just a little girl, but at the same time she's not a child; her innocence has gone, and you can't put it back. It's not something you can let yourself think about; I mean what must have happened to her. And that boyfriend of her mother's hasn't even been charged. Who'd believe Becky, standing up in court? Every other sentence she utters is a lie. She'd probably just stand there not saying anything, with her head down, trying to pull her hair over her face to hide from it all. But everyone knows he did it. Sometimes I think to myself if the chance arose; if I came across him in a deserted street I'd just finish him off for good. And her useless mother just stands by him; she's chosen him and to hell with Becky. And the number of times she comes to visit Becky and she's got a black eye.

Robert Marsden

## Michelle

I've tried with Becky, but I just can't get through. I don't care
what they say, I think she shits deliberately. She must know
what she's doing when she hides her pants under her pillow
and smears the stuff on the walls. There are times, little spells
of a few days, when she's normal; it's heaven, and we all say
how great she is and clever, and then, just when you think it
might be safe to bring your boyfriend home, it starts again,
and it can be ten times as worse as before, or that's how it feels
after a break. I can't understand it; it must be deliberate. We
have these family meetings now where we talk about it; how
we all care about Becky and want to help her with this
problem. Sometimes I think she just needs a good smack.
It's amazing how Mum keeps so patient with her. If you ask
me all these therapists have weakened her brain and she's got
no common sense left. She used to smack us when we were
kids and it never did us any harm.

## Janice

Becky does these drawings during her therapy sessions. Lots of
red, with people in fires or drowning, and always pictures of
the family, with herself on the outside, and Dad as a monster
figure. It's obvious really, isn't it? She has no control; its a
reflex action, like blushing, she just can't help it. The therapist
says it's like when you're so angry you just blow; you can't
help it. I still don't understand it properly. They tell us that the
shit is maybe a way of protecting herself. Perhaps he won't do
it if I'm dirty and unattractive. Apparently, sometimes the
excrement is part of the actual abuse. There's a whole seedy
world out there that we have no idea about. God knows what
you'd find if you lifted the roofs off some of these houses.

The worst time was probably a couple of months ago. It had

all got on top of us, to the point that Michelle was going to leave home. There seemed to be no end in sight, though everyone said we were doing a great job, if we could just hang on in there. The four of us had a talk, and decided we needed to get away together without Becky; a normal weekend together. So they arranged some respite for Becky with some other foster carers, and off she went without a backward glance. We all stayed in this little cottage in Robin Hood's Bay. It's a higgledy piggledy sort of place that looks as if it's sliding into the sea: pretty, with lots of funny little buildings with hiding places that the smugglers used to lie low in. It didn't work very well. I couldn't stop thinking about Becky. Every time I saw a child or a pile of dog dirt, and even when I didn't. I think I drove the rest of them mad. Will you stop talking about Becky? they kept saying. And I just couldn't do with sex, haven't been able to for weeks. Poor Doug.

## Doug

There was something about the grey misty weather that seemed to get inside us all. Janice could hardly crack her face into a smile; felt guilty as hell for leaving Becky, I suppose. And she tensed up when I tried to give her so much as a cuddle. The kids were great; they seemed to know it was up to them to salvage something. It was as if they went back ten years. John chased Michelle along the beach with a wet bit of seaweed, and she screeched at him, pretending she didn't like it; worried about getting her white jacket dirty. It seemed to do them good; in the bar they got to talking about how things were when they were little. Like lying in bed together waiting for Santa, but falling asleep of course before I came in with the presents. And each of them swearing the next morning that they'd caught a glimpse of him. Then we all looked up at Janice, and she was just crying, and couldn't explain why. She wanted to phone, but I wouldn't let her. I still don't know if she made a call without telling me.


## Michelle

The weekend away was a laugh in some ways. John and me became friends again. He's all right really, but I wish he'd do something about his appearance; that ragged old denim jacket and his greasy hair; you can see people looking at him. We got into this thing in one of the gift shops: have you remembered to take your valium today, John? and when is it you see your probation officer again, John? Mum and Dad didn't think it was very funny, but John and me thought it was great; you should've seen the faces on some of them women.

I suppose it made me realise how important Becky is to Mum. She was so cut up about leaving her. Probably too important, but that's Mum. And I suppose we're big enough to look after ourselves now. I just wish she'd stop doing it; she's meant to be very bright.


## Janice

She didn't make one mistake when we were away. We brought her some fossils back that we'd bought in a little shop. And she gave me a present. She gave me a real hug and a kiss and gave me this beautifully wrapped gift, all done up with Christmas paper and ribbons she'd found somewhere. She was so excited she wanted to help me undo it. There were several layers of paper all carefully sellotaped up. We had to get the scissors. I don't know why I was surprised really; she obviously thought I'd be genuinely pleased. Inside the parcel was a lump of shit, carefully wrapped in several layers of toilet roll.

# ABOUT THE AUTHORS

**George Anderson** was born in Twechar and has worked as a journalist in Dundee and Aberdeen. He now lives in Leith, works for SNH, and performs blues with The Arhoolies.

**Linda Anderson** lives in Edinburgh, and, when not writing, she teaches computing and produces school drama. She spent five years living in Nigeria, where she taught in a remote school. Previous publications include 'Pandrops' in *New Writing Scotland* 14 and 'Saving Mr Uguru', broadcast by BBC Radio 4.

**Iain Bahlaj** is 21 and lives in Fife. His previous publications include stories in *Front & Centre, Fife Fringe, Chapman*. His first novel, *Tilt*, is due for release in the near future, published by Pulp Books.
Email address: iainbahlaj@hotmail.com

**Alan Bissett** is 24 and a student at Stirling University. His first published short story was in last year's Macallan anthology. He is now editing the forthcoming Polygon collection *New Scottish Gothic Fiction*, and has just finished his debut novel *Boy Racers*, and writing the first and last chapters of *Product* magazine's six-part serial *Without You I Am Nothing*. He is on the judging panel of this year's Canongate Prize and fully open to corruption. He recently accidentally turned down a Young Achiever's Award from the Queen.

**Anne Bree** lives in Ayrshire. Her work includes children's books, newspaper articles, film scripts and an autobiography. Her alter ego is singer, academic and political activist, Anne Lorne Gilles. Her previous publications include *Seinneamaid Comhla* (CNSA); *Padraig Am Bus Trang* (CNSA); *Calum Agus Maired* (Acair); *Taigh Iain Ghreot* (Acair); *Am Mongaidh Frangach* (Acair); *Nighean Chiallach Mar Thu Fhein* (Acair) Forthcoming publications: *Song of Myself* (Mainstream); *Songs of the Gael* (Birlinn); *An Cur-Seachad Diamhair . . .* (Acair).

**Sophie Cooke** graduated in 1998 with an MA (Hons) in Social Anthropology from Edinburgh University. She lives in Glasgow and works as a freelance journalist and artist.

**Linda Cracknell** lives and works in Highland Perthshire. She came to live in Scotland from Devon about ten years ago. Her first collection of short stories will be published in October 2000. She has had individual stories published in a variety of places since August 1998 when Linda's first published story won the Macallan/Scotland on Sunday short-story competition.
 Acknowledgement: 'Life Drawing' © Linda Cracknell, 2000, published

# About the Authors

in *Life Drawing*, 11:9 imprint, Neil Wilson Publishing (2000), ISBN 1–903238–12–7.

**Meaghan Delahunt** was born in Melbourne, Australia, and has lived in Australia, Greece and Scotland. Her publications include short stories in a variety of literary magazines, with her first novel, *In the Blue House at Coyoacán*, to be published by Bloomsbury in January 2001.

**Chris Dolan** returned to Glasgow after living in Spain. He writes for the stage and screen as well as prose, is a consultant for UHESIO, and is a director of the Edinburgh International Book Festival. His previous publications include *Poor Angels and Other Stories* (Polygon); *Ascension Day* (Hodder Review); *Sabina* (Faber & Faber); *The Angel's Share* (Borderline) as well as short stories in Polygon, Canongate and Egmont collections.

**Anne Donovan** lives in Glasgow. Her short stories have been published in various anthologies and broadcast on BBC radio. Winner of the Macallan/ Scotland on Sunday short-story competition in 1997 and a Canongate Prize winner in 1999. Her collection of stories, *Hieroglyphics and Other Stories* is due to be published by Canongate in spring 2001. Currently in receipt of a SAC bursary, she is writing a novel.

Acknowledgement: 'All that Glisters' © Anne Donovan, taken from: *Hieroglyphics and Other Stories*, (Canongate Books, Edinburgh, 2001).

**Michel Faber** was born in Holland, grew up in Australia, and settled in the Scottish Highlands. He writes all day while cats look on. Previous publications: stories in *New Scottish Writing* (1997), *Snapshots: 10 Years of the Ian St James Awards*; *Shorts Volume I*; *The Printer's Devil*; *Chapman*; *Northwords*, *Story*; *Black Book*; and others. Short-story collection *Some Rain Must Fall* (Canongate); novel *Under the Skin* (Canongate). Short-story collection won Saltire. Novel sold to fifteen countries. Still grumpy.

Acknowledgement: 'Fish' © Michel Faber, taken from *Some Rain Must Fall and Other Stories* (Canongate Books, Edinburgh, 1998).

**Jim Glen** has had short stories and poetry widely published and broadcast on radio. He was awarded SAC writers' bursaries in 1991 and 1999. Currently working on a first novel.

**Diana Hendry** has had stories included in anthologies and read on Radio 4. Previous publications: *Making Blue* (Peterloo Poets); *Strange Goings-On* (Viking); *Harvey Angell* (Red Fox); *Double Vision* (Walker Books); *The Very Noisy Night* (Magi); and short stories in *God: an anthology of fiction* and *Sex, Drugs, Rock'n Roll* (both Serpent's Tail). She has published two collections of poetry. Her junior novel, *Harvey Angell*, won a Whitbread Award.

# About the Authors

**George Inglis** was born in 1958 and lives in Houston. He works in Glasgow as an information/administration worker. Previous publications included in *New Writing Scotland*.

**Michael Mail** was born in Glasgow. He currently lives in London where he is a director of an educational charity. Previous publications: short stories published in *Caledonia* magazine and *The Scotsman* newspaper, among others. Having won last year's competition, he is now working on his first novel.

**Morag McDowell** has been published in Ireland and works as a manager for British Airways Holidays. She was born in Glasgow and lives in Brighton.

**Hannah McGill** was born in Shetland and grew up in Lincoln. Previous publications: journalism in *The Scotsman*, *The List*, *The Sunday Herald*, *Product*. Fiction in the *Edinburgh Review*. She now works as *The Scotsman*'s TV critic and is writing her first novel.

**Seonaid McGill** was educated at Ardrossan Academy and the University of Glasgow (MA Eng. Lit.). She works as a freelance copywriter and is the mother of three daughters.

**Farquhar McLay** was born in the Gorbals in 1936. He went down with TB doing national service with Cameron Highlanders in 1954. He has been writing ever since. Previous publications: author of many radio plays and talks in 1950 and 1960. Edited Glasgow anthologies *Workers City* (1988), *The Reckoning* (1990), *Voices of Dissent* (People's Poems, 1986). Poems and short stories published widely in magazines and anthologies. Currently writing a novel, which is near completion.

**Donald Paterson** was brought up in Tain, Ross-shire, and now lives in Elgin and works in Aberlour. Previous publications: a story 'God's Dove' published in Cencrastus in 1984. He has only recently returned to writing after a sixteen-year gap, and is currently working on more short stories and a novel.

**M. S. Power** wrote the *Children of the North* trilogy of novels which was televised by BBC2. Previous publications: *The Crucifixion of Septimus Roach* (Bloomsbury Publishing, 1989); *Summer Soldier* (Bloomsbury Publishing, 1990); *Dealing with Kranze* (Mainstream, 1996); *Nathan Crosby's Fan Mail* (Orion Publishing, 1999). He lives in Galloway.

**Wayne Price** was born in south Wales and now lives and teaches in Edinburgh. Previous publications: stories in many journals and anthologies, including *Stand*, *Panurge*, *New Writing Scotland* and last year's *Shorts* anthology. He has been writing and publishing stories since 1985 and is working on a second novel.

**Dilys Rose** lives in Edinburgh with her family. Previous publications: *Madame Doubtfire's Dilemma* (poetry); *Our Lady of the Pickpockets*, *Red*

*Tides; War Dolls* (all solo collections of short stories); *Pest Maiden* (novel). She currently teaches creative writing part time at Glasgow University, and is working on a second novel, more stories and, to her surprise, poems.

**Alexander McCall Smith** is the author of numerous books, both fiction and non-fiction, including most recently a novel set in Botswana, *Tears of the Giraffe* (Polygon, 2000). His collection of short stories *Heavenly Date* (Canongate) was short-listed for the McVitie's Prize. His books have been widely translated.

**Ali Smith** was born and grew up in Inverness and is living in Cambridge just now, working on a play and a new novel. Previous publications: *Free Love and Other Stories* (Virago, 1995); *Like* (Virago, 1997); *Other Stories and Other Stories* (Granta, 1999); and forthcoming *Hotel World* (Hamish Hamilton, 2001).

**Alan Spence** is a Glasgow-born novelist, short-story writer, poet and playwright. Books include *Its Colours They Are Fine, The Magic Flute, Stone Garden* and *Way to Go*. Awards include People's Prize, Macallan/ SoS Prize, McVitie's Prize. He is writer-in-residence at the University of Aberdeen.

Acknowledgement: 'Nessun Dorma' © Alan Spence, taken from *Stone Garden*, (Phoenix House, imprint of Orion Publishing Ltd, 1997).

**David Strachan** was educated in Huntly and St Andrews, trained as a pilot, variously employed in America and South Africa, taught in Edinburgh, Glasgow and Dundee, and is married with a son and daughter. Previous publications: short stories published and broadcast in Kenya, play performed in Nairobi. Short story in *New Writing*, play performed by Mandala Theatre Co., and poetry published in *The Scotsman*.

**Robert Marsden** was born on Tyneside and has lived and worked in Scotland for twenty years. He has now settled in the Scottish Borders. This is his first published work.

While very effort has been made to compile accurate information about the authors and to trace and credit all copyright holders, *Shorts* is produced to a very tight schedule. The Publisher will endeavour to rectify any inaccuracies in any future edition.